Lines

We

Shouldn't

Cross

Cece Raven

Playlist

SUPERCROSS & MOTOCROSS TRACK
SECTIONS DEFINED

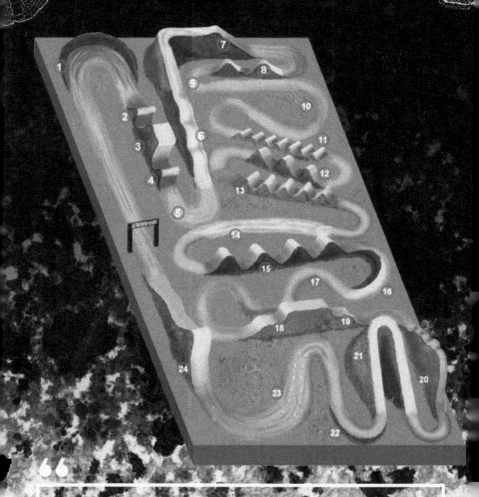

1. BERMED CORNER	9. SHARP TURN	17. S CURVE
2. STEP ON	10. SWEEPING TURN	18. STEP UP
3. TABLE TOP	11. WHOOPS	19. STEP DOWN
4. STEP OFF	12. TRIPLE	20. STEP OVER/DRAGON BACK
5. FLAT CORNER	13. RHYTHM SECTION	21. DOWN HILL
6. ROLLERS	14. SAND SECTION	22. TALLADEGA CORNER
7. SKI JUMP	15. QUAD	23. SPLIT LANES
8. DOUBLE	16. OFF CAMBER	24. BOOTER

 **Motocross Dictionary**

AMA:
American Motorcycle Association. The governing body for MX in the USA.

Bottom Out:
To use all of the bike's suspension. Can be heard with a metallic clank.

Braaap:
Can be used when describing going all out. You can use it in pretty much any situation. Comes from the beautiful sound a 2 stroke engine makes while riding it fast. Brraaaap!

Case:
You case a jump when you land with the front wheel on the back of the landing and the rear wheel on the front of the landing, resulting in a very hard impact. The motor and frame hit the dirt because of the impact.

Crossrut:
When the front and rear wheel are not in the same rut.

Enduro:
A style of riding done in the woods.

Holeshot:
To holeshot means that you reach the first turn in the lead. One of the best feelings in racing!

Huck-a-buck:
When the bike is riding you, you are bucked all over the place. Usually happens in the whoops.

Monkey Butt:
Your rear-end after you have ridden miles of trails.

Nac Nac:

A trick performed while airborne in which both legs are positioned on the same side of the bike and one gets extended out from the bike.

Plastic princess:

Describes a rider, or their bike (often both), that is too precious to get dirty. You recognize them in the pits with their perfect plastics, shining tires and fresh gear.

Rutted or Ruts:

Used to describe track conditions. "That corner is so rutted out." Tires have been digging into the dirt causing long ruts. This can be very hard to ride, especially if you're not used to it.

Sandbagger/Sandbagged:

Someone who is riding in a class that is slower than their own capabilities. The sandbagger does this to have a better chance of winning. Not cool!

Sag:

Refers to how much a suspension compresses when the rider sits on the bike. Sag is often used as one parameter when tuning a suspension for a rider. Manages the effectiveness and plushness of the suspension.

Shock:

A part of the frame that controls the movement of the rear suspension.

Soil Sample:

Getting a face full of dirt.

Supermini:

This is a class designation. Supermini includes the fastest kids that are still on minibikes (typically 85cc to 105cc engines).

Whip:

Movement when jumping when you push the back of the bike out to the side. Do this by entering a jump at a slight angle, turning the bike to the side.

Whiskey Throttle:

When a rider gives too much throttle and then starts to slip off the back of the bike, this causes their hand to just pull on the throttle even more and eventually the rider goes out of control. Big crash!

Yama-Thumb:

The infamous blistered inside of the right thumb from the stock grips and handlebar. This is well known to us blue riders.

For more terms and racing facts go to the website below!

Cc: https://www.mx-gear.com/motocross-terms-slang/

Trigger Warnings

Hello Dear Readers,

It warms my heart so much that you have decided to read my debut novel, Lines We Shouldn't Cross. Although reading can be an amazing way to escape reality or be healing from our own personal journeys, I value your mental health. Please take into consideration the following trigger warnings before you choose to continue reading.

In this book, there's mentions of an abusive ex, relationship trauma, loss of a parent, abandonment, attempted sexual assault, cheating, bondage, a parent in jail, and a loved one in the hospital. If anything stated above is triggering for you please consider the safety of your mental health before continuing.

One more thing before you dive into Winchester Bay. LWSC contains explicit content and is rated for ages 18+.

If you have decided to continue reading, thank you so much and I hope you love Claire and Dustin as much as I do!

To the women who aren't afraid to stand up for themselves, and to the friends who stand-up for you when you don't have the strength to.

Preface

I'll never ignore my instincts again.

I knew something was wrong. I could feel it in every fiber of my being. And now I've probably lost her.

Fuck. Fuck. Fuck. Please be alive.

I repeat in my head as I slam my palms into the steering wheel of my Ford Bronco.

I swear if that fucker touches one piece of hair on her beautiful head. I'll end him.

I'm driving ninety down highway 101, when I look out my rear view, and see a swarm of red and blue fluorescents flash by.

There are very few moments I've been thankful for this small town, and this is definitely one of them.

It's a damn good thing the cops are going to get there before me, because if they weren't...

They would be zipping up a body in a black bag tonight. And it wouldn't be her's or mine they'd be hauling out.

I'll never forgive myself if I'm too late.

Hang on, Angel. I'm coming. Please, just hold on.

Part One

DuneFest

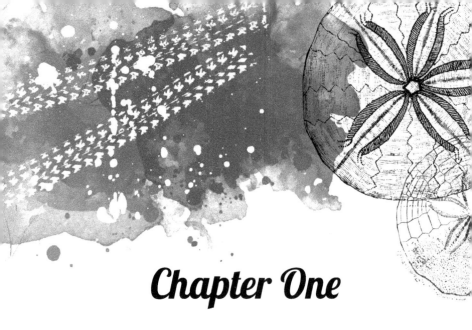

Chapter One

Claire

I don't think anyone has ever explained how inanimate objects can control your emotions. I realize how stupid that might sound to some. But to the people who do understand, when you lose that item, you're left feeling empty or sad over something that breathes life into you but doesn't actually breathe. And it makes absolutely no fucking sense.

That an entity like a house, birthday card, book—whatever it is—can be so influential to a person's life. For some, it may be a note from a grandparent who has passed, or a music box they've had as a child that still soothes them to sleep even as an adult. For me, it's my childhood home.

"You all set, Mini?" Dad shouts from the truck as I step onto the front porch. He's called me Mini for as long as I can remember. Him, this house, and that nickname are the few things that have been constant in my life.

Although I'm excited for this move, leaving the cottage behind is going to be hard. All my memories are here.

Resting my hand on the railing of our porch, I let years and years of memories resurface.

On this lawn is where I took apart and put together my first engine. Where countless water gun fights and mud puddles took place, followed by our staple of hot dogs and mac & cheese for lunch. When I got older the conversations got more serious, and the traditions changed, but none more important than the next. If anything, our moments became more meaningful. More significant.

On these planks of worn white wood, the mutual safe haven for Dad and I, we would sit on this porch and talk about our day while playing a game of UNO. Where he would hold me in his arms and let me cry after a rough day. Where we would share lemonade in the summer and hot cocoa in the winter.

In this driveway, I said goodbye to him—tears streaming down both our cheeks—before Han and I jumped into her shitty Prius and headed off for University of Las Vegas. This home is where weekend trips back to Reno turned into expecting George Strait to be blasting from the shop doors every time I showed up to visit. So many memories. Memories I'll cherish for the rest of my life.

This house also holds a lot of moments I wish to forget.

It's where I first opened my heart to a boy, and he turned into someone I no longer recognize.

I don't want to think about that. I just want to enjoy the happy memories. Reminisce on the things that shaped me to be who I am today. Until eventually, I will have to say goodbye to the bright red door that used to welcome me home.

I take the last step off our porch—or I guess now I should say *the* porch—of the cottage on Windhaven Avenue. Reluctantly letting go of the railing, I turn and jog towards him.

"All set!" I reply.

My backpack slung over my shoulder and in my other hand I grip the handle of my suitcase. The wheels click along the cracks of the front walkway, as I hustle down to his white F-150. My dad has owned this truck since the day I was born. The only thing different today, is that it's hauling a U-Haul behind it with all our belongings neatly stacked inside. In the bed sits my black and gold Hawk DLX 250 and his red Apollo DB-36 250.

Happiness on two wheels.

The only thing keeping me sane this last year and a half, is racing and my father.

For as long as I can remember, he has always been able to read my mind. Been able to sense my feelings before I could even explain them. He knew I desperately needed an escape. Needed to move away from this city; and I never even had to say a word to him.

Dad loves Reno and leaving is not going to be easy on him. But he'll do it for me. That's just the relationship we have. We would do anything to make each other happy and we tell each other everything.

Well... almost everything.

I pull the passenger door open and jump in. "Thank you so much for this," I grab the seat belt and pull it across my body, sliding it into the base with a satisfying click. "I promise I'll get back on my feet when we get to Reedsport."

"Don't worry about it." He lightly shakes his head at me. "I've loved having you around, take as much time as you need. I know you'll figure it out." Grabbing my shoulder with his hand, he gives me a playful shake. "I love you kiddo."

"I love you too."

This last year has been *hard*. Right after the summer following graduation, I headed straight for UNLV.

Biggest mistake of my life.

I was only there eight months before running home.

Dad was pretty disappointed in me.

If only I told him the truth of why I left, then he would completely understand. But I can't tell him yet... not until there are thousands of miles between us and Las Vegas.

Now that he has accepted I'm not going back to college, I know that he is more than happy to be sharing a roof again. Truth is, Dad would totally be content if I chose to live with him for the rest of my life. To me it just feels like I've taken a step backwards. In Las Vegas, I had my own apartment, my own car. I began to enjoy that piece of freedom. I felt successful. Now I'm back to square one.

God, I'm such a failure.

How many times have I said that to myself throughout these last several months? At this point it feels like my brain is a scratched vinyl rotating on repeat, and the hand dropping the needle can't even prevent it from spinning.

I've always been strong, stubborn. Just like my father taught me to be. So why did I run away at the first sign of conflict? Why did I let someone else's actions determine my future? I don't know. I'm still trying to figure that part out.

I will make sure that changes when we get to Reedsport.

I've been trying to find a job and get out on my own but everywhere I applied, I could never get past the first interview, or I wouldn't hear back at all. At this point, I've heard every excuse in the book.

"You're just too qualified for this job position."

"We don't have the funds right now to be able to support the pay your qualifications would require." I didn't care what my pay was, I just wanted the job. I told them that, and in their return email they said they had already filled the position. Adding another rejection to the infinite list of my failures.

My all time favorite excuse was, *"We just aren't looking for someone of your...stature."* Meaning they didn't want a woman working in their mechanics shop.

I was raised around every vehicle you could imagine. I know the ins and outs of every engine on the market—and not on the market. My dad works at a shop called *Born Ready Auto,* well he had been, up until last week. Being a single parent, babysitters and daycare was not in the cards for him. So where did little Claire end up? You guessed it. Working right alongside him, sitting on a rolling mechanics creeper, and a spill tray next to me, starting from the day I could walk. And before that I was sitting in a baby bouncer chewing on a socket wrench only a few feet away from the service bay. The only reason I know that is because there is a wallet sized print out of that exact moment plastered to the dash inside his Ford.

I just want to get my hands dirty and work on anything with an engine for the rest of my life. But sometimes you don't get to work at a place that feels like home, that makes you happy, and helps build your future. Sometimes you just have to get a job as a stepping stone to success—that's what I'll be doing in Oregon.

I already have an interview at a local diner in town called Big Fish Cafe. A waitressing job will just have to do, for now. Until I can make some connections and hopefully get into the local mechanics shop.

Dad picked Reedsport mainly because it holds one of the biggest Motocross competitions in the country. DuneFest.

Taking some time on the sand is just what I need to get my mind off of all the stuff that has happened within the last year and a half. If I'm being honest with myself, I need this move more than I need to breathe.

We stop at the gas station to grab snacks, drinks, and fuel before hitting the freeway. After we fill up the truck and are about to pull out of the parking lot, he breaks the silence.

"Do you want to call Han before we take off? We've got a six hour drive ahead of us."

"I just sent her a text saying we just got gas and are about to leave."

"Alright then, on the road we go. How is she?"

"She's doing good. She decided to pursue a teaching degree."

"That's awesome! She'll do great in that field."

I nod. "I think so too. She's always had a heart for kids."

Han is my best friend. We moved to UNLV together, to start—what was supposed to be—the best four years of our lives.

She wasn't as forgiving as Dad was about me leaving Vegas. Honestly, I couldn't blame her, though. It was my fault she was mad, and she had every right to be.

I packed up all of my belongings—or at least what I could fit into my 4Runner— and skipped town overnight. I never went back. When she messaged me the next morning, I told her I had a mental break, couldn't bear to be without my dad, and realized college wasn't for me. That was so far from the truth. I also told her to sell whatever I had left there and keep the money as if it would make up for my betrayal.

I know it makes me a shitty friend. The fact that I just up and left the one person—other than the man sitting next to me—that I can count on. Especially since I left her with a mediocre excuse and can't even put my own shit aside to spare her the honesty. I guess running away seemed like the logical explanation at the time. I promised myself I would tell her the truth when I got back to Reno, but then I dragged myself into this mental hole of assuming no one would believe me, or make a bigger deal out of the situation than need be, and now it's been almost a year. It feels pointless to tell her the truth now, since we've gotten past it... for the most part.

Still, the hardest part of this whole situation was leaving Han–lying to her for so long. She'd understand if I just told her the truth, but I can't yet. I honestly don't know when I'll be able to. Maybe this will be just one of those things I take to the grave with me.

"Where's our first stop again?" I ask.

He checks over his shoulder before we merge onto the freeway, leaving Reno behind us. I can't help the twinge of pain that strikes through my heart as we leave 'The Biggest Little City in the World'.

"Medford, Oregon. From there it's only a three hour drive. We will leave early in the morning from the hotel, probably around six. We will need a few hours to unpack and get what we need for DuneFest. Then the next day, we'll head to Winchester Bay to camp for four days."

"Are we going to finish unpacking and getting the house ready after DuneFest?"

"Yeah... It's gonna be a busy next couple weeks. Are you ready, Mini?" He looks over at me expectantly. Waiting for the predictable answer that has plagued our family for generations.

I roll my eyes at him. "I was born ready."

This saying has been passed between us ever since my first race in Reno when I was five years old. Before he said it to me, Grandpa had been saying it to him. So, when a job opened up at a shop called Born Ready Auto, he said it was fate.

"Ain't that the truth." He says with a smirk on his face. Clearly proud of himself, and possibly me.

All jokes aside, I am ready.

The beginning of a new chapter.

A new start.

Hopefully this one will be better than the last.

Chapter Two

Dustin

"DuneFest is only three days away. Are you looking forward to another championship title?" Axel questions.

I yank on the tie down. Making sure our bikes are loaded correctly, and secured onto the bed of his Tacoma.

I stand up and cross my arms over my chest, staring down at him from the back of his truck. "It would be more exciting if I got to kick your ass again this year."

Axel scoffs and shakes his head as he continues to check the straps on his side. I knew Axel wasn't going to be competing for the SandMaster title this year, but it still sucks. I'm going to miss riding next to my brother.

Last year, he told me it would be his final race. I guess a part of me was hoping he was joking. Apparently he has other priorities like running his business, and someday he wants a family. I just couldn't imagine a life without racing. Since I was four, my entire life has consisted of pouring my blood, sweat, and tears into Motocross. The future I'm building for myself is adding ten more championship titles to my already five back to back victories, and someday going pro.

Due to my racing career, there isn't a person in town who doesn't know my name. I plan on riding that high and being on the sand for as long as possible.

"Mom is coming this year right?" I ask him.

"She said she was, but you know how her shifts can get at the hospital."

Mom has missed out on a lot these last couple years. The hospital had taken a big hit a few years back and lost a bunch of employees due to some lawsuit— she won't go into much detail— and since then she hasn't been able to be as present in our lives. She's missed out on the last three DuneFest trips because of it.

This year the hospital is covered and has finally caught up with hiring employees.

"I hope she can make it."

"So do I," Mom says from the front porch of my parents house. Leave it to my mother to be able to hear everything inside and outside of her house. Must be a side effect of raising a teenage asshole. *Oh, did I say asshole? I meant, Axel.* Closing the front door, she walks over, and gives both of us a hug.

"I have a feeling this year is going to be the best year yet." She raises her eyebrows at me. "I love you boys. I'll see you in the morning." Her hand is behind her head as she waves at us and walks away. Her keychain—filled with god knows what— jingles around her fingers.

Axel and I promised her we would keep the tradition of Saturday morning breakfast. A weekly occurrence in the Price household. After we moved out, she had been so sad, this was the least we could do for her.

"Love you too, Mom," Axel and I say at the same time, causing both of us to send death glares at each other. She chuckles, then climbs into her car, and pulls out of the driveway.

As if on cue, Dad pulls in right behind her. They share a quick wave and blow each other a kiss through their car windows, then Mom disappears down the street.

My parents have worked opposite shifts ever since my older brother was born. Which means for the past twenty seven years, the only time they get together has been on the weekends, and that's not including Saturday morning breakfast and Sunday morning PFCDs- Price Family Cleaning Day. When we were kids we would only clean my parents house, but now we work as a team to bust out both mine and Axel's, along with theirs. Leaving only the evenings for them to spend any time together.

I can tell the loss of quality time is weighing on both of them. They will need a change soon.

Dad's truck door slams shut, drawing my attention. "How's it going boys? Are you all packed up?"

I've been ready for weeks.

"Yeah. Just strapped down the bikes and *my* bags are loaded into the back." I glare at my brother. "I can't speak for everyone in our family, though."

Axel shoots both hands into the air. "Damn, I'm almost ready. Don't kill me just yet."

Dad laughs. "I'm just glad it's not me on the other end of that look." He turns his attention towards me. The look of business and no play. *Here we go.* "Dustin, how are you preparing mentally for this year's race?" He used to race competitively when he was my age. There are still a few of his trophies showcased in his office, right alongside mine and Axel's. Mom got pregnant with Axel shortly after they started dating. Instead of being able to focus on Motocross and hopefully make it into the pros, he gave up that dream to provide for his family. There wasn't a day that passed where he didn't tell us it was the best decision of his life– choosing his family over his wants. Even with all that in consideration, there were still times when I felt so much pressure from him that I couldn't help but feel like he was trying to live out an old dream through me. I still sometimes struggle with why I put so much pressure on myself.

Is it because I want it? Or is it because I feel like I owe it to my father?

"I'm ready, just like I am every year. Kicking Axel's ass on the sand this last week has really given me that extra boost of confidence." I wink at my brother and he rolls his eyes. Dads stare is stone cold, wiping the smile off my face real fast.

"This ain't a joke. If you walk away with another SandMaster title, it will be your sixth championship win in a row. There will be riders coming from all over the country to try and take that from you. Your head needs to be in it all the way."

"I understand."

I ride better when there's less pressure on my shoulders. I know that he pushes me so hard because he wants me to succeed. Sometimes, I wish we could just enjoy the sand again. For fun, without the weight of the competition hanging on our shoulders.

"Good." He gives me a quick nod of approval.

"I've got to head down the shop real quick. Big Rich asked me to meet up with him." I hitch a thumb over my shoulder. "Apparently he has some news for me."

"Did he mention what it's about?"

"No, just some news about this year's race."

"Alright. Just make sure when you get back home, you write up a game plan. We need to be prepared for anything this year. We don't want another incident like DuneFest 2019."

Axel and I both wince.

DuneFest 2019. An inexperienced rider was thrown into the wrong racing bracket by their parents, causing a ten bike pile up. Dad scolded both Axel and I for not noticing sooner and notifying the judges. I'm still not entirely sure how he made it our fault. The reason my brother and I wince is because of the tongue lashing we got from our father, and the memory of all the injuries after that race.

"I'll make sure it's done by tonight,"

"Good." Dad nods again and heads inside.

I walk down the front lawn and jump into the driver's seat of my Bronco. After I roll down my window, I shout at Axel, "You better be packed when I get back, or I'm leaving you alone with him at DuneFest!" I pull off the curb, onto the street before Axel can snap back one of his snarky remarks. Unfortunately, I am unable to get out unscathed when I look in my rear view mirror and notice he is flipping me off. I can't help the big grin that takes over my face as I head towards Jeremy's Automotive and Off-road.

Dad never pushed me to get a job, he said training and winning race competitions was enough. He told me that as long as I was focusing on making it pro, he would help me financially. I think he doesn't care as long as I have a future that provides a nice retirement for him.

I wanted a job anyway.

I am twenty-three, after all. I need to be on my own. Plus, it was perfect timing, Axel's roommate just moved out and had an extra room available. We have been talking about living together since we were in middle school. We may butt heads all the fucking time, but that doesn't mean he isn't my best friend.

Getting a job was easy. Nobody was going to tell the SandMaster that he couldn't work at the local mechanics shop. The job was mine before I even applied. Perks of living in a small town. Another bonus is that the shop is only five minutes away from my house. Ten minutes away from my parents.

I pull into the parking spot next to Big Rich's red Jeep Wrangler.

Big Rich runs DuneFest. He oversees every part of the annual event. Without him I don't think DuneFest would be coming up on its 20th anniversary.

I enter through the back garage of Jeremy's. Only employees —with the exception of Big Rich—are allowed through the back entrance. As I walk in, I notice Liam and Micheal working on a set of 250s, probably getting them tuned for the race. I give them a quick nod and head towards Jeremy's office.

Once I get through the garage, I make my way past the warehouse storage room. Where rows and rows of parts are arranged by size and alphabetical order; plus, the specialty rows towards the back of the warehouse that hold the equipment for dirt bikes, four-wheelers, and side by sides.

I reach the back of the shop when I hear a boom of two voices through the brown metal door leading into Jeremy's office. It wasn't hard to tell which one belonged to Big Rich and which one belonged to Jeremy.

"He needs to know... we will tell him we aren't concerned and just want to give him extra time to prepare, a little more so than the previous years," I hear Big Rich say.

"I don't know man, I think you're going to jinx him if you don't just let him ride like he does every year."

Jeremy is tapping his pen on his desk as I open the door.

They both stand simultaneously.

This is fucking weird.

Big Rich walks over to me and puts his hand out, as I take it, he pulls me in for a half hug. "There he is, the man of the year, or should I say the last five years."

"How are you doing? It's nice to see you,"

"I'm doing good." He glances back at Jeremy, he shakes his head and Big Rich shrugs. This entire situation is bizarre. "Listen, I just wanted to let you know I've got some information from Debbie, our booking coordinator for DuneFest... there's a new rider this year." They share a look.

What the hell is going on? They are never this on edge.

"There's new riders every year. You're not gonna tell me it's Jett Lawrence. Are you?" I chuckle.

"God no! I mean that would be great for publicity... but no. The new racer is from Reno and apparently they have an EnduroCross title." Big Rich turns and takes a seat in the fold out chair across from Jeremy's computer. "They're going to be good. I know you've trained all year, but we figured we'd give you a heads up."

Even if my new competition has won an EnduroCross title, I'm not scared. It'd be nice to get some decent competition out here, besides my brother. And he's not even competing this year.

This new information is actually exciting.

I'm still confused on why they have their panties in a wad, though.

"Thanks. Is that all?"

Big Rich opens his mouth to speak, but Jeremy cuts him off, "Actually, would you mind lending Liam and Michael a hand on those 250s. They belong to the Linetti twins, and I really don't want to hear shit from Joe just because you didn't work on them."

"Sure, no problem." I look directly at Big Rich and raise my eyebrows. "Are you sure that's all?"

Again, he goes to speak but Jeremy cuts him off, "Yes, that's all."

My brows furrow at the extremely odd interaction this has been. Obviously Big Rich has something he wants to tell me but Jeremy doesn't think it's important, or doesn't want me to know. "*Okay?...* I guess I'll see you guys later then."

"Bye."

"See you later."

I turn and walk out of Jeremy's office and head towards the vehicle bays.

I wonder why they are all worked up about a new rider.

After finishing up on the pair of 250s, I head back to the house.

I see Axel's headlights flash through the front window about an hour after I get home. I check the time and notice it's close to eleven o'clock at night.

I ordered pizza for dinner and picked up some Coronas on my way home. Tonight we will be hanging out, then tomorrow we will train together, and the next day I've got a competition to win.

Axel walks through the front door and slides the straps of his waders off his shoulders. "Oh, thank God! You ordered pizza... and you got beers. Fuck, I could marry you right now,"

I cringe. "I'm flattered, but I'm pretty sure that's illegal in Oregon. Plus, I love you but I could never fuck you."

"Don't make it fucking weird." Axel smirks, then sits down on the leather couch, and cracks open a beer. "What did Big Rich want? To kiss the race-king's ass again?"

I scoff as the smell of fish and sea water rushes through my nose and makes me want to vomit. I'm instantly on my feet. I swipe up the pizza box and rush to the recliner across from the coffee table, ignoring Axel's explicits. "You need a damn shower man. You smell like shit."

He looks down at himself. "What? I smell like every strip club on seafood Sunday."

"Blaming your ex-girlfriend for your poor hygiene is a low blow."

Axel stares at me slack-jawed for a second before we both start busting up laughing.

In between catching his breath he says. "Answer my question, then I'll go take a shower-"

"And wash the couch," I add.

He rolls his eyes but agrees. "And wash the couch."

"Big Rich didn't say much. Just mentioned that there's a new rider from Reno, with an EnduroCross title, racing this year."

Axel chokes on a bite of pizza. He must have snagged a piece before I swiped the box. "Shit. Are you nervous? I know how much DuneFest means to you." He stands and heads towards the stairs.

I shake my head and open the box to grab another slice. "Nah... it's still my title. My town. My race."

"I see your ego is still intact," he says as he slugs me in the shoulder then reaches into the box and steals another piece before running up the stairs.

"You fucker!"

"You might want to prepare for a loss. You have to be just as good at losing, as you are at winning!" he shouts at me from upstairs.

"Where the fuck did you get that from? Is it on this pizza box?" I lift up the grease stained cardboard and pretend like I'm looking for this mysterious piece of advice my older brother just gave me. There's four years between us, but it's never felt like it.

He laughs. I can barely hear him as he shouts over the sound of running water. "I'm just looking out for you lil bro."

"Thanks, but I don't need it!"

I'm not scared.

Whoever this new racer is...

He will learn who I am soon enough.

Chapter Three

Claire

The last five hours of driving from Reno to Oregon was... boring. It has been mostly flat.

However, this trip with Dad is just what I needed. We laughed, sang karaoke, ate way too much beef jerky, and drank way too much Gatorade. Through it all, I could feel the little broken pieces of my soul putting themselves back together.

We only have an hour left till we arrive in Medford, and the last part of this drive is the best. We are passing through a couple of towns called Yreka and Ashland. As soon as we hit the mountain range I roll down my window, and take in the deepest breath of fresh air. I never knew air could smell so good. It smells like pine trees, evergreens, lake water, and the smallest hint of campfire. If I could, I would bottle up this feeling and these smells, and breathe it in for therapy on my worst days. I rest my forearm on the edge of the car door and lean my head out the window letting the scene and smells wash over me. The crisp morning air rushes over my skin causing my hair to bellow behind me as I close my eyes.

How long has it been since I have taken a deep breath?

I have been longing for this alone time with my father. Ever since I moved back in with him, he has been slammed at work and then we planned for our move. So really it's just been one thing right after the next.

My dad is my best friend, and as a child it seemed like we had more time together. Like we had more opportunities to mess around and have fun. Whether that was riding or working on one of his project cars or simply watching Fast and Furious together. I miss those times. I miss the days when everything was easier and I didn't have a weight hanging on my shoulders.

We are staying at the Super 8 Motel. Nothing impressive, but perfect for Dad and I. The upside is it does have a water slide so I guess that's pretty fancy in some people's books.

Our hotel is actually a little outside of Medford, in a small town called Central Point. In order to get there we have to drive through Main Street. It is adorable, the city is lined with old school brick buildings filled with boutiques and local restaurants. The street is bustling with people talking and hanging out in the summer sun.

It makes me anxious to think about living in my own small town.

"It says turn right here." I let him know. As the passenger you are always the designated navigation system. And heaven forbid if you accidentally miss a turn.

We pull into the small parking lot and I jump out to unhook the U-Haul, while Dad grabs our bags and checks us in.

It's about six in the evening, so we scour the internet for a local restaurant to grab food at. We end up choosing a place called The Point Pub & Grill. It's towards the end of Main Street, but we park further up the road so we can walk along the sidewalk and stop in to visit some of the local shops.

It feels good to be on my feet and not sitting in the truck. I lost track of how many times my ass fell asleep on our drive over here.

After we spend some time exploring Central Point, we head to the restaurant.

As soon as we walk through the glass doors, a waitress leads us to our seats and Dad takes the chair across from mine. "How are you feeling?"

I shrug. "Good, actually. I thought I would be more sad to leave Reno, but honestly it feels nice to be out. Plus, Oregon is beautiful. I think I was born for the mountains." I look down at my menu and search for what I want to eat for dinner. "How are you feeling?"

"I don't know yet." He sighs and takes a drink of his water. "I am excited but a piece of me will always belong in that big-little city." He looks over at me and smiles. "I raised you there in that cottage and those are my favorite memories, it's hard to leave them behind."

I return his smile but ignore the sentiment.

If I think about it too much the anxiety comes barreling back, and I don't have the heart to tell the man sitting across from me that there are a lot of things I am thankful to leave behind in that town. And how I feel selfish for letting one traumatizing memory ruin all of the adventures we've had.

A waitress comes over and takes our order. I choose the Chicken Bacon Mac & Cheese and Dad decides to get the Beer Battered Fish.

I'm scanning over the pictures of the truck I plan on purchasing when he breaks the silence. "Let me see the pictures of the truck again."

"How did you know that's what I was looking at?" I hand him my phone.

Without blinking an eye, he says. "Your features twist into the same expression mine does when planning to break apart a vehicle."

He starts flipping through the pictures when the waitress returns with our meals. I catch the way she stares a little too long at my father and roll my eyes in response.

"Is there anything else I can get you?" she says in a sultry voice, her attention never leaving my dad.

He smiles up at her and I swear her knees falter. "No." He looks over at me for confirmation, I shake my head. "That's all. Thank you."

Once she is out of sight, I take my phone back from my father. "Will that ever end?"

"What do you mean?" He smirks at me fiendishly and takes a bite of his food. His face lights up. "Holy shit, that's good!"

I take a bite of my food and raise my eyebrows in response to the explosion of flavors on my tongue. "My god, yeah it is!"

With our bellies full and satisfied we head back to the hotel to wash up and get some rest.

In our room we play a couple rounds of UNO, watch a few episodes of Prison Break, and then we get some much needed sleep.

The morning light seeps in through the hotel curtains waking me up before my alarm. I roll over onto my side and check my phone before I get up and get ready for the day. The blue light from my screen causes me to squint.

I notice I have a few missed calls, a couple from Han, one

from an unknown number, and a handful of texts.

I click on Han and I's message thread.

Hannah Banana

Hannah: Did you make it to Medford alright?

Hannah: hello!! you know I am prone to panic attacks when it comes to you..

Hannah: I promise I will call the police department on your ass if you don't respond by the morning!!!

Hannah: your officially on my shit list

Hannah: I can't even use the right *you're* because I'm so mad at you

Fuck, I am the worst friend on the planet.
I sit up on the bed and text out a reply.

Me: I'm sorry. Please don't kill me. I was so distracted by hangin out with Dad, I left my phone at the hotel during dinner.

Me: Then passed out shortly after we got back. We are alive and about to get breakfast then head out. Ilysm and I'll make it up to you. I pinky swear.

Her response comes back instantly.

Hannah: A good mafia romance will suffice as an apology..

Hannah: just so you know I will not forgive you if it happens twice.

Me: *googles good mafia romances*

Me: I'll do one better and call you when I get settled into the house in Reedsport.

Hannah: I want the Dark Verse series by Runyx. Tell google to fuck off. Fine I guess that's okay. Love you long time.

Me: Love you long time.

I set my phone down on the side table then throw the white comforter off my body. When I look across the room I notice Dad is already gone—probably to go grab breakfast. I hop off the bed and get dressed.

I walk into the bathroom to fix my hair and do my best to not smell like I have been traveling in a car for the last day. When I look into the mirror, I see my curly hair sticking up in every direction, some areas flat against my head and some so tangled I swear a small animal lives inside.

I sigh and grab my spray bottle. Wetting it down— almost completely—I comb through it then squirt some of my curl cream into my hands and run it along the strands.

Well, that's as good as it's going to get.

I stare back at my reflection and take a deep breath. Gripping the countertop, I take a few minutes to really look at myself. I know I should be reciting self affirmations of some shit like that but the only thing that comes to mind is... *coward.* Tears begin to build in the corner of my eyes and I shake them away. After snapping myself out of the feeling, I shove all of my cosmetics into my travel bag and begin to clean up from last night.

After I pack up the few things I had laying around, I zip up my suitcase.

I'm stripping off the bed sheets when I hear the beep for the hotel door and shortly after, Dad steps through. He has a coffee, bagel, yogurt, and a banana from the hotel's complimentary breakfast in each hand.

Shutting the door with his foot, he acknowledges me from across the room. "Good morning."

"Good morning." I respond as he walks over and hands me my breakfast. "Thank you."

"No problem. Are you all packed up and ready to go?"

"Yup! Did it first thing after I woke up." I take a sip of my coffee and hum my approval. Black with a little bit of honey, just how I like it.

"Sweet, let's go then. We can eat in the truck."

"Sounds good."

We leave all the sheets and blankets in a pile in the corner, and in a separate pile we leave the towels. We accumulate our trash, grab our suitcase, return our key cards, and head down to the truck. After we hook up the U-Haul again, we set out for home.

Home.

It still doesn't feel real that we will be living on the beach or any other place besides Reno.

He eases us onto the freeway and the weight of what we are doing finally settles in. This time tomorrow I'll be waking up in a new home, a new room, a new town. Not Reno. I'm trying to sort through the feelings coursing through me. I can't decide if I am riddled with feelings of excitement and happiness, or stress and anxiety.

"Last stretch, Mini. Just three hours till we will be in our new house."

"I can't wait to see it in person."

Dad purchased the cutest faded blue beach house I have ever seen. It is a three story house stacked up on a hill. There's a wrap-around deck on the second level that overlooks the mountain range. The driveway has a stone wall leading up the bottom level of the house and its entire floor is a garage and shop area (perfect for working on our bikes). The third floor is my room. I have my own bathroom and a small living area attached to the right of the staircase. There's two small windows overlooking the town, and a window in my bedroom where I can see across the street.

I sold my 4Runner right before moving. I pitched in half of what I made for a down payment, because we both loved the house so much. With the move being last minute, Dad couldn't afford it on his own. He told me he would pay me back in less than a year, but I am not worried about it.

I searched for weeks on *Marketplace* for a new vehicle and happened upon a Kentucky blue and white 1969 Ford F-250. I am not mad. This is a trade I will welcome any day. There are a few things Dad and I will have to fix, but neither of us complain about digging into an engine. Plus, the salesman—Rodney—said it'll drive and that's all I need it to do for now.

"Do you need to pick up your truck today? Or can you pick it up after DuneFest?"

Leave it to my dad to be able to read my thoughts, *again*.

"I *mean*... I'd rather pick it up today but it's not on the top of my to-do list."

"I can drop you off at the shop when we get into town. You can pick up your truck, and then just meet me back at the house to unpack."

"That sounds great! Thank you."

"No problem, you already have the address to our house right?"

"Yeah. I already programmed it in my maps as, *home.*"
Home.

There was that word again. I don't know if this will ever feel real, or if these feelings will ever settle.

I feel a light shake on my shoulder, waking me from my sleep. "Mini, we are here."

I must have fallen asleep for the last hour of our trip.

I didn't think I was that tired, but I guess all the overwhelming thoughts and feelings put me on my ass.

I rub the exhaustion from my eyes and sit up to peek out my window. The 'Welcome to Reedsport: Gateway to the Dunes' sign flashes by as we drive into town.

"We made it... it's beautiful," I say as I soak in the view around me.

"It sure is."

Downtown Reedsport is just as cute as Central Point, maybe even a little bit more. Old style buildings line both sides of the main road. Every few feet, lamp posts with the most beautiful arrangement of pink flowers tower over us. In front of us—just behind the town—all kinds of beautiful green trees transcend toward the sky.

"What's the name of the shop you're picking up your truck from?"

I reluctantly take my eyes off exploring the town and grab my phone from my back pocket. Pulling up my conversation with Rodney Price, I scan through our texts for the shop name.

"Jeremy's Automotive and Off-road. It's from a private seller and this is where he told me to meet him,"

"Do you want me to stay behind with you to make sure everything goes smoothly?"

"No. It's okay, it may be stupid but I trust him. He gave me a complete rundown of the truck in extensive detail and sent me a handful of pictures."

"Okay, just call me if you have any issues."

"I will."

Another perk of a small town, it takes less than five minutes to get anywhere. Before I know it, Dad pulls into the shop. I give him a kiss on the cheek, grab my bag, and jump out of the truck. I wave back to Dad through his rear view mirror as he pulls out of the parking lot and drives out of sight.

I'm only waiting a few minutes when a man pulls up next to me in a big black lifted Chevy, and right beside him is a younger man—only a few years older than me— in my new Kentucky blue baby.

The older man, I'm assuming Rodney, walks over to me and extends his hand.

"Hi, I'm Rodney Price and this is my son Axel." He gestures to the younger man standing beside him. "Are you Claire?"

I take his hand and introduce myself. "Hi, yes. I'm Claire Gates. It's nice to meet you guys." Then I turn to Axel and shake his hand. "So this is her?" I point to the truck behind them.

"Yeah, it belonged to my younger son before he decided to buy a Bronco," Rodney replies.

"Well, that worked out great for me." I step to the side of Rodney and walk over to the truck. Hopping into the driver's seat, I pop the hood, and turn it over. The check engine light flashes. "I see that the check engine light is on. Do you know if it is the catalytic converter, emissions system, or sensor?"

"I'm sorry, I don't. My brother was the one who drove it, he would have a better idea. In the glove box, there should be a run down from the last time it was in the shop."

"Have you swapped out the engine at all? Or I guess, do you know if your brother did?"

Axel shakes his head. "Not that I know of."

"So it most likely has the original V8 engine with a three speed automatic transmission?"

He huffs out a breath. "You would know more than I would." He looks over at Rodney.

"Yes, it has the original engine."

"Impressive." I hop out of the truck and walk up to the front. My next mission is checking the alternator. "I ordered new brake pins because I noticed in the picture you sent me they looked a bit corroded." With one hand braced on the hood I point to the battery's positive terminal. "I guess possibly a faulty voltage regulator with corrosion on the battery as well?" I look over at Rodney and he shrugs his shoulders. Turning my attention back to the truck, "Along with some cosmetic damage on the grill and rear bumper. I ordered replacements and the new parts should be here by next Saturday. You mentioned it was idling pretty high in our messages, so I went ahead and bought a new air filter and ordered some throttle body and air cleaner. I'll clean out the throttle and replace the air filter, then she should be as good as new." I slam the hood shut and look over at them. "Is there anything else I should know about?"

Axel whistles and exchanges a look with Rodney. "You know your stuff, don't you?"

"I've been working on cars, trucks, bikes, 4-wheelers, basically anything with an engine since I was old enough to hold a wrench," I inform Axel, who is still staring at me like he is discovering a new species of woman.

"I'm happy to know she's in good hands, she's been in the family for awhile," Rodney tells me. An unidentifiable emotion on his face. Sadness? Gratitude? I can't tell.

I do my best to reassure him just in case. "She will be, sir. I appreciate you selling her to me."

He exhales a sigh of relief.

I couldn't imagine all the memories this truck may hold for their family. It must be hard for him to let go. I wonder if like my home in Reno, this truck is one of those inanimate objects that hold significant memories for him.

Rodney signs the papers over to me and I give him cash. We shake hands one more time, they welcome me into town, and then I watch as they climb into Rodney's Chevy and take off.

After they disappear down the street, I climb into my new ride and start her up. As for me... I'm heading to my new home.

Home.

Still so weird to process. The only place I've ever known was Reno. Now, I guess I will have Reedsport as well.

The truck drives great all the way to the house and I know this was a good buy just by how the truck feels under my hands. With some minor fixes, we will have a long life together. It's refreshing to see everything about this move going smoothly thus far. Hopefully it continues to go that way. I pull into the driveway, just as I see Dad walk out of the garage.

"That truck is beautiful, just like its driver," he says as he approaches my new ride and opens the door for me. I hop out and stand next to him.

His compliment causes my face to light up. "Thank you."

He places his arm over my shoulder, and we both look up at our new house.

"Mom would have loved this place," I say out loud before I can realize the full gravity of this moment.

I'm not the only one leaving memories behind in Reno.

That's where my parents met.

Where they bought their first home as teenagers.

Where he brought me home from the hospital. *Alone.*

I see his shoulders slump a little as he smiles softly. "Yes... yes she would have."

Even though Mom isn't here, I can still feel the love she had for us tucked into every piece of our lives. I only feel that way because my dad has done such a good job sharing pieces of her with me, and he never made me feel uncomfortable to ask questions. In fact, he reveled in the opportunity to talk about her.

I envy the love they used to share, that he still has for her. I only hope someday I will be just as lucky to have a love like theirs.

I would like to see him move on eventually, though. He deserves to be happy. It has been way too long since he has even attempted dating.

"We better get to it, we've got a lot of work ahead of us if we want to be ready for DuneFest." He unhooks the lock from the U-Haul and slides the door open.

"I packed all the supplies and things we would need for DuneFest right in the front. And as you can see, I also used the tool box and storage cabinet as a barrier to keep things from falling forward as we were driving,"

"Smart thinking, Mini. That'll make separating the things we need immediately, and the stuff we can take care of later, a lot easier. But we still have to unload all of this so we can return the U-Haul by nine tonight."

"We better get busy then." I smile at him.

The first things we unload are the supplies we will need for DuneFest and we set them closest to the garage door for easy access. Then we unpack box after box after box. We put mostly everything into the garage and shop area. The only things we bring into the house are our beds, the kitchen table, and basic necessities we will need for the night. The rest will have to wait till after DuneFest.

I step into my bedroom for what seems like the millionth time today. Although, this is the first opportunity I have had to really look around. I walk over to my window and pull open the blinds. It seems a little stuffy in here so I crack it open. I will never get used to the way the air smells here in Oregon. It smells like something straight out of Bath & Body Works.

Even though the view from my window is mostly taken up by our neighbor's house—who I plan on introducing myself to later—I can still see the river in the distance and our whole street is surrounded by evergreens, pine trees, and these beautiful bushes with striking orange flowers on them. I haven't been in Reedsport long, but if I had to choose one word to describe it, it would be *beautiful*.

Dad and I head out to drop off the U-Haul and stop by the grocery store to stock up on food for the four day camping trip at DuneFest. I thought that we would just be tent camping, but Dad surprises me when we pull into the grocery store parking lot and he parks next to a camping trailer with a 'For Sale' sign in the back window.

A woman in her late thirties jumps out of the truck that is currently hauling the trailer. She is beautiful. She has gorgeous red hair, her eyes are golden brown, and tiny freckles dot her nose. She has a natural glow to her and I can't help but notice how Dads breath gets caught in his throat at the sight of her.

"Hi! Are you Jesse?" Her voice feels like bubbles. I don't even know if that makes sense, but it's accurate. "I'm Tattie! It's nice to meet you, welcome to Reedsport!" Dad goes in to shake her hand but instead she puts her arms out wide and goes in for a hug. "Sorry, I'm more of a hugger than a hand shaker. And who might you be?" She turns to me, pulling me into her embrace. She smells like chocolate chip cookies.

I think I'm in love with this woman.

"I'm Claire, it's nice to meet you."

"Claire." She rolls my name around in her mouth like she is tasting it. "That's beautiful,"

"Thank you. I love your hair."

"Thanks, I was born with it." Her voice is playful as she throws her hair over her shoulder. Exaggerating every movement.

It's then I notice Dad hasn't said a single word, so I elbow him in the side. It seems to do the trick and he snaps out of his trance. Tattie giggles at the interaction.

"So... um... I have the cash with me in the truck. I'll just take a quick look at the trailer then we can sign over papers and everything else," he says. I pinch my lips together trying to hold in my laughter. I've never seen Dad this flustered. It's cute. He walks past Tattie and straight to the trailer. He turns around so fast he almost trips over his own foot. "Oh... and it's nice to meet you too, Tattie." I'm unable to hold in my laughter at the fact that this thirty-nine year old man is still just as flustered when faced with a beautiful woman as a teenage boy. I send him a thumbs up. He just glares at me in response.

Tattie and I chat while Dad checks out the trailer. She tells me about a few spots in town that we have to check out, like the lighthouse and the pier. I know it's unlikely, but if everyone in town is as welcoming as Rodney, Axel, and Tattie, then we are going to be more than happy here.

They finish up exchanging paperwork and cash. Then she gives both of us one more hug. This time something changes in Dads expression as they hold onto each other a little longer then a usual hug should last.

He must notice it as well because his facial expression changes from one of bliss to one of alarm. "Well we better get going," Dad says as he pushes Tattie away. I shake my head in disappointment.

"It was nice to meet the both of you. I hope to see you guys around town!"

"You too! Thank you Tattie." I say in response.

Dad and I climb into his truck. The trailer loaded up on the tow hitch behind us.

"She's beautiful."

Dad is spaced out, his eyes are locked onto his dash. "Mhmm..." He shakes his head a little. "Wh—what did you say?"

"*I said*, she's beautiful."

"Oh... yeah," he responds as he turns the key in the ignition.

"You know, I was wondering if we were going to get food for this trip or just starve instead?" I give him a sly smile. I'm messing with him and he knows it.

He looks at me from the corner of his eye and chuckles. "It's that obvious, huh?"

"Just a little bit," I say as I hover my pointer finger over my thumb. "You should ask her out."

"I'll think about it." He turns off the truck and pulls his key out of the ignition. "Let's go get some food."

I don't push him anymore because I know that's all he'll give me.

We stock up mostly on snacks and drinks. For dinner we will have hot dogs and hamburgers. They are the easiest to make while camping. But on the last night we will have taco salad in a bag which is a right of passage if you're camping with the Gates. And also, absolutely delicious.

After shopping, we swing by a local restaurant and grab some take out. We make it home just after eight. Now we are sitting down at the table, enjoying some Mexican food.

"How are you feeling about the race tomorrow?" Dad asks me as he takes a bite of his burrito. Opening day of DuneFest is the Infiniti Huck (a jump competition). This is when riders will show off their Heelclickers, Airplanes, Whips, Nac Nacs, and if you can get enough air, Cliffhangers, or Superman's. The FreeStyle Show is the following day. After that, ShortCross, the one I'm looking forward to the least. On the last evening of DuneFest, is the Night Race, an all out battle through the sand. The challenge: you have to ride by the guidance of the sunset and lights of your fellow riders. I'm most excited about that one.

"I'm ready. I'm just excited to ride, I don't really care about winning. Taking home an EnduroCross title was amazing, but after all that training and pressure, it really took the fun out of it for me." I take a deep breath. "I'm just ready to ride for myself again and DuneFest is the perfect opportunity for that. And if I come home with a trophy, it'll only be a bonus."

DuneFest doesn't only offer a handful of Motocross competitions, there's also corn hole, concerts, Pit Bike races, the Tire Toss, Barrel Racing, and the Drag Strip. After the stress of leaving UNLV, not being able to find a job, and moving to another state;I cannot wait to be camping on the sand, the smell of gas, and the sound of roaring engines ringing in my ears for the next four days.

"It's nice to see you smiling and enjoying what you love again." Dad sighs. "I finally have my Mini back."

He's right, I haven't been the same since I moved back to Reno from UNLV. But just a few hours in Reedsport has already returned some of the light that I've lost.

After Dad and I finish up our food, I head upstairs to take a shower and get ready for bed. It's going to be so nice to wash away all the junk from today.

I walk into my bathroom and turn on the water. After I strip away my dirty clothes, I step into the shower. The warm water runs down my back and my entire body softens. Releasing all the tension I've built up from preparing for this move. I don't think I've taken a deep breath since we passed through the mountains in Ashland.

I really need some rest after these last couple of days.

I turn off the shower and wrap my towel around me. I walk from the bathroom to my bedroom and lock the door. Once I'm in my room, I strip off my towel and begin to wring out my hair. When I look up I realize I made a terrible mistake.

I freeze.

Shit.

I forgot that I opened my window earlier when we were unpacking to let some air in.

"Fuck."

Of course *he* lives next door.

Not only am I naked standing in front of my wide open bedroom window, but across the street is Rodney's son—Axel—staring right at me. His mouth dropped open.

The universe has a sick way of playing games.

As soon as we make eye contact he smirks, waves, and walks back into his house. I quickly wrap the towel around me.

Why the fuck didn't I do that sooner?

I run to the window slamming it shut and pulling the blinds closed.

Leaning against the window sill, I close my eyes, and mutter a few curse words.

Great. Just great.

Not only am I new in town, but now I'll be known as the naked neighbor.

Chapter Four

Dustin

Today is the first morning of DuneFest.

Axel and I have been up since four. He packed his bag after he got home from work last night, and we were about to leave the house when I got a text from Mom saying she and Dad wouldn't be leaving until five. So, my brother and I are sitting around the kitchen island eating some last minute breakfast.

"I can't believe you saw our next door neighbor naked! And that you didn't tell me until this morning."

Axel smirks into his cup of coffee. "It's not that big of a deal."

I raise my eyebrows at him. "Oh sure... so we are just going to pretend you weren't blaring Mariah Carey while taking an extra long shower last night."

He chokes on his coffee, spitting it back into his cup. "I don't know whether to be appalled or impressed that you know Ms. Mariah is my go to." He reaches behind him and grabs an apple, throwing it at my head. I catch it before it can hit me.

Turning it over, I examine the apple in my hand, then take a bite.

"Was she hot?"

"I think you already know the answer to that."

"This was the same girl that bought my truck?" I saw it parked across the street last night. It's weird to think that it will still be within walking distance, but it is no longer mine.

"Yeah, I was honestly pretty impressed by her. She knew her shit when it came to trucks. Apparently, she has been working in a shop with her dad for a long time."

"Hmmm..."

"I know that look." He shakes his head. "She's not your type, man. She is confident, independent, and you like the type of girls who are..." He squints, filtering through that peanut sized brain of his. "How do I put this... oh yeah! Needy."

I scoff and throw my half eaten apple at him. "You're wrong."

"Gross, why did I catch that?" He lets the apple core drop to the ground like it's carrying a disease.

"I'm not looking to date anyone right now, anyway."

"Or ever."

Axel's right, but I'm not gonna tell him that.

I don't have time for anything else. I am focusing on myself and my future. It has been that way since I was in high school, and it's not going to change now.

The two girls that I did date wanted more from me. They needed more attention, they wanted me to focus on building our relationship, *blah, blah, blah*— shit like that. And I just couldn't give that to them. Plus, we live in a small town. Every girl my age I've known since we were children, and there is *no one* it would actually work out with.

I have plenty of time to find my future wife later on. For now, it's all about me and Motocross.

My phone vibrates on the kitchen countertop. I pick it up and I see I have a text message from Mom.

"Mom just texted saying they are loaded up and ready to head out."

"Let's go, then." Axel dumps the rest of his coffee into the sink and grabs his keys off the counter.

He is hauling the bikes in the bed of his truck, and I will be following behind him in my Bronco. Since I have the canopy on, I set up a bed in the back. That's where I'll be sleeping for DuneFest, and Axel has a hard shell tent attached to the roof of his Tacoma. It's the perfect set up because we won't take up much space on the sand, leaving more room for our parents' camp trailer.

I lock up the front door and jog down the steps to our driveway. Before I climb into the driver's seat, I glance across the street. I notice that the camping trailer I spotted last night, and my old truck, is gone. I'd seen their bikes strapped up, and I'm assuming they are headed to Winchester Bay for DuneFest. The drive is only fifteen minutes, but you want to get there early because camping on the sand is first come first serve.

Good for them.

My mind can't help but wonder who the mysterious girl in the upstairs window across the street is. I'd be lying if I didn't admit that I might be a little envious that Axel was outside last night grabbing the mail, instead of me.

As expected, it is only five-fifteen in the morning and the bay is already booming. There are hundreds of camping trailers, trucks, RVs, and pop up tents on both sides of the sand. Making a one way path down the bay. Set up right before the tracks is a booth, that's where we will need to get our wristbands. But first we need to find a spot that will be able to fit all of us.

Luckily, it is still early enough that we are able to find a good spot closer to the front. We unload everything pretty quickly. After we get the pop up tent set up, the first order of business is unloading the bikes. Once they are on their stands we begin to unload everything else.

While Mom heads over to the check in booth, Axel, Dad, and I get to work. We do a complete rundown to make sure that my bike is in the clear for the race.

I am in the middle of adjusting my suspension when Big Rich walks up to me and claps a hand on my back. "There's our SandMaster."

"Hey, Big Rich. How's it going?"

"Going well, all the racers are checked in and we are about to announce the start of the Infiniti Huck. I just wanted to tell you that the new racer is right over there." Big Rich turns and points. I follow his finger to a set up across the sand and off to the right. Which just happens to be home to my old truck.

Of course.

"They are number 87, last name Gates. Figured you might want to introduce yourself."

"Thanks, I appreciate it."

"No problem, good luck out there, man. Not like you're gonna need it." He gives me another pat on my back and then heads back the way he came.

After I finish tightening the suspension on my bike, I wipe my hands off on a rag, and head over to introduce myself. I'm already dressed head to toe in my classic mint and gray Fox riding gear. Mom picked out this set for me because she says they look good with my blonde hair, and something else about how they bring out my green eyes; but I really don't care either way. Mom always missed out on these kinds of things with having two boys, so letting her pick out my racing gear was the least I could do.

I am ready to race, all I am waiting for now is the announcement over the intercom.

As I approach the pop up tent with the number 87 on it, I notice there is a woman sitting on a bench swapping out a rear tire for a paddle tire. On the bike stand is a black and gold Hawk DLX 250. I lean against the light post near her campsite and cross my arms over my chest.

Her black curly hair is tied into a braid that runs along her back almost reaching her ass. I follow the curve of her spine till I notice a little bit of ink poking out between the black tank top she is wearing, and the dark gray cargo pants she has on. It looks like script work but I can't tell from this distance. Her muscles pull tight along her shoulder blades and back as she tightens her suspension. I don't know which God made her but I think I finally have a reason to worship. When I look away from admiring her beautiful body, her eyes meet mine. They are the lightest blue I have ever seen, I already feel myself drowning in them.

"Can I help you?" she hitches her eyebrow at me.

Shit.

She is absolutely gorgeous and I have just been caught staring at her ass and tattoo.

Way to go, Dustin.

I shake my head trying to get out from under the trance she just put on me. "Uhh... yeah, sorry. I was looking for my new competition." I clear my throat. "I was curious if your brother or father is around?"

She furrows her brow, and I watch the light drain from her eyes. Her stare is cold, absolutely freezing. I'm pretty sure I just involuntarily shivered.

Somehow, I've already fucked this up.

And I find myself wanting to do whatever I can to get the light back into them, and mad at myself for being the reason they became so cold to begin with.

She turns her body to face me better and rests her hands on her knees. A spanner wrench in one hand and a dirty rag in the other. Her hands are covered in grease and black streaks line her forehead disappearing under the backwards hat she has on.

I have never been so attracted to someone in my entire life.

"You know they just left." She has a sarcastic tone in her voice. "But I could tell them you stopped by..." It takes me a minute to realize she is waiting for me to introduce myself.

"Sorry... Dustin."

"*Dustin.*" My name is laced with disdain as she repeats it.

For some reason, that makes me angry. Not because of how she said it, but because I have a feeling I made her say it like that.

I want to take her cheeks into my hands and kiss her full pink lips until she moans my name. I want her to only associate my name with passion and happiness.

What in the actual fuck is going on?

"Right, umm... well, tell them I said good luck, I guess." Somehow my twenty three years of speaking the English language just flies out the door.

"I will be sure to tell my *brother* and *father* you stopped by and said good luck." She says father and brother with a sarcastic tone, and I feel like I just messed up big time. The only problem is, I don't know how. The only thing I seem to be able to focus on is her.

"Uh... thanks. I guess I'll see you around."

She gives me a short nod, rolls those lustrous arctic eyes, and then turns back around to her work on her bike and bearings.

Clearly, I'm being dismissed.

I catch one more glance at her tattoo and the curve of her ass before walking away. I want to know what the rest of her tattoo looks like. Where does it stop? Does it go all the way up? Does it curve along her hips?

God, those hips.

I shake my head, again.

When I get back to our tent, Axel has finished swapping out my rear tire for a paddle, and stiffened the sag on my bike. He already has it fueled up as well. The only thing I have to do now is get a beautiful girl off my mind, and win a race.

"Hey, man."

"Hey..." I know my face looks all kinds of fucked up right now because my mind is running wild over the last few minutes trying to figure out what the fuck I did to receive the cold shoulder from Gates. Axel reads it instantly.

"What's up?" Axel questions as he grabs a rag and wipes the grease off his fingers.

"Nothing really... I just met our new neighbor and went to introduce myself—Oh shit!" My hand collides with my face and I drag it down to my chin in utter disappointment. "I didn't even ask her for her name. I totally brushed her off, I basically acted like she wasn't there."

Axel raises his eyebrows and chuckles. "Well, you're officially a grade A asshole. No wonder you've never had a girlfriend."

"Coming from mister one and done, himself."

He points a spanner wrench at me. "You got me there."

All of a sudden I remember that Axel saw her naked last night and my jaw clenches in response.

Am I jealous of him?

What is going on with me?

Chapter Five

Dustin

For the last four hours I have been trying to get my mind back on track.

I need to focus on the Infinti Huck, but everytime I close my eyes and try to bring my mind back to the race ahead, the only thing I can think about is *her*.

Her icy blue eyes, curvy hips, full lips, and that beautiful black hair that hangs down to her waist. Then I find myself uncomfortably hard in front of my family, and you can only readjust your junk so many times before someone assumes you have a disease or worse—you're a perv.

I've never felt like this before.

I don't like not being in control of myself.

Sure, there's beautiful women all over town, but not a single one has ever made me lose focus. My riding career has always taken precedence over my love life. I've always been able to compartmentalize my desires from my goals. But this woman has all my attention, she is the only thing I'm concerned with at the moment. And that's a big fucking issue.

"Hey, bro. Are you good? You look like you're gonna be sick." I have been zoning out a ridiculous amount of times in the last four hours. Probably from using all the remaining mental strength I have to shake off a girl I just met *hours ago*.

God, I'm pathetic.

"Yeah, I just need something to get her off my mind." I run my hands through my hair.

"Who? Claire?"

"So that's her name... Claire. It's beautiful." I say almost in a daydream.

He frowns at me. "What the fuck is wrong with you?"

I throw my hands out to the side. "Dude... I don't know! That's the problem."

Axel's eyebrows shoot up to his forehead as a few people walking by stop and look at me.

"It's a side effect of hitting puberty late," he explains on my behalf and shakes his head. "Nasty little anger issues."

I chuckle. "Sorry." I tell the strangers passing by. They roll their eyes at me, and continue on.

I have never snapped at Axel before.

Maybe I just need to apologize to Claire. Maybe I'm just concerned because I acted like a total douchebag, and that's completely out of character for me. I think I'm stressed because I don't want her first impression of me to be a bad one.

Yeah, that has to be it.

I'll go over there, I'll apologize, and then I can shake her off forever.

"I'm sorry, man. I think I just need to apologize to her. I feel like such an ass." I stand up from the camping chair I am sitting in next to Axel. "I'll be right back." I'm about to walk over to Claire's trailer when I hear Big Rich's voice come on over the loudspeakers.

"*We are now lining up all contestants for the Infiniti Huck. Please report to the check in table towards the front—next to the track. All contestants please have your numbers pinned to your riding gear. Be safe out there and best of luck to everyone."*

"I guess that apology is just gonna have to wait. It's time to race," Axel says as he stands up next to me. "Listen, don't worry about it right now. You need to go out there and focus on you." He puts me in a headlock and runs his knuckles along the top of my head. "Don't forget you owe me one for being an ass earlier."

I laugh and shove him away. "Victory beer on me."

"Now we're talkin'." He hangs his arm over my shoulder. "Let's go, you've got a competition to win." My parents have always been supportive, but my big brother is my rock. The one person who knows me better than anyone else.

Mom and Dad meet us at the starting gate.

The Infiniti Huck track is a course packed tight into the sand, running roughly three miles long. Coming right out of the starting gate there is a bermed corner about a quarter of a mile down, sending you to the right. Following that, riders will hit a step on, over a table top, and finish on a step off. This is where you'll see a lot of Nac Nacs, Heelclickers, and Whips. Then after that, you will hit a flat left corner that sends you to a set of rollers, followed by a ski jump. Right before the end is a sweeping turn that will lead you into a set of whoops. Finishing it off is a straight away—close to a mile long— leading you right into a booter. This is where you'll see all of the competitors sending it. Giving it their all. Where every rider will pull out the best trick in their book to hopefully win over the judges and take home a trophy. DuneFest coordinators conveniently placed the bleachers right in front of this jump. If the pressure of doing your best wasn't enough to jack up your nerves, adding the pressure of not eating a soil sample in front of hundreds of people will definitely do the trick.

There are many perks to being the SandMaster, but starting first for the Infiniti Huck is not one of them. That means I will have to go all out and not fuck up, because if I do? Well, then I've just given everyone else an easy chance at beating me. I have two laps to try and impress the judges. Two laps to try and secure a win.

I slide up my kickstand with the heel of my boot and walk my bike over to the starting gate. I swing my leg over, and sit down. It's then that I notice my dad walking toward me. I can't help but look past him, towards the rest of the competitors lined up and waiting for their chance to steal my title. I can't lie to myself, I know what my true intentions are. I'm trying to spot Claire, or the black and gold 250 with the number 87 on it. But I'm unable to see either of them.

I strap on my gloves, pull down my goggles, and start up my bike as my dad approaches me.

"You ready, son?"

"Of course, Dad. It's the same every year."

"Remember to stay humble." He scolds me. "It may be just like every other year but that doesn't mean the riders are the same. Nothing is ever given. It's always earned." His eyebrow arches. I nod to let him know I hear him loud and clear. "Don't forget to let the big dog eat," he says. Meaning, sit back and twist the throttle to let my bike get as much traction and power into the ground as possible before taking off.

"Always."

He gives me a fist bump and then heads over to the bleachers to sit with Mom and Axel. Once again I find myself scanning the crowd for any sign of *her*. No luck.

Any second now that green flag will drop and it will just be me and this bike, nothing else. No pressure hanging on my shoulders. No Dad breathing down my neck. Just me and the crackling of exhaust.

I take a deep breath, and watch as the man in the tower drops the green flag, releasing the starting gate.

I launch my front tire up and over the metal bar, setting myself up for a great turn into the bermed corner. I come out of the right and get ready to hit the step on. As I extend my legs to the right side and tilt my upper body backward, I fly over the table top. Giving the crowd an Up-Nac.

A few people whistle and chant my name.

I blitz over the whoops, and hit the straightaway.

I adjust my speed, making sure I achieve the necessary momentum to lift off the jump face. Centering my body on the bike, and firming my grip on the handlebars, I prepare myself for the stunt ahead.

As my front wheel soars off the lip, I extend my legs backward, pushing my body off the foot pegs. In one fluid motion, I release the grip on my handlebars, and disconnect my body from the bike. Defying gravity itself.

Arms and legs fully extended, my body parallel with the ground and my bike, I soar over the crowd with a Superman.

The whole audience roars.

Usually, I would save that stunt for the last lap. But I have new competition this year, and they need to know who I am.

As I watch the ground draw closer, I grip my rear fender, and align myself back onto my bike. I brace myself for impact, using my legs as shock absorbers, and instantly feel the thud of my tires as they kiss the sand.

On the second lap, I hit the table top with a Heelclicker, and finish with a backflip over the Booter. The judges score my run with a 9.8. Even better than I did last year, when I got a 9.6. It is impossible to get a perfect 10 from the judges here at DuneFest. They are hard asses with high expectations.

I roll my bike off the track. As soon as I cross the starting line, I'm swarmed by locals congratulating me. I give them my thanks and check the starting gate to see who the next rider is. The number 87 pinned to their chest catches my attention first.

It's Gates. I look up, and see their head is already turned in my direction. I make eye contact with their blacked-out gold goggles. I still can't see who their rider is. They give me a thumbs up, and then flip me off as they kick-start their bike.

What an asshole.

Either Claire didn't relay my message—or worse, maybe she told them how much of a jerk I was, and now he has decided to hate me. Either way, I'm not off to a great start with my neighbors.

I pull my bike off to the side, leaving it just behind the bleachers. Then I take a stand next to my brother as we get ready to watch my competition.

"Hey! Great job out there kiddo, 9.8, that's amazing!" Mom says as she pulls me in for a hug.

"Seriously! That's the highest score they've ever given out, even in my days." Dad was a damn good racer. He pulled some of the highest scores DuneFest has ever seen. That was until just now, when I managed to land a 9.8.

"That Superman you pulled was sick. Gates has no idea what he's getting himself into." Axel points out as we look back over to the starting gate.

"Thanks, guys."

9.8 is a damn good score, the best they've handed out in years, but for some reason I don't feel as confident about my run as I did coming off the track. Something about seeing Gates at the starting gate has me second guessing everything.

He exudes confidence.

Being naturally intimidating must run in the family.

The only other thing I can rely on now is him maybe casing it on the booter. A lot of riders their first time at Dunefest underestimate that drop. I am silently praying that Gates will make that same mistake.

The next few moments roll by in slow motion. Everything is silent, it's like the whole world is in a stand still. Or maybe it's just me not breathing.

I watch as they raise the red flag.

Next, comes the yellow.

Usually this whole ordeal lasts a few seconds but I feel like I have been sitting here for an hour...

The green flag drops, and off he goes. He hits the bermed corner, sand flies out behind his tire. He's going too fast. There's no way he will hit the step up, and not fly over the table top. He won't have enough time to do a trick. If he misses that first jump it will definitely cost him.

He hits the step up...

Sailing over the table top, he pops a Nine O'Clock Nac before he recovers and lands perfectly onto the step down. I could have sworn he was going way too fast to be able to pull that off. He should have hit the step off too soon, but he didn't.

He is coming up to the straightaway. He lines himself up, thrusts the throttle back, hits the booter...

And pops a fucking Superman Seat Grab.

Shit.

Fuck.

He is rubbing it in my face.

I glance over at Axel to gauge his reaction. His mouth is in a thin line. He looks just as anxious as I feel right now.

I don't even dare to glance at my dad.

He's entering his second lap. This time he hits the table top with a whip, and cruises over the whoops. Finally, he rounds out of the flat corner and straightens out for the booter.

It's going to be hard for him to top that seat grab.

The sound of his bike rings in my ear, as he thrusts his throttle back.

He hits the jump...

I suck in a deep breath as the anticipation crashes into my chest.

His feet slid up to the front of his bike, hooking underneath the handlebars, his arms stretched high into the air, back arched slightly.

My jaw drops as he flies over the jump right in front of us, accomplishing the hardest stunt in Motocross. A Cliffhanger.

And then proceeds to land it, perfectly.

You've got to be fucking kidding me.

You have to spend years just getting the balance right. Then another few years teaching yourself how to land it. If you can walk away with your confidence still intact, and no major injuries, then you have been more successful than most dirt bike riders. I have landed it twice throughout my entire career in Motocross, and I'm still not confident enough to pull that stunt at a race.

He pulls his bike off the track and pauses before the starting gate. The whole crowd is waiting for the judges to announce his score.

I can't hear a damn thing as I zone in on the scoreboard. I know there are hundreds of people around me talking and chanting, but right now it only feels like me, Gates, and the inevitable.

The announcer stands up. "Gates, number 87." *Oh my god these pauses are going to kill me.* "The judges have scored your laps for the Infiniti Huck at a... Perfect 10! Congratulations!"

The crowd goes ballistic, and I hear the whispering of small town gossip already flooding the streets before Gates can even walk off the track.

I look over at my parents.

Dads face is strained so tight I'm pretty sure he is going to pop a blood vessel, and Mom has a somber look on her face. I know I look defeated. Because I am. I just lost for the first time in five years.

"I better go introduce myself... for real this time."

"Do you want me to come with you?" Axel asks sympathetically.

"Nah.."

I walk over to Gates who is standing next to an older man. Who looks a lot like Claire, just more fucking intimidating. *I didn't even think that was possible.* He has onyx hair with streaks of gray, a short dark beard that lines his chin and jaw, and those same piercing blue eyes as his daughter. He is a big man. I mean *big* man. Stocky, probably about six foot three, looks like he hits the gym four times a day and takes steroids for breakfast. If that wasn't enough to make you shit your pants, tattoos run down both his arms and I can see traces of more ink peeking out from the neckline of his t-shirt.

He has his arms around the rider from the side. He is shaking their shoulders, and I can see him mouthing words that I assume are congratulations. I approach them and clear my throat.

"Hi, I'm Dustin. I came by earlier to introd—"

The rider pulls off their helmet and a long black braid falls out.

The only trophy I am taking home tonight is the World's Biggest Douchebag.

She tilts her head to the side and gives me a devilish grin.

"Not who you were expecting?"

Chapter Six

Claire

I could take home a hundred trophies from DuneFest, and my highlight will still be seeing this smug asshole's expression when I take off my helmet.

"Not who you were expecting?"

I don't give him any time to respond. Instead, I just push my bike towards our pop up tent. Dad walks alongside me, as we leave Dustin stopped in his tracks. I hear his footsteps approaching as he finally shakes himself out of whatever trance he was in, and runs to catch up with us.

"Hey... wait!"

I roll my eyes. "Dad, I'll catch up with you back at the campsite."

"Are you sure?" He looks over his shoulder and glares at Dustin.

Of course I filled him in on the egotistical rider who showed up to our tent insisting on meeting his new competition, and then continued to ask for my *dad* or *brother*. It did grind my gears that he didn't think *I* could be the rider, but that's not even the worst part in my opinion. No, the worst part was that he didn't even bother to ask for my name. Like I wasn't important enough for him to know.

"Yeah, I'm sure."

"Okay, I'll take your bike with me." He glances back at Dustin one more time. "Give him hell," he whispers into my ear.

I wink at Dad and turn around to find Dustin standing only a few inches in front of me, taking my breath away.

He pisses me off, and I want nothing to do with him, but my body is still being a traitorous bitch. Reminding me just how long it has been since someone stared at me the way Dustin is. It is easy to see the way his breath hitches and his pupils dilate when he looks at me, confirming that his body is working against him as well. I plan on being completely impertinent with him. I want to make him feel like shit for pushing me to the side and not giving me the respect I deserve. That anyone deserves. The butterflies in my stomach only fuel my frustration at this point.

I reach inside and gather my backbone. "What do you want?"

"I want to apologize." He rubs his hand along the back of his neck. He is nervous. *Good.* "For a few things actually."

"I'm listening."

"For starters, I'm sorry for not properly introducing myself to you, or asking for your name. Basically for coming off as a complete sexist asshole." *Well, at least he admits it.* "There's plenty of women riders here every year, I don't know why I didn't even think about asking you. Probably, because..." He shakes his head. "Never mind. Either way, it's not an excuse and it was extremely disrespectful. I guess I was just caught off guard..." he shifts on his feet. "Anyway, I'm just really sorry. Is there any way I can make it up to you? I don't want your first impression of me to be a bad one."

"Why do you care?"

His eyebrows pull together. "What?"

"Why do you care if my first impression of you is bad?"

"I... um... I don't really know why, if I'm being honest. Normally, I wouldn't care."

"Hmm..." I turn on my heel and start to walk off. One, that's not a good answer. Two, my body is stupidly attracted to this man and I know my nipples are about to give me away because they are hard as rocks.

What is it about being slightly degraded that has me all hot and bothered?

"Wait! That's it?"

I don't turn around when I answer him. "Were you expecting a different response with that shitty ass answer?"

He jogs to catch up with me. "Yes? I mean... no... *fuck*, I don't know."

I scoff.

"Come with me to the concert tonight?" I stop and turn to face him. "Let me make it up to you."

"What part of this conversation made you think I would say yes to that?"

"The part when you stopped and turned to look at me." *Fuck, those beautiful green eyes.* He throws his hands out to the side. "Come on, Gates. What do you have to lose?"

My damn dignity.

What's that saying again?

Treat em' mean, keep em' keen.

And here I am, ignoring the most classic red flag there is.

I'm also trying to push aside the fact that I love how he just called me Gates as a nickname.

His eyes are sparkling, his muscles are straining against the fabric of his racing jersey, and the devious grin on his face tells me for some reason I know I will be going to that concert tonight.

He takes note of the shift in my expression, and assumes that's a yes. "I'll be by your tent at ten. See you then," he says and starts to run off.

"And what if I'm not there?!" I yell back at him.

He shrugs and back pedals towards his bike.

God, he's infuriating.

Still, I can't stop my eyes as they travel along the planes of his body. He's lean, and tall, but years of riding have paid off on his arms, shoulders, and hands. The way his racing gear clings perfectly to those sculpted muscles should be a sin in itself.

After a generous amount of ogling over Dustin, I turn to head back to our campsite, and reality hits me. The nerves and anxiety come barreling forward at the idea of going on a date with a guy. But it's not a date, right? Just two people going to a concert.

Yeah, I can do that.

He's just trying to apologize for being a royal ass, anyway. I mean, I don't have any friends here yet, and it wouldn't be so bad to make connections with someone who lives here and has ties to the racing community. Having some other company besides my dad—even though I love him— will probably be good for me anyways.

Okay, breathe. Not a date, just two people going to a concert.

I hate that I've left JT in the past and he still has control over this part of me. It's been over a year since we broke up, and I haven't been able to emotionally heal from what he did.

I can still feel his hands wrapped around...

Shaking the thought away, I let out a heavy sigh. Dustin is *not* JT, and this is *not* a date.

I was so in my head that I didn't even realize I walked right past my campsite. *Damn it.* I turn around and slam right into a hard body.

"Shit... I'm so sorry" I look up and realize I ran straight into Dustin's brother—Axel. The last time I saw these eyes, they were staring at me while I was naked.

His hands are on each one of my biceps as he slowly backs me up. He is very gentle for such a large man. He has bright green eyes just like his brother. His hair is dirty blonde like Dustin's, but his is long and pulled back into a bun. Where Dustin is clean shaved along his strong jaw, Axel has a beard. For brothers they couldn't be more different, but you can still tell they are related. If I could describe Axel in one word it would be...Viking.

"No, don't apologize it was my fault."

The tension is palpable between us.

Do we talk about the fact he saw me naked? Or do we avoid it altogether? Personally, I prefer the latter.

"Alright, well I better get going." I nod and point over his shoulder towards my campsite.

"I want to apologize for the other night." Oh, so we are going to talk about it. *Great.*

"You're not the one who needs to apologize," I shake my head. "But let's not worry about it. Let's just pretend like it never happened. Easier for both of us."

"If that's what you want."

I furrow my brow, and tilt my head. "Is that not what you want?"

"I just don't want to get off on the wrong foot. If you want to pretend like it didn't happen, then we can do that. If you want to talk about it and work out an understanding, then that's cool too." So he's just genuinely a nice guy, and not trying to flirt. Good, because I hate love triangles and I doubt he knows that his brother just asked me to a concert with him about ten minutes ago.

Even though it's *definitely* not a date.

"Thank you, but I would like to pretend it didn't happen. Less embarrassing for me."

"Okay, sounds good. See you around," He pats me on the shoulder and then walks past me. "Oh... hey, Claire?"

I turn and look at Axel. "Yeah?"

"Welcome to Reedsport." He winks at me and then continues to walk off.

Welcome to Reedsport, indeed.

Dustin could learn a few things from his brother.

Luckily, I didn't walk too far away from our trailer. When I get back, Dad already has my bike on its stand—fueled up— and ready for the next competition.

He is drinking a beer with his feet kicked up on the seat, a plate of hot dogs on the table to his right, and George Strait blaring in the background. He looks so happy.

I giggle at the scene in front of me. "You look like you're enjoying yourself."

"This is how life is supposed to be *everyday*." His head is extended over the back of his chair as he blindly reaches for a hot dog. "The beach, dirt bikes, beer, hot dogs, and country music." He takes a giant bite and stands up. "How'd your talk with that entitled douche-pickle go?"

"First off, nobody says douche-pickle. Second... I'm going with him to the concert tonight." I basically spit out the words, hoping that if I say them fast enough he won't hear me.

"You think that's a good idea?"

Damn. Plan didn't work out as well as I'd hoped.

"Yes. Mainly, so I can make some connections here in town. Plus, he did seem genuinely apologetic about this morning."

"I don't like it. But I trust you to make your own decisions. What time is the concert?"

"It's not until ten tonight,"

"Alright, well let's have some fun until then."

Dad and I spend the rest of the day checking out all of the events at DuneFest. First, we hit the drag strip to watch the kids ATV race, which is seriously adorable and some of the children here are absolute badasses. While watching the amateur race, Dad and I reminisce on some of the memories we share from when I first started racing. He had every single one of my trophies on a display case inside of his office at the house in Reno. He plans to set them up the same way in the spare bedroom of the new house. I know it must have been hard on him, raising me all alone. I couldn't imagine being a single parent. I will always admire him for that.

We bounce around to a few more events. I kick his ass at cornhole, and he schools me at poker.

When we get back to the trailer, we decide it is time to eat. Dad grills some hamburgers while I make us a salad. When dinner is done we sit down at the little plastic table we bought earlier this morning.

Before I know it, ten o'clock isn't too far away.

The feelings of anxiety and excitement wash through me all over again. I know my dad can feel the shift in my energy by the way he is looking at me.

"Hey, Mini. You okay?"

"Yeah, just a little nervous that's all." I pick at the salad in front of me.

"This is a big deal. It's your first date since JT."

"This is *not* a date!"

He throws his hands up. "Okay, not a date."

I didn't mean to snap at him like that. But if I even think about dating, it makes it hard to breathe. And I've spent all day trying not to make a big deal out of tonight.

"I'm sorry." I hang my head. "I just don't know Dustin that well, and I need this to be just two people hanging out."

I've been talking myself down from the emotional ledge I've been standing on, by reminding myself that tonight is only about him making amends for his previous behavior. One step backwards, and I'll stumble off that ledge and lose myself to anxiety coursing inside of me.

"It's okay. I get it." He looks down at his plate and takes a deep breath. "After I lost your mom it was impossible to think about anyone else. It was just easier to focus on you and be there for whatever you needed. That way I never had to think about moving on, or someone else filling her shoes. Every time I thought about dating it would make me want to throw up, cry, or punch something. The only person I wanted was your mom, so I put it off, and well... you're twenty-one now, and I've never had a girlfriend. I'm not saying I regret it. I enjoyed being selfish about my time with you. But I can't help but think that you deserved to have a motherly figure, and it's my fault you missed out on that." He looks up and makes eye contact with me. "I can't help but feel like I am the reason you're struggling." He sighs. "Anyways, what I'm trying to say is. Don't wait, Claire. I wouldn't change our past, it was beautiful, but it was *so* lonely at times. I know you're holding back the truth about what happened between you and JT. But you need to leave him in the past, and let someone love you like you deserved to be loved. Whether that's Dustin, or someone else. You're too gorgeous, amazing, kind, stubborn, and strong to let some asshole ruin love for you."

My eyesight is blurry as I jump into his arms, almost knocking both of us over. "Thank you."

I don't know how he always knows exactly what to say. But he is right, I deserve to give myself another chance at being happy.

"Of course, Mini. I love you."

"I love you too."

"What do you think about going to that sunset family ride before the concert? Could be just what you need to calm the nerves."

"Absolutely."

I love my father.

I get up to put on my riding gear. Before I step through the door of our camping trailer I turn and look at him. "Hey, Dad?"

"Yeah?"

"You deserve someone too."

He smiles and I can see the tears building in his eyes. "Go on, get dressed. I'll get the bikes ready."

I nod and head inside.

Leave it to a member of the Gates family to be able to give advice but not take it. Sometimes, these bull-headed genes are our own worst enemy.

My dad has given me the world and he deserves to have someone in his corner. Someone other than me. He deserves happiness and not to be lonely anymore. Maybe he just needs a little help putting himself out there.

He has held me through every step in life, and I plan on doing the same for him.

When he's ready.

Chapter Seven

Dustin

"You really think that's a good idea, son?"

You know how there's always at least one sound that instantly grinds your gears anytime you hear it?

Yeah, that's my dad's voice for me.

"She just kicked your ass at the Infiniti Huck, and you have to win the next three comps or you can kiss your SandMaster title goodbye."

We *were* enjoying the other events that DuneFest hosts. Now, it is only a couple hours before the concert, and I have just broken the news to my father that I will be going with Claire.

My only intention for approaching her after the race was to introduce myself, but when I noticed *she* was number 87, the only thing that mattered was making up for my mistake.

As soon as I saw that fire in her eyes and that stubborn smirk take over her beautiful mouth, my motives changed.

"Honey, I think it's a great idea. Dustin deserves to relax and have some fun." Mom threads her arm through Dad's and gives him a smile.

She is beautiful, and I am absolutely certain she is the sweetest human on the planet. She also knows this concert tonight will only help my focus, not hinder it.

Getting my father on board is another story.

"Truthfully, I'm going whether you want me to or not. I was only letting you know out of courtesy because I've lived here long enough to know how fast gossip spreads. And I'd rather you hear about it from me than someone else."

"You're an adult. You make your own decisions. But I still think this is a bad idea."

"Noted. Now can we eat some dinner?"

"Absolutely!" Mom says in a cheerful tone.

I think we are both thankful for the change in subject.

We sit around the table inside of my parents' camping trailer and enjoy dinner together despite the little bit of awkwardness still lingering in the air.

The minutes tick by, and I swear the last two hours are the longest I have ever lived.

I will never agree with him, but Dad might be right.

I can only think about one thing, and that's Claire.

I know I should be focused on the tournament; focused on keeping the SandMaster title, but the only thing capturing my attention right now is trying to decipher the feelings that ignite in my chest when I talk to her.

I haven't been this excited or nervous since my first DuneFest tournament. So, I don't know what is better for me right now. More time with her...or less.

Even if I thought backing out of the concert was the best option for my racing career, I'm not going to.

I may not have dated anyone since middle school, and I may be in over my head, but I am not stupid enough to pass up another chance with her. Hell, I know I am lucky to have this one in the first place. Especially after I made a huge ass out of myself. To be honest, I wouldn't be surprised if she gave me a big 'fuck you' and disappeared before I came by to pick her up tonight.

But that look she was giving me.

I may be rusty in the ol' relationship department, but no one's looked at me like that before.

Behind the determination and stubbornness, I saw want and desire, and I'd do anything—make up any excuse—to feel even an ounce of the passion that Claire has hidden behind those icy blue eyes.

I use my parents' trailer to get dressed. Seeing that my bed in the back of the Bronco is not a great option, unless I am trying to flash half of Reedsport.

I didn't bring a lot of nice clothes with me, but I think what I picked out is decent enough.

It's August, so the weather is warm. It will cool down some this evening but overall it will be hot outside. I am wearing a t-shirt with my favorite band on it, AC/DC. I slip into a pair of navy blue shorts, and lace up my black high top converse. It is about fifteen minutes to ten. I need to leave now or we will be late for the concert. I jog down the stairs leading from the bathroom into the living room, and grab my hoodie. I'll bring it for Claire in case she gets cold.

When I step outside, Mom and Dad are sitting in their lawn chairs talking and drinking a beer. They both turn and look at me when I open the door.

"You look very handsome, Dustin."

"Thank you, Mom."

"Have fun tonight." She stands up, and gives me a kiss on the cheek before heading inside. Leaving Dad and I alone.

We share a look.

I don't have time for this awkward silence, so I speak up first. "Well, I gotta get going or I'm going to be late. Will I see you in the morning for the FreeStyle comp?" I know he will be there. I only ask him in an attempt to keep the peace. We don't always see eye to eye but I still love my father, and I would like us to be on the best terms possible.

He doesn't respond.

Instead, he stands up, pushes past me, and goes inside.

"Awesome. Great talk," I say to myself.

Despite his history with Motocross, he never forced me into racing. He let me choose it for myself. But when I did decide to start, let's just say...he never let off the throttle.

It's always business or training, and no play.

It's become so serious that I'm starting to lose my drive.

And frankly, seeing Claire's face after she won the Infiniti Huck trophy...I'd lose this whole damn competition to see that smile again.

I jog over to her campsite.

As soon as I reach their pop up tent, I see her Dad sitting in a plastic chair. There's a beer resting on his knee as he looks me up and down and I swear I can feel sweat leaking down to my ass crack.

I don't blame him.

If I had a daughter, and they were going out with a guy, I'd give him hell too. No matter how old they are.

"Hi! I'm Dustin Price. It's nice to meet you sir." I walk over and stick out my hand. He stands up and slides his hand into mine. Returning a very *firm* handshake. His grip is a little tight—honestly it kind of hurts—but I'm not gonna wince when he's testing me.

I never got a good look at him after the Infiniti Huck race but at this distance I can see he has a pretty large scar over his left eye. If the tattoos, onyx hair, and shear size of him weren't intimidating enough let's just add a fucking scar to the mix.

"Jesse. Jesse Gates."

I don't know where to go from here. I've never had to introduce myself to the father of a woman I am interested in before. I'm silently praying Claire bails me out, but I know that's the cowardly option. I'm just nervous I'll say the wrong thing and fuck it up. And if I say nothing at all? That might be worse.

I decide to go with the safest bet.

"How was your first day at DuneFest?"

"Good."

Short, no emotion.

Okay, not a great start.

"Listen, it's simple. If you're worth her time, she'll tell me." I nod and go to speak but he beats me to it. "*Then* we can worry about small talk. But for now, if you hurt her... I'll break every bone in your legs, and you can kiss racing goodbye." I gulp.

Don't forget you're a man too.

I need to prove to him that I won't be a waste of her time, and that I intended to keep her safe.

Did I really just give myself a pep talk to talk to another guy?

"Sir, I have no intentions of hurting your daughter. Quite the opposite actually." He gives me a look. "Oh god! Not like that... I just mean, I plan to keep her safe." *This. Is. Going. Fucking. Fantastic.* I shake my head. "Let me put it like this. If anything happens to her while she's with me—even though I will make sure that nothing does—I will personally hand myself over to you. If anything happened to her, I wouldn't be able to live with myself, and you'd be doing me a favor."

His eyes narrow at me as he weighs my words. I know he is trying to decide if I am telling the truth or not. My first intention might have been to gain some points from Jesse, but I meant every word. I would give my life for Claire, and I just met her. He seems to believe me in some capacity because his body relaxes.

Just as Jesse is about to say something, the door to the camping trailer creaks open. And when she steps out... she looks absolutely beautiful. I can't help the fact my mouth drops open and I have to shove down every inappropriate comment I want to make.

She deserves to be admired, respected, and adored.

But I have other things in mind as well.

Her long black hair is in tight wrings as it falls deliciously around her perky boobs. She is wearing a cropped black tank top with thin straps. Her black jeans cling to her hips, and waist, in the most flattering way possible. To top it all off, she is wearing a pair of black high top converse.

Fuck, if she wasn't already perfect.

I realize I have been a little too speechless drinking her in and feel a pair of eyes burning into me. Jesse has his arms crossed over his chest, and is glaring at me like I'm about to become an episode of *Criminal Minds.*

Claire chuckles, then walks over to me.

"Are you ready to go?"

"Absolutely. You look *so* beautiful."

"Thank you. I don't really have anything to wear." She looks down at her outfit. "I definitely didn't plan for this." If this is her casual look, I hope to God I'm around when she decides to go all out. To hell with that, I'm going to give her a reason to get all dressed up.

"You look perfect, Mini."

"Thanks, Dad." She gives him a hug.

"You two have fun tonight. But not too much fun." He looks at me over her shoulder. I nod in return, knowing damn well I will do whatever Claire wants. I have a feeling she's not one to sleep around on the first date anyways. If I can call this a date. For her, it might just be two friends going to a concert, or just me making up for being a dick earlier.

We walk side by side down the makeshift road in the sand. The walk to the stage is short, but I try to go slow, so I can soak in this time with her.

The way the light from the moon hits her gorgeous features is nearly killing me. The blue light bounces off her black hair and makes a ring around her head.

She looks like an Angel.

My Angel.

Did I really just say that? What the fuck?

Not my Angel, not yet, but I am going to try and make her mine.

"The conversation with my dad didn't go too badly," she says, shaking me out of my thoughts.

"Wait, you were listening to that? To all of it?"

"Oh, absolutely! You think I would miss out on that fun?" She has a devilish grin on her face. "Absolutely not."

"I've got my eye on yo-"

Smack.

I stumble backwards.

"*Ow...* shit!"

A sharp burn takes over my left temple.

I look up to see what the cause of my injury is..

A fucking tree branch.

I reach up and put a hand on the side of my face. Sure enough, I can feel a small bump forming under the skin. I was so focused on her that I wasn't paying attention to where we were walking.

I already screwed up my first impression with her, and the second one isn't going so well either. If the night continues to go like this, I can kiss any chance with her goodbye.

My face turns red and hot. Not from pain, but from embarrassment.

"*Oh...*Oh my god. Are you okay?" She lifts her hands up to touch my temple and inspect my wounds. The feeling of her skin on mine sends lighting throughout my body, and for half a second I consider faking an injury just to keep them there.

She plucks a leaf out of my hair, removing the evidence from the attempted murder of the Douglas Fir assassin.

"Yeah, I'm fine. Thank you."

She nods, then doubles over in laughter.

Her laugh is so infectious and pure. God, I'd do anything to keep that smile on her face.

There's little tears forming in the corner of her eyes as she tries to gather herself and speak. "I'm so sorry. I mean, I'm happy you're okay. I just... I'm... I'm sorry." She tries to spit out in between giggles.

I laugh along with her. "I'm glad you find my pain amusing."

She reaches up and rubs at my temple one more time.

Our eyes meet.

The breath gets knocked out of me. Just like the first time those icy blues met mine, I feel myself drowning.

She pulls her hand away.

I'm already cold without her touch. My mind is running wild trying to find an excuse for her to put her hands on me again. But none of them are appropriate for this moment.

Stop thinking with your dick.

I need to make this night special if I plan on keeping her interested. I'm lucky she walked out of that trailer door, and I plan on making sure she doesn't regret that decision. But I seriously need to step up my game if I'm going to make that happen.

The past two interactions we've had I have made a complete fool out of myself. Strike one was assuming she wasn't the rider and now mindlessly walking into a tree branch— nearly knocking myself on my ass—is strike two. And everyone knows what happens on strike three...

"Who's playing tonight?" She asks, pulling me out of my pity party and back into the moment.

"A local band, I believe their name is Sick Obsession. I think they play rock music."

"I noticed your AC/DC shirt. Is that your favorite band?"

"Yeah, it is. I listen to them mostly when I'm working out."

"What's your favorite song?"

"Easy. T.N.T from their High Voltage album. My brother and I used to play it before every race to amp each other up."

"You don't do that together anymore?"

"This was the first year we didn't. He decided last year he was going to be done racing to focus on his crabbing business; it didn't feel right to keep the tradition without him."

"I'm sorry... It sounds like you two created some great memories though."

"We did," I say fondly, remembering all the smack talk and pre-gaming I did with Axel over the years. "Do you like rock music?"

"I usually listen to a lot of country music with my dad. But I do love AC/DC. I think my favorite album by them is Back In Black. Overall, I listen to more alternative rock though. Specifically early 2000s."

I chuckle. "Okay fair. Do you have a pre-race song?"

"Obviously, who doesn't?" We both laugh. "My pre-racing song is 'Headstrong' by Trapt."

"A classic. I like your taste."

She smiles.

My heart constricts in my chest.

Will I ever get used to this feeling?

Unfortunately, our stroll together comes to an end. We walk up to the booth, and I pull out my wallet to pay for our tickets. The lady asks for our IDs, after we hand them over, she wraps a neon 21+ band around both of our wrists. From where we stand, we can see the stage and the crowd is already piling in. I notice a few groups in the back sitting on fold out chairs or blankets, and realize I made a mistake. I didn't even think about the fact that we might want to sit down.

Damn it.

Major fuck ups: 3. Dustin: 0.

"Shit... I'm sorry I didn't even think about grabbing something for us to sit on."

"That's okay, I don't mind getting dirty if I have too." She winks at me.

Is she flirting with me?

Maybe I haven't screwed this up after all.

At this moment, I wish I had read 'Flirting For Dummies'.

"Do you wanna grab something from the bar?" I ask.

"Yeah, I could go for a drink."

We head towards the little pop up in the back. While we wait in line, we share things with each other. Mostly just the basics. Her favorite color is forest green, she eats Oreos and milk for comfort food. She likes scary movies, dogs more than cats, and her closet consists of basically black clothing. I've been dying to ask her about her life in Reno, and her EnduroCross title, but I figure that is a conversation for another time. Instead, I ask her about her dad. They seem to have a tight relationship, and I remember him calling her 'Mini' earlier. I'm curious about how the nickname originated.

"I noticed when we were at your campsite, your dad called you 'Mini'. Is it because you're a mini version of him? Or is there another reason?"

"That's funny you asked. Most people just look right past it." She smiles at me. "When I was little, probably about twelve or thirteen, I won a few competitions on a 112cc. The age range and bike power is classified as the SuperMini. Ever since then, he has called me Mini."

"So what you're saying is you've always been a bad ass."

She giggles. "Yeah, pretty much."

We finally get to the front of the line and the bartender— an older man— asks us what we would like to drink.

"Can I have a Corona and lime, please?"

I pull my attention away from the man and look at her.

We have matching shoes, she drinks my favorite beer, she's a damn good rider, her body is magnificent, and she's not afraid to put a motherfucker in his place. *Plus,* she's agreed to go out with me.

This is too good to be true.

I take in this moment.

I admire her gorgeous features, accentuated by the flood lights surrounding us. The energy I feel pulsing between us. The reaction my body has to her touch. The commonalities we both have.

She was made for me, and I for her.

I want to brand everything about her into my memory. I never want to know what it feels like to not have her in my life again.

I could survive off this feeling. Survive off of her.

I know how utterly ridiculous that sounds since we haven't spent more than twenty minutes together, and maybe I'm naive. Maybe I'm reading into this more than I should be. But I have never met anyone more perfect than her.

The way she makes me feel is electrifying and that has to be more than an attraction. More than lust.

It's then that I realize I've been lost in thought for a little too long. Both her and the bartender are waiting for my drink order. She has a smirk on her face like she's reading my every thought, while the older man is getting impatient with me. His face is the poster of irritation.

"I'll have a whiskey on the rocks, please." I say in a rush, trying not to look like a complete creeper. Then it hits me.

Why did I just order that? I never drink whiskey.

We grab our drinks and start to walk towards the stage. I eye my cup and spin it in small circles. The ice inside smacks against the plastic.

"Hmm…" There's a confused look etched across her beautiful features. "I didn't peg you as a whiskey drinker."

"What did you peg me as?" I take a drink.

"A sex on the beach kind of guy."

I choke on my drink and spit it out.

Excuse me what?!

She caught me so off guard.

I turn and look at her.

Her eyes are shut and her mouth is open. There's little droplets of whiskey sliding down her features. One bead is delicately hanging onto her eyelashes, about to drop onto her cheek. My brain replaces the whiskey with something a little less appropriate and I feel myself harden at the thought.

That is not the current circumstances.

I shake my head, making the thought fly in and out of my brain faster than a 500cc riding a straightaway on peat.

Damn it, say something! Anything! Apologize!

Instead, I just stand frozen in disbelief.

This kind of shit only happens in movies.

A couple standing next to us watches the whole thing unravel and starts cracking up laughing.

"I'd be so livid with you!" the woman says as they walk away from us. Ultimately, waking me up to the reality of my situation. Humiliation floods over me as I realize she is trying to wipe the mess off with her hands, and I need to find a way to help her clean up.

This can not be fucking happening.

"Oh my God… I'm so sorry. Here." I slip my hoodie over my head. I use it to try and help her wipe off the copper liquid.

Instead, she takes it from me and begins patting at her face. If I didn't fuck up this date when I embarrassed myself by running into a branch, not bringing chairs for us to sit on, or creepily staring at her while ordering drinks, I sure as hell fucked it up now.

I know I'm inexperienced when it comes to dating, but I didn't realize it was this bad.

When she's almost done cleaning off her face, she pulls my hoodie down and stops mid-wipe, just over her nose. The only thing I can see is her eyes, and she's giving me a look that I can't decipher. Then she places the hoodie back into my hands.

I look down, too embarrassed to meet her gaze.

I'm nervous to see what expression is going to be staring back at me. Afraid she will tell me to 'fuck off' and start walking back to her campsite. It's not like I'd blame her if she did.

I finally build up the courage to look at her, and I see a huge smile on her face.

"I told you I didn't mind getting dirty. But I didn't quite mean it like this." There's that beautiful laughter again.

The thought of her leaving lifts from my shoulders, and relief floods over me.

God, I don't deserve any time with this woman.

"Again, I'm so sorry." Embarrassment still heating up my cheeks, I turn my head to the side.

"Really, don't worry about it. We are humans, we make mistakes and accidents happen. It's not a big deal. Besides, I don't mind the smell of whiskey. Hey…" She grabs my chin and turns my face so my eyes meet hers. The warmth from her touch rushes through my body. I can tell she is being honest by the way she is looking at me.

She lets go of my chin and smiles at me.

There's a semi wet strand of hair hanging in her face. I tuck it behind her ear, running my thumb along her chin. Her breath hitches. It feels good to know that I have the same effect on her that she does on me.

If there's ever a right moment, this sure as hell feels like it.

I'm about to pull her in for a kiss when she points toward the stage, eyes still locked with mine.

"It looks like the concert is about to start."

I reluctantly pull my eyes from hers, and look in that direction. "Yeah, I guess so."

Excitement in her voice, she grabs my wrist, and pulls me through the crowd. "Let's go then!"

We push our way to the front, weaving in and out of the bodies surrounding the stage. Her eyes light up as soon as she sees the band up close. Something lands at my feet, I look down to notice she dropped the dark green scrunchie that was around her wrist. I bend down, and slip the small piece of silk into my pocket. If anything, I can use this as an excuse to see her again.

Anticipation pulses in the air around us. The music causes the ground we stand on to vibrate, and the lights start dancing.

I can feel it all. But the energy between us is deafening. Consuming.

Everyone else is enjoying the show. Enjoying the band as they perform a killer set.

I'm enjoying her.

The tight curls of her hair bouncing up and down. The beer in her left hand swaying as she waves her arms in the air. Her lips move perfectly as she tries to figure out the words.

The fact that I haven't scared her off yet is nothing short of a miracle.

The band is finishing the end of their set now. But I don't want this night to end.

I wish I could freeze time and spend a few more hours here with her. Or better yet, reverse time—start over—so I can change the events that transpired and not make a fool of myself.

I don't even know if she realizes what she's done for me in this small amount of time we've spent together. She has given me a night of peace and freedom. Freedom from the pressure and expectations my father has placed on me.

I know when I return to my campsite the same disapproving glare will be on his face. I can't remember the last time we actually had a conversation about anything other than racing. It's always shop talk with him.

Would he even know that I took a culinary class and can make a killer homemade gelato?

I doubt it.

I'll worry about the stern talks and criticizing scowls later. For now I want to enjoy the time I have with the girl next to me.

She says something to me, but I can't hear anything over the music.

"What?!"

She stands up on her toes and leans in to whisper in my ear. I'm not much taller than her. I'm 6'2 and she's probably about 5'9. But this is the first time I've been close enough to breathe her in. She smells like cherries, a hint of vanilla, and whiskey. No doubt from when I spit my drink all over her face.

Rookie move.

Those sparks of lighting come flooding back under her touch. I have to fight the urge not to grab her and pull her into me. I want to bury my face in the crook of her neck. I want to lick all the sensitive parts of her skin. Kiss her until she moans my name.

My cock twitches in my pants at the thought of her pinned against me.

"Thank you so much for this."

"Anytime, Angel." I whisper in her ear.

She takes a step back.

For a split second, I feel like calling her by that nickname was a bad decision, but then her gaze softens.

She turns back around to enjoy the music. Then, she slowly steps in front of me, her ass grazing along my groin. Pulling her closer to me, I follow her lead and let her decide how she wants our bodies to move together.

I could get used to this.

My arms fall on top of her shoulders. Her free hand wraps around my forearm. We spend the rest of the concert entwined just like this.

I spend the rest of the night with an Angel in my arms.

Chapter Eight

Claire

Dad was right.

I deserve to move on, to give myself another chance. Even though neither of us have said this is a date, and before I was so adamant on not putting pressure onto this night, I've completely changed my mind. In fact, I think I'd be hurt if Dustin told me otherwise. This concert has been one of the best nights I've had in a long time.

I know he must be embarrassed by the accidental insinuation of giving me a 'good time' to my dad, running into a tree branch—almost knocking himself on his ass—forgetting chairs (which isn't a big deal), and spitting whiskey in my face.

Truthfully, I find it refreshing. It means he's human. And it also means that he is just as nervous as I am. Which is comforting for me. I just don't want him to feel bad, all those little things don't bother me, but I know he probably feels like this entire date is a shit show. When I tell Han the details of this night, she will probably agree with him.

In between every few songs we would go and get refills on our drinks. His first drink was a whiskey on the rocks, but he quickly changed to a Corona and lime for the second round. He didn't want to irritate the bartender more, so he just blurted out the first drink on his mind. I admired him for being honest. I definitely think a beer is more his speed. I also think it's kind of cute that we both prefer the same drink, and have matching converse.

I'm a few beers in and that warm feeling is starting to spread. It could be that, or the grinding of our bodies. I put my money on the latter.

Earlier, when I lifted my hand to touch his temple after he ran into the branch, I felt an overwhelming feeling of lighting and warmth spreading throughout my body. All I wanted to do was touch him again. If the feel of his skin on mine made me almost lose myself, I wonder what kissing him would feel like. The thought alone sends warmth to my core, and my lower belly pulses with anticipation.

I shut the thought down quickly before my anxiety takes over. After he accidentally spit his drink in my face, we had a moment when we almost kissed. I wanted it so badly, but my memories from the past came crashing into me and I got scared. I know Dustin is *not* my ex. He would not hurt me like JT did, and I want more than anything for Dustin to erase that memory and replace it with a better one.

I just need a little more time.

Maybe at the end of the night, and a good amount of self encouragement, I'll be more comfortable with the idea of letting him kiss me.

The band just finished their final song, a cover of 'The Rock Show' by Blink 182, and the whole crowd starts chanting.

"Encore. Encore. Encore!" I yell as I pump my fist in the air. Truthfully, this band isn't my favorite, but I'd do anything to drag this night out. Unfortunately, the band doesn't return and everyone starts packing up their things.

"Damn, I was really hoping they'd sing at least one more song," Dustin says as we turn to start walking back to our campsites.

"Me too."

"Do you need to head back right away, or can I show you something first?"

I give him a skeptical look. "You aren't going to try and murder me, are you?"

He chuckles, "Maybe, maybe not. But that's just part of the adventure isn't it, Angel?" He winks at me. I love that he decided to call me by a nickname. I love the way that it rolls off his tongue, how his rugged voice makes it sound sensual.

"Why did you choose to call me Angel?"

He stumbles with the change in subject and turns to look at me.

"Do you not like it?"

"I don't know... I just want to know why you chose that nickname over the others."

He lets out a long breath.

His eyes become intense as he stares right into mine. "When we first left your campsite... right before I ran into the tree, making a fool of myself." I smirk at the memory. "I was admiring the way you looked under the moonlight. The shadows and soft blue of the light played on your features so perfectly. You're already so beautiful but the way the light hit your gorgeous black hair, it left a similar look to a halo above your head. At that moment, I decided you were an Angel. My Angel..." his eyes go wide as he realizes what he just said. "For the night, of course." My heart swells at his confession, at his brutal honesty. I know it takes a lot for him to tell me that, especially on a first date.

This is a date, isn't it?

No one is that romantic with someone they would prefer to call a friend.

The air between us grows intense as he tries to gauge my reaction. I can feel the nervousness radiating off of him.

I guess I should let him out of his misery.

"I love it. And I also love it when you call me Gates. But I think I love Angel a little more." His face relaxes and the air between us returns to its natural warmth. "So, about this place you want to take me. Is it a local hookup spot?"

His eyes widen and he laughs. "No, nothing like that. There are a few places around town that are, if you'd like me to show you." His gaze drops down my body. And that familiar warmth settles in my core and my nipples harden under his stare. *I should have worn a bra.* Reading my thoughts, his eyes linger on my breasts. It takes everything in me not to jump into his arms.

Then the panic sets in. The memories from my past taking over and ruining this moment. I cross my arms over my breasts and turn away. Worry crosses over Dustin's face and his posture shifts. I hate that I made him feel like he did something wrong, yet I can't tell him about my past. I haven't told anyone the truth. Maybe, he will be the person I share my burdens with one day, just not tonight. I can't scare him away, not after the night we just had.

Feeling the shift in my mood, Dustin changes the subject. "This place I'm taking you to– it's better at night time. I come here when I need to think or just... get away, I guess. And I figured since you just moved here and a lot comes with moving—especially from your hometown—that you could use a place like that as well." Tears threaten in my eyes as we walk along the sand. The fact that he's willing to share his safe place with me is almost too much to handle. I don't know what I did to deserve his kindness.

My first impression of the man standing next to me is completely different from the impression I have of him now.

"What are you thinking about?"

"I was thinking about how different you actually *are* compared to the asshole I pegged you to be when we first met."

He laughs. "I can't blame you, but I'm glad you changed your mind."

I smile at him.

He walks us through a path between two large patches of coastal grass, leading up to the beach and the ocean. The water is in high tide now, and it's crashing against the shore. It's absolutely beautiful. I haven't been able to check out the ocean yet. Since we've been here it's been nothing but one task after the next.

We have been walking along the beach in silence just enjoying the scenery. I have a feeling Dustin is just allowing me to take it all in. Usually, I'd be trying to find a way to fill the silence. Making awkward conversation just to make the other person feel more comfortable. Oddly, there's no pressure between us. It just feels normal... right. No expectations to meet. Just two people enjoying the night.

"It's not too far now, just up there." He points to a cliff a little ways off in the distance. Surrounding it are boulders piled on top of each other, giving the illusion that the beach abruptly ends.

As we get closer, I realize there's a natural made archway that makes a perfect path to the other side of the beach. As we make our way through, I run my hands along the rock. It's cold and damp, and I can feel the thrum of the ocean along its wall, like it's humming its own melody. It's absolutely magical. Even though I spent my whole life in Reno, this place already feels more like home.

Dustin has shared with me this piece of serenity and I don't want to be scared anymore. There is just something in the way he makes me feel, like I am safe, secure. I want to open up for him. Show him that I feel the same way he does. The only reason I have been hesitant is because I am worried about getting hurt again. But so far, he has given me every reason to trust him, it's my turn to give a little back.

He's not far away from me, enjoying the same sensation of the ocean as I am. His hand has been slowly brushing mine as we've been walking along the beach, and I know he wants to reach out. But he's been respecting my space after I basically shut him out the last time we were flirting with each other.

Before I can talk myself out of it, I reach out and grab his hand. Intertwining our fingers. That familiar warmth returns instantly. He looks down at our hands, then back up to me.

"Thank you for sharing this with me. It's beautiful."

"It sure is." By the look in his eyes I know he's not talking about the ocean. My cheeks flush and the tips of my ears feel hot. "This isn't even the best part." He's got a sly smirk on his face as he tilts his head toward the exit of the tunnel. "Come on." My hand in his, he takes us through. Just as we reach the end, my mouth drops open.

I cannot believe what I'm seeing.

There's hundreds of sand dollars and various other shells lining the beach.

"Oh my God." I pull my free hand up and cover my mouth in utter disbelief at the sight in front of me.

"Pretty amazing isn't it?"

Still stunned, I'm only able to give him a nod in return.

"Not many people know this, but the coastline in Oregon is actually considered a highway. People ride their quads, dirt bikes, trucks, and all kinds of vehicles along the beach. The sandbar between the cliff and the ocean is too small to ride along, and the tunnel too narrow for any vehicle to get through. Leaving this section of beach untouched. I think that's why these shells have lasted for so long."

We carefully step along the sand making sure we don't crush any shells.

"Some people come by and collect a few for themselves. But at this point I think it's an unspoken rule that this place is a sanctuary and everyone treats it with the utmost respect." He bends down and picks up a sand dollar that is still perfectly intact. "Open your hands." I do what he asks and put my hands together in the space between us. "Many people believe that by opening a sand dollar it releases peace into the world." He cracks the shell in half and five bird-like pieces fall into my hand. "It's more of a religious thing, but I love the representation anyway." He turns each delicate piece over in my hand to make it resemble a flock of birds in mid-flight. "Sand dollars have five jaw apparatuses, that's what you're holding in your hand. A lot of people say they represent doves. The story is, after God flooded the earth, he sent a dove with an olive branch as a symbol of peace. Meaning the world was re-born. So when you crack open a sand dollar and five doves fall out..."

"You're releasing peace into the world."

"Exactly."

As I examine the beautiful white pieces in my hand, I let everything he said settle deep into my soul.

I really could use some peace.

I think he is more aware of my emotions than I give him credit for. He must feel the war raging inside me as I battle between my past, and the feelings that are surfacing for him.

"Can I keep these?" I ask.

"Of course. Consider these your new representations of peace. If you ever feel like there's no hope left, or the world is caving in around you. Just remember that you are in control. You determine your fate, your life, Claire. Don't let anyone take your peace."

I'm on the verge of crying for the second time tonight.

I look down again at the little birds in my hand, an overwhelming realization hitting me at the same time. "This is the best date I've ever been on." Oh, shit. Did I just call this a date?

My eyes widen at my lack of self control.

Damn it.

What if that's not how he sees this night? But the flirting, the sparks between us, the way he looks at me. I couldn't be making that up in my head, could I?

The smile he gives me and the way his face lights up, gives me the answer I need.

"Even though I spit my drink in your face?" he plays.

I laugh. "Especially because you spit your drink in my face."

A flash of teeth and a loud laugh roars through him. "You're going to give me a run for my money aren't you?"

"Always."

I look into his emerald eyes as he looks into my icy blues; the trees meeting their first frost.

"As much as I hate to even mention it. It is midnight, and we both have a race in the morning. Do you want to start heading back?"

I nod. "Yeah, that's probably a good idea."

The walk back is peaceful and dark. The moon and our phones are the only source of light.

We are both so focused on our path that we don't talk much.

For me, I am overwhelmed by my own thoughts. With everything that's happened tonight I'm trying to get a grip on my feelings, and let go of some of the anxiety I've built up when it comes to dating. With Dustin it feels so natural, real, easy. The more we allowed each other to get comfortable, the more beautiful the night became.

Unfortunately, we reach my campsite, and an unexpected feeling of disappointment washes over me.

Dustin grabs my hand. "I had a great time tonight."

I stare at him as my heart begins to race.

All the feelings I have been carefully hiding away come rushing back as my mind shoves insecurities at me.

I *refuse* to let my past ruin this moment for me.

I look down at his lips and unconsciously bite my own.

When I look back up, his eyes are dark. Zeroed in on me.

I'm watching the rise and fall of his chest when he grabs me by my hips, and pulls me into him. I'm caught a little off guard, and brace myself against his strong chest.

I swallow as he moves one hand from my hip, and traces the line of my body. Slowly moving his way up my side and settling his fingers under my chin, his eyes dance with fire as our body's press into each other. His hand continues to travel along the side of my face, until it's in my hair, and he's gently cradling my head.

"Are you gonna kiss me or not?" I tease.

He chuckles and shakes his head. "Are you always this bossy?"

"I guess you're just gonna have to find out."

He tilts my chin so my eyes are level with his.

"I am going to kiss you now. But, before I do. I want you to know that I am going to take my time with it... with you. I've been waiting all night for this moment. I'll be damned if I rush this, and don't take every second I can to taste you. To enjoy the way your cheeks pink with heat, and the way your breathing causes your body to press deeper into mine. I'm going to take my time with you, Claire Gates. Simply because I fucking want to."

My breath hitches.

He smirks at the way my body responds to his words.

Then his lips crash against mine like he can't bear another minute without the taste of me.

Even though I asked for this, it takes me a minute to catch up, but then I slide my tongue into his mouth. He responds and slides his against mine. I drag my hand up and run my fingers through his hair. He moans into my mouth. He brings his other hand up and cups my face on both sides, deepening the kiss. We stay tangled up like this while the world drowns out around us. He hardens against my stomach, I feel myself getting wet in response. "Fuck." He says against my mouth. He pulls away slightly and presses his forehead to mine. Nothing has ever turned me on as much as kissing Dustin has.

There's no denying our connection now.

Reluctantly, I take a step back.

He grabs my wrist and pulls me into him. He grabs the back of my thighs and hoists me up to straddle his hips.

"I'm not done with you yet." He repositions his hold on me so that I'm sitting on his forearm, and grabs the back of my neck with his other hand. Our lips meet again. "Even if you're only mine for tonight, I am going to *savor* you, take every piece of you that I can. Are you okay with that?"

Fuck, yes please.

I nod.

"Say it, Angel. Tell me you're mine."

"I'm yours."

He smirks. The passion in his eyes makes it look like he is coming down from a high. His lips crash against mine as he moves my hips up and down on the bulge in his pants. "Can you feel how much I want you?" *God, I love his dirty mouth.*

"Yes."

He kisses me again, this time slower and less rushed. Then he sets me down slowly, keeping our mouths connected. When my feet touch the ground, he cradles my head in his hands again, and peppers my face in small kisses. I rest my head on his chest and he wraps me in his arms.

"You were well worth the wait," he whispers into my hair. There seems to be a bigger meaning behind what he just said, but I'm not sure what.

"You were well worth the pain."

He stills and pulls me away from him.

"What do you mean by that?"

My eyes are beginning to water and I don't have the energy to explain the depth of that statement right now.

"I better get inside. I'll see you at the Freestyle Comp tomorrow, yeah?"

There's concern etched into his handsome features.

I can tell he doesn't want to let it go. In spite of that, he agrees anyway. "Yeah."

I stand up on my toes and kiss his cheek. "Goodnight, Dustin."

Then I turn around and walk to my camp trailer. I can feel his gaze watching my every move, I bathe in the warmth it gives me. I look over my shoulder before I pull the door open, he waves at me before I slip inside.

I lean against the frame for a moment and take in everything that just happened. For the first time in a long time I feel...whole. I smile as tears run down my face.

This time they aren't tears of sadness but tears of joy.

I'm so fucking happy.

Chapter Nine

Claire

"*Ah!*" Han yells.

I grimace and pull my phone away from my ear.

"You kissed him? I'm so happy for you!"

I balance the phone between my head and my shoulder as I slip on my riding boots.

"It's not that big of a deal, Han."

"*It's not that big of a deal?*" I can practically see her head bouncing side to side as she mocks me. "Did you really just say that?"

"Will you stop yelling?"

"Only after you admit this is a big deal! This is your first kiss in a *year*. A whole ass year!" She pauses. "I'm surprised you remembered how to kiss."

"I'm surprised your lips haven't fallen off yet from how much you kiss."

"But it's just so fun," she whines. "*Admit. It.*"

"Fine." I roll my eyes. "It's a big deal." I smile into the phone. "You're acting like I'm the only woman in the world that's experienced heartbreak before."

"You're the only woman in the world going through a heartbreak, that I actually care about. So, to me you are."

"Careful, or you'll turn us into a soap opera." I warn her.

"God, I would kill to be on One Tree Hill."

I shake my head. "I've got to get going, the competition is about to start."

"Okie dokie. But I will make you spill every detail later! I know you can't see me but imagine me pointing a very serious finger at you."

"And I'm pointing a very serious finger at you too." I say in my best attempt at a sweet voice.

"*Ha. Ha.*"

I giggle. " You know I love you."

"I love you, too. I'm very happy you guys made it to Reedsport safely. Good luck today!"

"Thanks, Han."

As soon as I hang up with Hannah, an unknown number starts calling me.

That's weird. It's probably just a telemarketer.

I press decline and continue to strap up my boots.

In about twenty minutes the Freestyle competition is scheduled to start. And all I can think about is how Dustin's lips feel on mine, and every little detail from last night. This morning I realized he never asked for my phone number, and I never asked for his. For some reason, I'm still obnoxiously checking my phone.

I did rush out of there last night despite how much I wanted to stay. There is still a piece of me that's hesitant to let another man in like I did with JT. I just want to take things slow. I want to learn all about him first; his likes, his dislikes, how he likes his coffee—if he even likes coffee—what are his goals? Does he have any other passions besides motocross? What's his family like? *Oh, God.* The thought reminds me of a very unfortunate situation, his brother saw me naked.

Humiliation floods over me all over again. I hope that's not a big deal to him. How would I feel if it is? Fuck it, it's not like I did it on purpose. And who is he to blame me for an accident or make me feel bad?

Although, a part of me would be sad. There's something special between us. I don't know if I have the right words to explain it. But it's there, and it's real, and it's impossible to ignore.

My mind is all over the place.

What is going on with me?

I shake my head as I stand up and walk over to my bike. I need to get out of my thoughts and into the race ahead of me. I drop my bike off the stand, and see Dad walking over. We debriefed a little bit this morning on how last night went. I basically told him not to hate Dustin, and that I'm willing to give us a chance.

I'm not going to divulge too much information, he is still my father after all. He is probably just as thankful as I am that I have Han so he doesn't have to hear all the intimate details anyways.

"Hey, Mini. I'm heading over to the starting gate. We've got about twenty minutes till race time."

"I'm right behind you, I just have to grab my helmet, goggles, and find where I misplaced my damn hair tie." I scan the sand around us for any sign of it.

"No worries. I'll see you over there."

"Sounds good."

Where is that damn hair tie?

I've been looking everywhere for the last five minutes, trying to track it down, when I hear someone walking up behind me. I spin around, and smile as soon as I see who it is. The way his racing gear clings to his muscles, and how the mint green brings out his eyes, takes my breath away. The sun brings out streaks of gold in his dirty blonde hair, and his face is clean-shaved, showcasing his strong jawline as he holds a pair of paper coffee cups in the crook of his arm.

"Looking for this?" Dustin says as he holds up my dark green scrunchie with his other hand.

I put my hands on my hips and narrow my eyes at him. "Why do you have that?"

He tilts his head to the side. "Someone might have dropped it last night, and I may or may not have kept it." He smirks at me. "After all, I needed an excuse to see her today."

"And here I thought you were trying to strengthen your odds this morning by stealing my lucky hair tie. Lord knows you could use the help."

He scoffs. "That mouth is gonna get you in trouble, Gates."

"I hope so," I tease.

He sets the cups down on top of the work bench to his right. I admire the way his riding shirt clings to his muscles as he crosses his arms over his chest. I send my personal thanks to the god that sculpted him.

"Is that so?" He lifts his eyebrow playfully then closes the gap between us. When he is close enough for us to share air, he places his hands on either side of my neck and pulls me in for a kiss. I sink into his embrace. The warmth returns to my body and his touch becomes a familiar feeling. His other hand drops to cup my ass as he plays with the back pocket of my racing pants. At this moment, I forget everything that is going on. The only thing that matters right now is this moment with Dustin. Not the competition, not my past. Nothing.

Our kiss gets interrupted by the screech of the loudspeakers as a man on the intercom announces the last call for the Freestyle Comp.

"We have about fifteen minutes before we need to head to the starting gate, would you like to have some coffee with me?"

I nod. "I would love to."

He smiles and grabs our cups as I follow him over to our small plastic table.

I take a sip of the liquid strength. It's a little sweet for me, but still good enough.

"See, this is my problem." Dustin says after I take a drink.

"What's your problem?"

"I don't know enough about you." The look in his eyes makes me shift in my seat. It feels like he is stripping me bare. "I don't know if you feel the same way, but to me it feels like I have known you my whole life and I can already tell when you don't like something." He gives me a knowing look.

I laugh. "How did you know?" I thought I did a good job schooling my features of disgust, but I guess not.

"Don't take this the wrong way..."

"Anytime someone says that it's basically an opening for an insult." I take another sip and then set my coffee down on the table. "Tread lightly, Price."

His green eyes shine under the threat. "Oh, I am. Trust me." He scouts his chair closer to mine. "Usually, your features are all hard lines and I see the way you put on a mask of indifference for everyone else. But when you drink that coffee," he motions to the cup sitting on the table beside us, "and try to hide your distaste– your features relax." He runs his thumb along my bottom lip and stares at my mouth. Those familiar sparks of lightning return. "So don't lie to me, Angel, because I can tell when you... *enjoy* something." His eyes snap to mine and this time I grab him by the collar of his shirt and smash his mouth against my own.

One of his hands braces against the back of my seat as the other cradles my neck. His tongue darts out and licks at the seam of my lips. I open for him, and desire instantly builds in my core. I run my hands up under his shirt to feel the hard lines of his abs and warmth of his skin, I moan at the feeling. He takes a hold of my lip with his teeth as he gently drags them along the skin.

Panting, I catch his stare. His chest rising and falling just as quickly as my own. "We better get going."

"Mhmm."

He laughs and has a satisfied look on his face because none of my smart ass remarks come out.

I sit in utter disbelief as he stands and begins to walk towards the track.

"Good luck out there, Angel."

I shake my head and snap myself out of it. "Watch your back, Price." I say as he runs off.

"Took you a moment to catch up. Welcome back."

"Fuck off."

He laughs then takes off across the sand. I get distracted by watching Dustin jog away and lose track of time.

Shit, I need to go.

I grab the handlebars of my bike and start walking towards the starting gate.

If I'm not more careful, I'm gonna start falling for this man. I can't help but feel like I already am.

Do I want that? Am I ready for another relationship? I don't know. But I'm willing to find out.

Dustin ended up winning the Freestyle Competition. He came in with a couple of nice Nac Nacs and a Heelclicker. Then finished off his last round with an Airplane and a Hart Attack. I was impressed to say the least. He's a damn good rider. I tried to ignore the rush of pride that took over when I looked up at him on the 1st place podium.

I got 2nd place and a rider named Dominic Linetti got 3rd. If I wanted to go for SandMaster, I would have to win the next two races to be able to walk away with the title. I didn't come here to win another trophy, I only came here to spend some time with my dad. The fact I get to do something I love is just a plus.

What I am enjoying is the silent competition that Dustin and I have going on.

The local news takes some pictures of us for the paper and after they are finished I step down off the podium to say congratulations to him.

He smirks at me. "Seems like your head wasn't quite in it this time, Gates."

I glare at him. "I didn't want to completely demolish your reputation. I would *hate* to see the 'Race King' lose some of his adoring fans."

He winces at the nickname. "If I am the Race King, then you are the Race *Queen*."

I like the sound of that.

We look like little raccoons as we stare at each other. The goggles block out a perfect band over our eyes, and the wet sand speckles our faces. He wipes a small amount of dirt from my cheek and then leans in to kiss me when someone interrupts us.

"Dustin! Over here." I look over and see Rodney waving him over. I smile at him, he gives me a tight-lipped nod in response.

That's odd.

"I better get going, he is going to want to recap and prepare for ShortCross. Can we maybe meet in a few hours? Maybe go for a walk on the beach? Or get lunch in town?"

"I'd love that."

He smiles and presses a gentle kiss to my forehead. "See you around, Gates."

I smile as I watch him run over to his family. He looks over his shoulder at me and winks.

I run my hands over my arms, feeling giddy for the first time in—well, my whole life. I have felt instant attraction before, but this... this feels deeper and stronger.

I'm about to go grab my bike when I notice my dad is chatting with a certain red-headed lady. Instead, I walk over to them.

"Hey, Tattie."

"Oh! Hey, Claire. Great race today! You did amazing."

"Thank you." I smile at her.

"I was just inviting you and Jesse over to my campsite this evening for dinner. We do a huge shrimp feed, and a bunch of locals stop by and bring food. It'd be great for you guys to network with some people in town."

"That sounds awes–"

Before I can finish my sentence Dad interrupts me. "I was just telling Tattie that we wouldn't be able to make it because... we had that thing." He raises his eyebrows at me.

Oh, hell no. I'm not getting you out of this, old man.

I smirk at him and his eyes widen as he shakes his head.

I won't completely humiliate him.

"We can take care of that later." There is, in fact, not a thing. I turn to Tattie. "We will be there. Thank you for the invite."

He looks at me and takes a deep breath.

"Oh, awesome! I'm so excited you guys can come. It'll be fun, I promise. It starts at seven tonight. I'll see you then!"

"Bye, Tattie," I yell back at her as we walk towards our campsite.

When she is out of sight, he stops me by placing a hand on my arm. "What are you doing?"

"What do you mean?"

"You know what I mean."

"The only thing *I'm* doing is making connections in a new town we just moved to. You and I both have to make friends at some point. Plus, I really like her. So what are *you* worried about?"

He narrows his eyes at me and his jaw clenches. "Fine, you're right. Maybe I'll meet someone from the shop there."

"There you go!" I say as I clap a hand on his shoulder.

This will be a great opportunity to make more connections. I would be lying if I wasn't hoping that maybe Tattie and him will get a little extra time together.

If Dustin isn't already planning on going with his family tonight, I want to ask him to come with me.

What is a shrimp feed after all?

After we get back to the trailer I prop my bike up on its stand and excuse myself. I'm headed over to Dustin's campsite when suddenly I hear my name. I turn around and it's Rodney, Dustin's father.

"Hey, Claire."

"Hey, Rodney. How are you?"

"I'm doing good. Nice racing out there yesterday and today."

"Thank you, I appreciate that. I was actually looking for Dustin, do you know where he went?"

"Actually, I wanted to talk to you about that."

"Okay..."

"Dustin needs his head in the game. I don't know if he told you this, but if he wins this year, this will be his sixth SandMaster title in a row." I nod my head. He did tell me that at the concert last night. "AMA scouts are looking at him and he needs this year's title. I don't mean to be rude, but ever since you came along, his head has not been in it. Respectfully, I would like you to reconsider whatever you're about to say to my son and maybe just wait until after DuneFest is over." This is not how I expected this conversation to go. Rodney was so nice when he dropped off my truck. This side of him is intense. Honestly, I feel bad for Dustin if this is the type of expectations his dad has been putting on him. I care about him, and ultimately, I care about his family too. But nonetheless, he doesn't deserve this, he's an adult. He can make that decision on his own if he wants too.

But if I am that much of a distraction to him, I don't want to get in the way of his future. Truthfully, who am I to say what he needs when I only met him yesterday. Maybe his father is right... *in a way*.

"Don't you think Dustin could make that decision on his own?"

He nods. "Dustin is a great man. But he often leads with his heart. A strength and a weakness. He'll throw everything away for you if he thinks it'll make you happy."

"We only met yesterday. I have a feeling he's more level-headed than that." I argue.

"Were you two not late for the competition this morning?"

Shit, he's right.

It was only a few minutes, but we were both late. I've never been late for a competition before, and I'm assuming Dustin hasn't been either. Especially with how strict Rodney is.

"Look, I'm sure you're a nice gal. I also think whatever is going on between you and my son can wait till after DuneFest." He rests his hand on my shoulder. I smack it away. He scoffs. "You need to think about Dustin's future. I'm sure you understand what I'm saying." I do know what he's saying. He wants me to throw the race on purpose, to secure Dustin's position for the pros.

"Hey! Do we have a problem here?" my dad's voice echoes from behind me.

I cross my arms over my chest, and glare at Rodney.

He looks at him and then looks back at me.

"No, I don't think we do. Do we, Claire?"

I'm not one to back down. Normally, I'd speak up and fight but I have a feeling that Rodney might be a little right, and I can't ignore that. Especially if Dustin's future is on the line.

I give him a venomous glare. "No, we don't. *However*, if you ever put your fucking hands on me again, we will have one." To hell with impressing Dustin's father. I know he won't be happy when he finds out about this interaction, and that will be Rodney's problem not mine.

"I think it's best if you leave now," Dad tells him.

Rodney nods, and walks off.

"What a prick. Are you okay? What did he want?"

"I'm fine." I take a deep breath and stare at the direction he disappeared to. "He wants me to let Dustin focus on his future. He thinks that in order for him to do that, I need to leave him alone until after DuneFest."

"What are you going to do?"

I look down at my hands.

They began to shake when Rodney put his hand on my shoulder. "I'm going to win this damn competition to prove him wrong. He thinks I'm the distraction, well now he's going to have a bigger issue." I pause because saying this hurts more than I expected. "And I'm going to leave Dustin alone, until DuneFest is over."

If the scouts are looking at Dustin that means they are already interested. I know for a fact it won't matter if he wins this year or not. He's already won five titles, they'd be stupid not to take him at this point.

If that's even what he wants for his future.

Rodney should know that if he's been supporting his son all these years. Meaning the conversation with me was just to be controlling. This plan might bite me in the ass, Dustin might never forgive me for shutting him out these next few days. Even so, his dad needs to learn a lesson, and I'll gladly be the one to teach him.

It's closing in on seven o'clock and my nerves have hit an all time high. This was supposed to be a fun night. We were supposed to be meeting new people in town, and hopefully making new friends. Now, all I can think about is how I'm going to tell Dustin I can't continue to see him. Just thinking about it makes my heart hurt. I don't know if I'll be able to keep my composure when it's actually time to tell him.

I probably should just be honest with him, tell him that Rodney cornered me and said I'm the reason he lost his first competition in five years. Not that I'm just a good rider, and the first decent competitor that Dustin's been up against in half a decade. *No,* that can't be it. It has to be that I'm just a girl distracting a man from his future.

Ugh. What a pig.

"We can skip it, you know?"

I swear Dad hears my thoughts.

"No. I need to take care of this. Either way it'll be now or later, and at least at the shrimp feed there will be people around. It'll be harder for him to talk me out of it."

"I'm proud of you. The decision you're making is hard. Plus, I'll always have your back. You know that."

"I hope I'm making the right decision. Honestly, none of the options I have feel entirely right. I'm just going with what I think is best for everyone."

"Every choice we make in life never feels like the right one. You just have to trust your heart. "

"I know. Thank you."

"Of course. Come on, we better get going."

We walk the short distance to Tattie's campsite and I try to rein in my emotions. When I see the layout in front of me, I pause. Her campsite is huge. She must help coordinate DuneFest somehow because her space is about twice as big as the rest of them. Between two camp trailers there's four or five pop up tables pushed together. A large, white, plastic wrap runs all the way down making the illusion that it's one very large table. There's chairs of all colors and sizes surrounding it on both sides. Little bowls that seem to be holding condiments are placed in front of each, and there's four plastic butter trays put at each individual set up.

Dad bends down and whispers in my ear. "What did you get us into?"

"I have no idea."

I've never seen anything like this before. It seems like organized chaos.

"Oh my gosh! You're here!" a familiar bubbly voice shouts at us from behind a massive pot to the left of the table. Tattie has a huge pair of gloves on and a giant stirring stick. She sets down her cooking arsenal, and rushes over to give us both a hug. "I'm so happy you made it!"

"*Yeah.* What exactly is going on?" I question her.

"You've never been to a shrimp feed before? Or some people like to call it a shrimp boil."

Dad and I share a glance and then we both shake our heads.

"Oh, what a treat!" she claps her hands. "I'm so happy I get to be your first! My sister Debbie and I host this every year. Debbie runs admissions for DuneFest by the way." *There it is.* Now the big campsite makes sense. "A shrimp feed is where you boil kielbasa, corn, potatoes, and shrimp altogether in one big pot." She counts each food on her fingers. "Then we pour it along the table and everyone digs in. There's no silverware or plates, which I think is the fun part! We all sit around, talk, and have drinks. The clean up is super easy because all you have to do is roll up the plastic wrap and throw it away!" Dad and I both have a skeptical look on our face, and Tattie giggles. "I promise, it's fun! Come on, I'll introduce you to Big Rich and Jeremy."

There's already a handful of people here.

Simultaneously stirring the food and introducing us to everyone, Tattie makes us feel right at home. Like we've lived here our whole lives.

The two people I was looking forward to meeting the most were Big Rich—the head honcho for DuneFest—and Jeremy, who owns Jeremy's Automotive and Off-Road. The best mechanics shop in the city. I'd be lying if I said I wasn't putting on all the charm when I talked with him.

He is the ticket into my dream job, after all.

I notice Dad is chatting with Ian, the head of education and training at the Lower Umpqua Hospital here in Reedsport.

Back in Reno, Dad was the manager of a mechanics shop during the day and at night he worked on the hospital transport team. He worked both jobs so that he could pay for my college degree. Sadly, there were no spots available at the mechanics shop here, which he would have preferred. But he did take the position as a hospital transporter. He has been considering getting his nursing degree lately, and I really hope he does. It would give him a better schedule, and pay.

Aside from all of that, it's nice to see him making connections.

Unfortunately, my ignorant bliss is interrupted a little too soon. I'm about to go over and talk with Tattie again when Dustin and his family walk in. My heart drops in my stomach. All of a sudden it's hard to breathe. Part of me was hoping they wouldn't show up. This is going to be a lot harder than I was expecting. Nothing could have prepared me for this feeling. His face lights up when he sees me and he smiles, but this time it feels like daggers straight to my heart. I glance over at Rodney, and he nods at me. Anger rushes through me, and I have to turn away to stop myself from punching something– or crying.

I know Dustin is walking over to me, but I'm not ready for this. Not yet.

He grabs my arm gently. "Hey, is everything okay?"

Luckily, I don't have to run because Tattie announces that food is ready and tells everyone to grab a seat.

"Yeah, I am going to go find my dad though. We'll talk after. Okay?" I refuse to meet his beautiful eyes as I talk to him.

"Claire?" There's worry in his tone and I look up for just a second. *Terrible mistake.* "What's going on?"

"Nothing, everything is fine. Go find your family." I shrug out of his grip and walk away.

I take a few hurried breaths as I search for my dad, and pray Dustin isn't following me. Once I find him, people are already picking out their seats and beginning to sit down.

I wait for Dustin and his family to pick their spots then purposely pick two chairs, for Dad and I, at the opposite end of the table. I chose to sit on the same side Dustin is on so I don't have to see him across the table. I don't know how I'm going to do this. How am I supposed to lie to him?

Before I can worry about it too much, Tattie and her sister Debbie—which look absolutely nothing alike—start pouring the food on the top of the white plastic wrap, and everyone digs in. This is very different and I kind of love it. Everyone's laughing and reminiscing on past years. Country music plays in the background. The food is absolutely delicious, even though I have only been picking at it, and the energy from the table is infectious. Everyone we've met tonight has been so nice and welcoming. Still, it has done little to ease the tension in my shoulders.

Everyone eats a little too fast and now my clock is running out of time.

When everyone's finished, Dad and I help toss the white plastic wrap out and put condiments back in coolers.

Trying to avoid Dustin the rest of the night has been excruciating. As much as I'm thankful this night is almost over, I'm also dreading it.

Visitors are starting to head back to their campsites and the party is ending. Dad and Tattie are talking about local hikes as we sit at the table outside of her trailer when Dustin walks up to me. I can already feel the tears threatening to surface when he says my name.

"Hey, Claire." He nods at all of us. "Jesse, Tattie, do you mind if I steal her for a moment?" He looks at me.

Why is this so hard?

Dad puts his hand on my knee and gives it a gentle squeeze. A gesture of reassurance that he has my back.

"Of course not," he says in a sympathetic tone.

I stand up and follow Dustin just outside of Tatties campsite. We are both quiet.

"Did I do something wrong?" he says at the same time I say, "I think we need to slow down."

"I'm sorry if I... wait what did you say?" His brows furrow in confusion as he catches up with my proclamation.

"I think we need to slow down. I think... I think it would be better if we were just... it's just... we just..." *Get it together, Claire.* I take a deep breath. "I am new in town and I think we need to be friends for now."

His eyes start to gloss over and he bites his tongue.

Fuck, this hurts.

"Did I do something wrong?" He asks again.

"No I just... I'm not... I'm not ready for any kind of relationship yet." I'm stammering so hard. The fact that I'm able to form coherent sentences is a miracle. No amount of self reassurance could have prepared me for this.

"I don't understand."

"I'm sorry. It's just better this way. You have to trust me."

"No, that's bullshit. There's no way I made up how great last night, or this morning was in my head." His eyes are trying to scan mine but I won't—can't— return his stare. He's searching for the passion and warmth we shared, but it's not there. If there's one thing I'm good at, it's putting up walls when I need to. "What happened?"

"I just realized this isn't what I want, and you need to accept that."

"No, fuck that. Something happened. Tell me."

"Dustin we are frie…" I begin to plead with him but he cuts me off.

"Don't *fucking* say friends to me." I flinch at his tone. "Shit, I'm sorry." He runs his hands through his hair and lets out an exasperated breath. "There's more here. I may not have a lot of experience in relationships but I know what I felt, and what I feel… in here." He puts his hand over his heart. "I saw it in you too. I know you feel the same way." There's pleading in his eyes and I'm about to say fuck it and forget everything. Screw his dad. Screw this race. But I can't.

The side of Rodney I saw tonight tells me he won't take no for an answer. That he is the type of man that has to learn the hard way. Dustin deserves better than that, he deserves to make his own choices. I know that sounds hypocritical of me at the moment, because ultimately I'm not letting him have a choice now.

However, this is the only way I see it working out: If I win the SandMaster title, some of the pressure from Rodney will be lifted off of his shoulders. He will still have the opportunity to go pro, but this way, the choice will be his.

I could let Dustin in on my plan, except I have a feeling the first thing he would do is go straight to his dad and defend me. Rodney is an asshole, but I don't know if I'm ready to throw a wrench in their relationship yet. If I keep going down this path with Dustin and we end up dating, there's no way his dad wouldn't catch wind. If he chooses not to take an offer for the pros, then Rodney will blame me, and I don't want that either.

This is my only option. Rodney learns his own lesson, Dustin gets a little more freedom, and I'm left out of the blame.

The only sacrifice? My heart.

I'm angry at the fact that I'm being put in this position. That Rodney put me here.

"Claire..?"

"*I don't! Okay?*" I look away from him. "You need to either let me go, or accept us as friends."

He shakes his head at me. "You can't be bossy when you're breaking my heart."

Damn it.

That hurt a lot more than I thought it would.

I know I'm being mean, I don't want to be. But what else am I supposed to do? He has to leave me alone until after DuneFest. Then I can explain everything to him.

If I don't ruin it all before then.

"Dustin, please."

His jaw clenches as disappointment twists across his face. "Okay, Angel. I'll respect your space." The use of my nickname is the last straw. I can no longer see clearly as my vision blurs. "You're hiding something, I can tell. Until you are ready to tell me the truth, I guess it's goodbye. " He shoves his hands into the front pockets of his jeans. For the first time tonight I met his gaze. "Have a good night, Gates." A tear falls down his cheek as he turns around and walks off into the dark.

When he's out of sight, I drop to my knees.

I let my wall down and the pain comes pouring out of me as I send my sobs into the quiet of the night. I cry until all the carefully put together pieces of my heart come crumbling back down. I don't know if we will be able to come back from this. I might have just made the worst decision of my life.

None of my feelings make sense to me right now. I just met this man, so why does it feel like I just broke off a serious relationship? Why does my heart feel like someone reached inside my chest and began hammering at it? Why am I crying so hard over only a few shared moments?

I'm about to welcome the cold sand as my bed for the night, when I hear footsteps, and Dad takes a seat next to me.

"Why does it hurt so bad?" I voice.

"Because you have a connection with him. Whatever form it is– relationship, friendship, or understanding. And you sacrificed that desire to explore what it could lead to by doing what you think is best for him." He pulls me into his side. "It's not always easy to do the right thing.

"I just met Dustin yesterday. It shouldn't feel like this. I've pushed away plenty of guys in the past, what makes him different?" The answer to that is easy. *The way he makes me feel.*

"I think you already know the answer to that question, Mini."

Pain riddles my body and I feel ridiculous for feeling this way.

"Come on." Dad scoops me up into his arms, and comforts me just like he did when I was little. I sniffle into his shoulder ruining his shirt with my tears and snot as he carries me back to our trailer. His thumb brushes along my back as he whispers to me. "It's going to be okay. He will come back. You have to trust what you're doing is right."

It's too late now. This has to work. And if it doesn't....

No, I can't think about that.

"I love you, Claire."

His words resonate in my soul as my emotions click from sadness to defiance. All this heartbreak can't be for nothing.

If I want to be successful, I need to push out the Angel and welcome the Devil.

Chapter Ten

Dustin

Fuck. My head pounds against my skull as I sit up in the bed of my Bronco. *What happened last night?*

There's suddenly a loud banging against my truck window and I scramble to grab a pillow and pull it over my ears.

Oh, god. Make it stop, please.

"Rise and shine, plastic princess," Axel yells as he smacks his fist against the glass.

"I'm gonna kick your ass when I get out of here," I groan.

"You've never been able to kick my ass. But you definitely aren't going to in your current state," he chuckles.

"What happened last night?"

"You don't remember?"

I can barely make out his face through the mud streaked window but it looks like there is concern written across it.

I'm trying to get a grip on the memories from last night but nothing is coming to surface. I need water. Maybe some bread– *ugh the thought of food makes me want to throw up.* I need coffee.

Yes. Coffee.

Coffee, good.

"No. Now, can you get me some coffee?"

Axel whispers something under his breath as he walks towards our parents camp trailer. I can barely make it out but it sounds like he says, *'This is gonna be fun'.*

I lay back down in the bed of my truck and bury my face under the blankets. I just need some caffeine, and maybe a talk with Axel, then I'll remember the horrors of last night. I already know I've probably done something embarrassing. I've only ever been this hungover one other time and that was my twenty-first birthday. I swore that day I'd never get that drunk again.

Apparently, I can't keep the promises I make to myself.

How much did I drink? What did I drink?

I roll over and grab my phone off the blanket. It's noon, I've got five hours till the ShortCross competition. If my dad sees me like this I'm screwed. I need to sober up fast and get ready to race. Just as I sit up again, I hear my tailgate drop open.

"Here." Axel hands me a paper to-go cup. I cradle the cup in my hands feeling the warmth spread through my fingers as the scent of vanilla fills my nose. The vanilla reminds me of Claire.

Fuck. Claire.

A memory comes rushing back to me as I remember being outside of Tatties campsite with her, as she broke off whatever it is we are... or were. Suddenly, the pain in my head feels small in comparison to the pain returning in my chest.

"Starting to remember huh?" Axel asks somberly.

I rub the back of my neck as I try to stop the tears that are threatening to return. "Yeah, man."

I scoot down the bed of my truck, and sit on the tailgate with Axel. The sun feels good on my skin, it helps me sober up.

I'm only wearing a pair of black sweatshorts, and I know I look just as shitty as I feel.

"What do you remember?"

"I remember Claire ripping my heart out after Shrimp Feed, then walking back here." I rub my forehead with my palm as I try to remember the rest. "I remember you handing me a beer, then we took a few shots of whiskey... June came over shortly after that and invited us down to the pier with her friends. A few more shots... then nothing." Axel nods his head up and down, confirming what I said.

He looks down at his coffee and picks at the black lid. "Do you want to know the rest?"

Fuck. Do I?

I remember Axel telling me all the shit I did the day after my twenty-first. I wanted to stick my head in the ground and bury it like ostriches do when they feel threatened. That would have been way better than having to hear I ran through Main Street buck-ass naked and jumped off the pier to go skinny dipping. Or waking up to see only one of my legs entirely shaved and a giant pink dick drawn on it with a sharpie. However, I do have to give the artist credit, the veins and ball hairs were painstakingly accurate—and quite beautiful.

I have a feeling whatever happened last night is going to hurt me ten times worse than what happened that day two years ago.

Mixing heartache and alcohol is never a good idea.

I let out a long breath. "Do I want to know?"

He shrugs. "It's a small town man. Either I tell you, or everyone knows and you don't."

Damn it.

"Alright, tell me." I brace myself for whatever Axel is about to say.

"Well for starters, it wasn't that bad up until the last twenty minutes before I brought you home. We went to the pier and the only thing you could talk about was Claire, how beautiful she is, and how good her lips felt; that no other girl in town could ever come close to her."

Okay, I can live with that. That's not too bad.

Axel must see the relief on my face, cause he smirks. "You were on top of the cooler shouting it, in front of half the local girls."

I cringe.

Okay, that's not so great.

I can still live with that though. Comparatively that's not the worst I've done. Plus, most of the girls in town already know I'm not interested and probably just thought I was being an ass for announcing it. I will be handing out a lot of apologies for the next few weeks.

"Want me to keep going?"

"Fuck, there's more?"

Axel nods solemnly.

"Yes." I hang my head. "Go on."

"You know April from Sugar Shack?"

"*Mmm...* Sugar Shack. Can we get a Bigfoot Donut?" Sugar Shack makes *the* best pastries in the entire world, I'd bet money on it. Their Bigfoot Donut is my absolute favorite. The sugary puff pastry is just what I need to cure this hangover.

"Focus man. You're going to hate this part."

Oh, God. No, no, no, no, no.

Axel reads my expression and I notice his mouth forms a thin line. Confirming my suspicions.

"I didn't. I couldn't. I wouldn't. No..." I shake my head vigorously.

"I swear I lost you for ten seconds. I was talking to June, looked over, and couldn't see you anywhere. When I did find you..." he pauses, waiting for me to tell him to stop. I can't. I have to know, no matter how bad it is. "Well... I don't know how to say this any other way... she was giving you head."

My ears start ringing and I swear I'm gonna pass out. Either from the alcohol still coursing through my veins or from the news that just hit me like a brick, I have no idea.

I've never hooked up with someone while drunk nor have I hooked up with someone and not remembered it the next day. I don't like this feeling. I don't care what other people do with their sex life. But for me, I only want to share myself with people I actually care about. Sure, April is a nice girl but I don't love her and I may sound like an asshole for saying this but I don't really care about her either. Plus, April deserves better than a blacked out counterpart anyways.

"Did you stop us?" I ask him, afraid of what the answer might be.

If I did anything else...

"Yeah, I did. And you owe me twice now because that was awkward as hell."

"Thank god." I drop my head into my hands. "Ugh..."

How could I let this happen?

How do I explain this to Claire?

Truth is, this whole night wouldn't matter if I never met her. I may not be proud of the choices I made, but I wouldn't feel bad about them either.

I guess I don't have to explain this to her. She did break it off. Still, there's a knot in my stomach and an ache in my heart. This feels wrong, even though it shouldn't be a big deal. Besides, it's not like we were dating. She told me she wanted to be friends. She made it pretty damn clear last night she doesn't feel the same way I do.

So why can't I let this go? Why do I feel so shitty?

Axel is sitting in silence, letting me battle my own thoughts and emotions. Waiting to see if I want his help or if I need to talk. I look over at him. "Why does it feel like this?"

I don't even have to explain. He already understands.

He takes a deep breath. "I can't speak for you, D. However, I can tell you about my own experiences and hope that helps." He looks out to the ocean, just past the row of campers in front of us. "No one besides Ray knows this," Ray is Axel's childhood best friend and basically my adoptive older brother. "and if you tell anyone, I'll kick your ass."

I laugh. "Understood."

"When I turned twenty-two... let's just say I let loose. As you know, I moved out of our parents house that same day and it felt so good to be an adult, to have my freedom, to be able to do whatever the hell I wanted. Peter and I had parties pretty much every weekend. Which meant a lot of girls came over. At first it was fun... the sex. Truthfully, I don't have any regrets. I was enjoying myself. But that's all it ever was with those girls. Until one night, this girl came over and I'd never seen her before. She had just moved into town. She was so gorgeous. Still is, to this day, the most beautiful woman I have ever seen. She is fun and silly. Strong, but vulnerable. Sweet but sour. Perfect. I have never laughed so hard or felt so... alive. We flirted all night together. Until, she led me upstairs and for that night she was mine." He takes a sip of his coffee and inhales. "With her it was different. There was a connection. A spark. I don't know how to explain it. It sounds stupid. But she gave me the same kind of comfort that Mom's lemon meringue pie does on Easter." Axel and I take a moment to appreciate the delicious memories. This is huge for Axel. He has a hard exterior and very few people know him past the surface. If he compares someone to his favorite memory, they really are special to him.

None of this makes sense to me though, because he hasn't had a girlfriend in seven years.

Maybe that's why. Maybe she got away.

I won't let Claire get away. I'll fight for her every damn day if I have to. Even if the only option I have is being her friend.

I'd spend the time she gave me learning about her until she was ready to let me love her.

Axel continues. "Anyway, suddenly after her, everything changed. I didn't want to just have meaningless sex anymore. I tried. Trust me. It just wasn't the same. I know without the girls before her, it wouldn't have led me to her, or given me the experience I needed to give her what she–"

I hold up my hand and interrupt him. "I don't need the details man."

He smirks. "Did you forget that I just caught you getting your dick sucked by a girl in the bushes only a few hours ago? I think we've passed that barrier, D." I cringe. I don't think I'll ever forgive myself for that. "The truth is, you find out what hurts them, hurts you. And when you hurt them... *Well*, that's the worst pain a man can ever feel. Letting the woman they love down." I have a feeling there's more to this story than Axel is leading on. He is definitely not the one to fall in love in one night, there has to be more history for him to admit that he loves this woman. But I'm not going to push him. He already confessed so much. That will just have to be a conversation for another time.

He does have me questioning myself though.

Do I love Claire?

I mean that sounds ridiculous. I just met her two days ago and at first she hated my guts.

After that night at the concert, the only thing I could think about was her. Hell even before that, when I didn't even know her name yet. Not just her body and her beauty, but her smile and her laugh. The way she plays around with me and her smart ass comments. The way she bites her lip when she's deep in thought. Her blue eyes that sparkle under the moon, and the way they turn to ice when she's frustrated. Everything about her. I know that she's ruined me. That I will be looking for pieces of her in every girl I meet.

I've never felt like this before. If I had to put a word on the way I felt for Claire, I guess the closest thing to explain it would be: love.

It's not like it matters now anyways. Something changed for her last night. She's hiding something from me. The words out of her mouth told me she wanted to be friends, but her body language told me it was hurting her just as much as it was hurting me.

I can't force her to tell me.

She put a wall up last night and every time I thought it dropped a little, it would turn to steel, and the sadness in her would turn to anger. If there's one thing I've learned about Claire in this short amount of time, it's that she's stubborn. When she makes up her mind you aren't going to change it. No matter how hard you try. No matter how hard *I* want to try.

What am I left to do?

Be her friend? Let her go?

Both options sound miserable. I guess if I had to settle for one, it would have to be friends. Even if she only allows me to have a piece of her, that's better than losing her completely. I just wish I would have realized that last night.

"Thanks for sharing that with me, Ax."

He sets his hand on my shoulder. "It's gonna be alright. Shit happens. Personally, I think this is mild compared to your twenty-first."

I roll my eyes. "Don't even get me started."

We both start laughing.

It gets cut short when we hear the door to the camp trailer next to us swing open, and my father steps out.

"Dustin, put a shirt on. We are going for a drive."

Good morning to you too, Dad.

I look over at Axel and mouth 'help me' before I respond, "Yeah, okay give me ten."

"You have five," he says before the door slams shut.

I don't know what his problem is but this isn't going to be fun. Times like this is when I wish I could go back and tell him that I don't want to race professionally. That I just want to do it as a hobby. Either way I know the pressure would have been put on shoulders to be successful in whatever I chose to do. Except, at least this way we would still have riding to share, and it wouldn't be so damn stressful.

Axel waves at me as he heads back to his truck. "Good luck with that." He gestures to the camp trailer.

I give him a fake smile and a thumbs up.

I hop off the tailgate and walk to the passenger side of my bronco. I shift through my duffel bag until I find something clean. I pull a dark green t-shirt over my head.

This will have to do.

Shortly after I finish pulling my head through the hole, I hear footsteps behind me. My heart leaps in anticipation as I turn around hoping to see Claire. My face drops when I notice it's April from Sugar Shack.

"Sorry to be a disappointment." Her tone and the way she bites her cheek makes me feel bad.

"It's not you... it's just—"

"You don't have to explain. Everyone heard you professing your love to the new girl last night."

"Her name is Claire." I bite back.

"Yeah... Claire."

I nod.

"Look, I just wanted to say sorry. I was really drunk and June convinced me to take *way* too many jello shots. My boss is a total asshole and tripled my workload this week. My ex was at a bar with my cousin and I just... you don't need to know all of that, and now I'm rambling but... uh..." She bites her lip and I can see tears forming in her eyes. "You're a nice guy. I heard your confession and I guess drunk me took it as a competition. That was so *very* wrong of me. You even called me Claire in the moment and I knew that should have been a red flag. Instead, I ignored it because I needed the distraction from my shit hole of a life and... I'm just sorry."

"Shit happens. If we are being honest I took way too many shots as well." I smile at her. "Things don't have to be weird between us. I was also very drunk... and I'm sorry." I clear my throat. "Your ex is a douche, and I would cut off your cousin if I were you."

She giggles. "Yeah, you're probably right. Anyway, I should get going. I just wanted to apologize and make sure everything was cool between us. We do live in a small town, after all."

She stretches her arms out to give me a hug.

At first I'm hesitant, but I don't want to embarrass her anymore. It's a friendly hug, two people realizing we made a poor decision while drunk and coming to an understanding.

When she pulls away there's a tear running down her cheek. I wipe it away with my thumb. "You deserve better. I can't give you what you want, just... don't go back to your damn ex, either." She nods and sniffles. "Bye, April."

"See ya, Dustin." She turns, starts to head back to her campsite, and abruptly stops, a frantic look on her face. She looks between me and whatever is causing her distress. I follow her eyes to a campsite across the sand.

Standing with her arms crossed, murder in her eyes, is Claire. No doubt, watching the whole thing unravel and thinking the worst.

She is so fucking sexy. Even when there's anger pouring out of every pore in her body. Her hair is in a messy bun on top of her head, tiny curls spilling out. She's wearing black sweatpants that hang loose on her hips showing off the small V that disappears into her waistline. A low cut tank top showing off her boobs and displaying her toned belly. The white from her top complementing her tanned skin. I don't know why, but the look in her eyes makes me hard. I know this is a completely inappropriate moment. Still, there's a part of me that wants to punish her for striking me with those icy blue eyes.

Damn it.

I throw up my hand between April and the death glare she's receiving from Claire. "It's not what you think!" I yell across the makeshift road. She tilts her head to the side and shakes it before she stomps back up the stairs to her camping trailer.

I go to run after her, I have to explain myself.

But before I can take a step, a hand grabs my wrist.

"Dustin, it's time to go," Dad says. A stern look on his face and I know there's no way I'll convince him to wait.

He's just going to have to.

I can't let her think the worst. She won't even want to be my friend after this. I have to explain myself before I lose her completely. My teeth grind together. "I have to go talk to her."

"It can wait."

I look over my shoulder for April but sometime between me yelling and my dad grabbing me, she must have ran off.

I would kill to trade her places.

"It can't. You don't understand," I plead. Hoping just once he'll listen.

He scans my face. "You're hungover. Give her time to cool off while you sober up. Trust me son, she isn't going to hear you right now, anyway."

How long has he been standing there? How much did he see?

I guess he's right. If I tried talking to Claire right now, I'd only be met with anger. Maybe if I gave her time to cool off, it would be easier for her to hear me out.

This whole situation sobered me up pretty fast. Nonetheless, my head is still pounding and I'm having a hard time thinking straight. When I make it up to her I want to give her all my attention, and I need to be in the right mind to do that.

"Alright, let's go." I say in defeat.

I don't understand how my life went from being absolutely perfect to utter disaster in less than a day. All I've ever done with Claire is fuck things up.

Maybe, I don't deserve her.

Maybe she was right.

I was angry and hurt at first when she told me she didn't want more. Now, I think she had seen things before I did. She knew I would cause her pain, that I would continue to fuck things up. If that's the case, I'm thankful she called things off. If I was always destined to make her suffer like this, then I'm glad we didn't get more serious. If this was all I did to her—hurt her, make her question me—then I was never worth her time to begin with, and she deserves so much better. Maybe this is why I was never meant to be in a relationship, because I would always be the thing that harms them the most.

I'll pull myself out of the equation before I let that happen to Claire.

Dad ended up taking me to Sugar Shack to talk about an offer from the pros. Typically recruiters will only scout you at AMA Pro-Am events, occasionally they'll show up to popular racing competitions just to get a better idea of who you are as a rider.

Apparently, David West— a recruiter—is going to be at the ShortCross Competition tonight. Dad wanted to make sure my head was in the game and that nothing was distracting me. I can't blame him for being concerned after what he witnessed this afternoon. As I had expected, he was also extremely disappointed in me for showing up drunk at two in the morning. I got an earful on behavior, respect, motivation, distractions– the whole nine yards. There was no '*I'm proud you made it this far son*' or '*You're going to kick ass today*'. Of course, no type of encouragement. I don't know what I was expecting. I should know better than that by now.

Hey, at least I got my Bigfoot Donut.

Out of all of the competitions, this is the one I dread the most. The ShortCross track is just a large oval with a bermed rim, roughly two miles long. There are 10-15 racers at a time. A total of six laps and you have to finish in 1st or 2nd place to be in the final race. Whoever wins the champions race, takes home the trophy. The reason I am not looking forward to the ShortCross competition is because it's not just me and the track. I will have to look out for other riders and watch my surroundings. If one rider goes down, they can take a whole lot of bikes with them.

Luckily, the conversation with my father was short because it was closing in on game time.

We are back at the pop up tent now with Axel and Mom. I am getting my racing gear on, and Axel is helping Dad adjust the suspension on my bike, as well as replacing my chain.

This is the second race in my entire career where I am more distracted than focused. I was stressed during my date with Claire and it was an entire shit show. Still, the events of last night pale in comparison to this morning. Somehow, within the last 24 hours I managed to fuck up the one potential relationship I could see working out and had drunken oral sex with a girl I have known since elementary school. The only positive outcome of this entire ordeal is I've realized why all these years I've never bothered with relationships. Maybe my father had been right all along. There is no place in my life for a woman right now. Even one as perfect and beautiful as Claire. Eventually, she will be a thing of the past and I will move on.

The only reason it hurts is because it's fresh. It's an open wound in the process of healing and eventually it'll scab over.

Then one day I'll have a scar, a memory of the past of what could have been. I just have to make peace with that.

Even if I come to terms with letting her go, I still have this nagging voice in my head begging me to apologize. I know it's the right thing to do.

Will she even hear me out?

I have to take the risk. I won't be able to live with myself if I don't. Plus, we live in a small ass town. Having to avoid someone is nearly impossible, not to mention the fact we are neighbors. It would be better for the both of us if I can make this water under the bridge.

Friends.

What a horrible word.

"Good afternoon ladies and gentlemen, this is your favorite DuneFest host, Big Rich. I'm calling all riders for the ShortCross competition, please make your way to the starting gate to get separated into your groups. Thank you, and may the best rider win," his voice blasts over the loudspeakers. Guess it's time to race, and not once was I able to focus.

I'll apologize to Claire after the Night Race tomorrow. Then we can move forward with being friends. It'll be the best opportunity anyways. The competitions will be over, and maybe we could spend the rest of the night hanging out.

The Night Race is the last competition for SandMaster, and my favorite. It's a straight, five mile race in the sand, and borders the ocean. It really is a beautiful scene. Although, it's the most challenging competition, in my opinion. You have to ride by the moonlight and the lights of the riders around you. If you're in front it's even more challenging. *What could be better?* Spending the day with Claire.

Damn it.

There goes the ounce of focus I had left in my reserves.

This is going to be so much harder than I thought. I just need to keep reminding myself that I'm not good for her. That the reason I'm distancing myself—that she is distancing herself— is because I will only continue to hurt her. I just need to focus on the SandMaster title.

Do I even want to win another SandMaster title?

The pressure from my father has been at an all time high, ever since we received the offer from the pros. Truthfully, my motivation to make riding a career has been dwindling away for the past couple years. I haven't had the heart to tell him yet.

He accepted Axel quitting way easier because he made it clear from the beginning that riding wasn't going to be his profession. It just sealed the deal last year when his crabbing business took off, giving dad proof that motocross wasn't his calling. But for me? I have no idea what I would do if I didn't race. I took one cooking class at the local community college in Italian cuisine and absolutely loved it. Is it my passion? Is it my calling? Did I want to pursue it? I have no idea. I can't just go up to my dad and say, *'Hey, I want to quit motocross. I know I'm only one step away from making half a mill a year, but it's just not for me anymore. Oh, what did you say, Dad? You want to know what I decided to do instead? Heres the best part, I have no fucking clue'.* I might as well chop off my own head and put it on a silver platter for him at that point.

"You keep thinking that hard and your head will explode," Mom says, shaking me out of the battle I'm having within myself. She is walking alongside me as I roll my bike from the campsite to the starting gate. Dad and Axel left earlier to find seats, she chose to stay behind.

My mom is a very short woman. More times than I could count, people would tell me I look just like her but with my dads height. She is also the most selfless person I have ever met. She constantly puts other people first, and would break her back for the people she loves. I admire her so much. If I had half the heart she does, maybe I wouldn't be in this position I'm in with Claire.

And now I've spent the minimal time that we actually get together wallowing in my own self pity.

"Sorry, Mom."

She shakes her head. "You don't need to apologize to me, sweetheart. You have a lot going on right now and I can see how much it's weighing on you." There's a tone of insinuation in her voice and for a second I think she is alluding to something other than the events of this morning. She rests her hand on my forearm and stops me. "I love your Dad very much, but he can be a very hard man. Sometimes, when he gets passionate about something, he develops a kind of tunnel vision. Forgetting that it's not just his life he's fighting for, but also that there is someone else involved. Ultimately, he just wants what's best... however that might look. Do you understand what I'm saying?"

I nod. "Yeah, I think so."

"Just try and talk to him, okay?"

"Okay."

I know that he won't hear me and will only apprehend the hundreds of thousands of dollars I am throwing away. Still, I'll try again for mom.

"Now. Go out there and win this race." She pats me on the back.

A few minutes later we walk up to the starting line, she gives me a kiss on the cheek and goes to find her seat next to Dad and Axel.

Meanwhile, I'm silently praying that Claire is not in the same group as me. Which is so strange, because just yesterday I was hoping I'd be right next to her. Watching her kick my ass to the finish line.

"Thank you racers for participating in the ShortCross Competition. I will read off the riders and their numbers at the beginning of each round. With that being said, here is the line up for group one. Linetti-46, Price-21, McGrath-1, Cranel-55,

O'Neil-186, Hanks-78, Smith-3, Murphy-28, Stevens-713, and Scott-23. Good luck out there."

I let out a sigh of relief as Big Rich's voice cuts out of the megaphone. I'm watching him in the judges tower as Debbie leans in and whispers something in his ear. The screech of the megaphone shouts over the crowd as Big Rich pulls it up to his mouth. "I'm sorry, I'm being informed that there is in fact one more racer in group one." *Please, please, please, please, please.* "Gates-87. My bad. Thank you everyone." *Fuck.* I look up at the sky, *couldn't you have listened to me just this one time?*

I slide my helmet over my head and walk my bike up to the starting line. I'm afraid to look down the line, but I need to see her, just once. Reluctantly, I lift my head and turn to the right. She's already looking at me, except I can't see her eyes because she's pulled down her blacked-out goggles. A part of me wishes I could see her eyes, and the other is very thankful that I can't.

We stay like this, frozen in time. Until the memories from the concert come flooding back, and it's brutally interrupted by the look on her face when she saw me with April. The pain in my chest returns, or maybe it never left and I've just welcomed it as a new friend.

I can't look any longer. I can't see her eyes, her plump lips, or her beautiful black hair. Still, the way her gear hugs her curves perfectly is excruciating and the anger in the way she grips her handlebars is tormenting me. I wish I was as brave or fearless as she is. She takes her pain and stares at it head on. Returning its deathly glare and making it cower under her strength. Instead, I succumb to its wrath. Letting it devour me whole, until there's only little pieces left.

I'm brought back to the moment when the rest of the racers kickstart their bikes. The roar of the engines takes over, drowning out my thoughts and forcing me back.

I guess it's time to race.

Chapter Eleven

Claire

I have been fighting my own emotions all morning.

I have extensive experience in pushing things aside so I can focus on the task at hand. I spent most of this morning separating the sadness, confusion, and frustration from the anger and determination I would need to win this next race.

All my carefully calculated planning starts to unravel when I look down the starting line at Dustin. I'm hoping that seeing his face will fuel my anger and give me more motivation to win the competition. But when his eyes land on mine—or I suppose my goggles—all I can see etched in his beautiful features is the same pain, regret, and longing that I carefully pushed away.

Then, the memory of seeing him hug that girl and wipe her tears the morning after I told him I wanted to be friends comes back in full force and all I feel is rage. Even though we are several feet away, Dustin must be able to feel my emotions because his head drops immediately.

I have no right to be angry with him. I'm the one who told him I wanted to be friends. I'm the one who decided to listen to Rodney and push him away.

Who am I to get jealous if he was with some girl?

We just met three days ago, I am foolish to believe he felt anything else for me than physical attraction.

But he was so convincing.

Fuck.

I thought I learned my lesson with JT. I promised myself I would see past the lies and manipulation the next time. Yet here I am, making the same damn mistakes I made when I was nineteen.

I won't let it happen again.

This morning when I was putting on my riding pants, I slipped my phone into my back pocket and found a rolled up piece of paper. It had Dustin's phone number written on it, in handwriting that looked like chicken scratch, with a note that said:

Claire,
Here's my number in case you decide you want to meet at a hookup spot (267) 436-5109
I hope you call or text. Good luck at the race!
P.S. I'd follow that ass anywhere (;

He must have slipped it into my pocket when he kissed me that morning at my campsite.

When I found it I laughed, cried, then crumpled it into a ball and threw it away. I might end up regretting that decision later when I finally let all this shit go, but in the moment it felt so good. Plus, it's not like he doesn't live across the street. If I needed his number I could go get it. Which is also extremely inconvenient. The fact that I would be trying to distance myself from this man and he's my neighbor is infuriating.

I seriously need to move on from this. We weren't dating, we had just met, I told him I wanted to be friends. I need to stop being angry. I have other things to worry about, anyway. Like landing that job interview, moving out of my dad's, and hopefully getting into the local mechanics shop. Maybe even opening my own shop someday. I don't have time for relationships or wasting my energy on a man who apparently isn't worth it.

So why am I still going to win the SandMaster title?

For me.

One last hurray. One last title. One last time to make an impression. If it helps Dustin, then cool; but I'm not doing it for him. I'm doing it for me.

It's time to race.

I look up at the tower in front of me. My breath fogging up the plastic of my goggles. The anticipation rolling over me as I wait for him to drop the green flag.

I take a deep breath, centering myself.

I pull back on my throttle feeling the thrum of my bike underneath me.

3.... 2.... 1.... Braaapp.

I launch my front wheel over the starting line, taking off for the first curve in the ShortCross competition. Dustin gets the lead, taking the hole shot.

Hugging the bermed corner, I'm on the outside following closely on his tail. My mask catches the sand that flings from his back tire.

I need to get on the inside.

We finished the first two laps and I'm still right behind him.

Four more laps.

I'm waiting for my moment. My opening. But Dustin is careful, calculated, a far more focused rider than he had been in the first two competitions. Making my assumptions correct that I needed to pull myself out of the equation.

Two more laps.

We hit the first corner and Dustin's rear tire gets caught in a crossrut causing him to go wide.

That's my window.

I downshift into 2nd, pin the throttle, and pull up side by side with him. Our bikes almost bump into each other.

Now's my chance.

In the second corner I lean right, hugging the inside, giving me just enough space to grab the lead.

I am vaguely aware of the other eight riders behind us, but when we race together, the whole world drowns out. I try not to think about it too much. I don't have time to worry about how racing with Dustin makes me feel. How being so close to him, sand shooting up behind us, the smell of gas and exhaust in the air, gives me butterflies.

I can hold this lead easily.

This is the final round for Short Cross. I pull this off and that gold medal is mine.

Coming around the last corner of the final lap, Dustin takes advantage of the straightaway, gaining speed.

The checkered flag comes into view.

Although we are going about 40 mph, when I see him out of the corner of my eye, it feels like we aren't going over five miles per hour.

We ride neck and neck until we cross the finish line.

Cheers and screams of excitement fill the air around us.

I slow down a little bit, letting my front tire catch grip in the sand. I engage my clutch, causing my rear tire to rotate. I let it slide out a little as I drop my left leg down and swing my bike in a circle. Smoke bellows into the sky behind me. The audience feeds off the adrenaline as they shout into the afternoon sky.

As soon as I jump off the podium, a swarm of riders come over to congratulate me on my victory.

"That was one hell of a race!"

"Yeah, nice job, Gates."

"Excited to have you in town."

"Thank you guys!" I say to my fellow racers as I smile down at the gold medal hanging around my neck.

I yelp as two hands grab each one of my hips and hoist me up onto their shoulder. I smile when I look down and see my dad's face lit up with pride. I'm sitting to the right of his head, just like I used to when I was a little girl. I am not an easy woman to pick up, but he still hoists me into his arms like I'm nothing.

He's been going to the gym everyday since I was a kid, my entire life I've dealt with girls my age drooling over him. This situation is no different. I return a scowl to every ogling woman I catch. I've spent years perfecting my bitch face. Partially for this reason, partially to protect myself. Fans and riders all around me are yelling and cheering. I decide to let it go for the moment, and enjoy the energy bouncing around us. I haven't been this close to winning a title since my EnduroCross championship.

I scan the crowd for a familiar face. He is standing outside the pile of bodies, his arms crossed over his chest, his face lights up when my eyes meet his. My arm stops in the middle of pumping the air, the wind getting knocked out of me as everything around me ceases to exist. It's just the two of us suspended in time before I jerk my head away unable to hold it any longer as the hurt threatens to resurface. When I look back over I see him walking back to his campsite. My nose crinkles in frustration as I blink back tears. I want more than anything to be able to share this moment with him. To return to our playful banter and silent competition.

I know at this moment no matter how hard I try to push Dustin away, my heart won't let me. It will never be the same without him. A piece of me will always care for Dustin. A piece of my heart will always be with him, no matter how hard I try to get it back.

I was kidding myself when I said I was racing for me. I may have needed to convince myself of my intentions so that I could focus on winning. But the truth is, deep down, I knew I was still racing for his freedom. That I still want what's best for him and a part of me hates myself for that. For allowing someone to get so deep into my heart again. The other part is damn proud of what I've done, what I'm still continuing to do.

My dad drops me back onto the sand. "I'm so proud of you, Mini," he says as he pulls me in for a hug.

"Thank you." I blush. No matter how old I get, hearing him tell me he is proud of me will always settle something in my soul.

"That was one hell of a race. I think it's time we go celebrate." He has a mischievous grin on his face.

"What are you up to?"

"It wouldn't be a surprise if I tell you. Come on, I'll walk your bike back."

I walk anxiously back to our campsite. My mind is swimming with possibilities about what he has up his sleeve.

I question him the whole walk and the man is a tight lipped, pain in my ass. There have been only a handful of times in my life that he has surprised me. Usually he is too impatient to wait and spoils the surprise. All the times that he has kept it quiet they have been huge events. Such as my first bike, my first car, my acceptance letter from UNLV, and our move to Reedsport. So whatever this is, it's big enough to seal his mouth tighter than the suspension on a 250 hitting a booter.

"Come on," I plead with him. "Just one hint?" I stick my lower lip out and give him my best Puss in Boots eyes.

"We are about three feet away from the campsite, you can wait."

I roll my eyes. "Ugh."

He's right. I guess, I can be patient enough to wait.

A few moments later we pull up to the campsite and my eyes light up in wonder.

Attached to the wall of the camp trailer is a white sheet. A few feet away, a projector sits on the plastic table we've been eating at. Fast and the Furious: Tokyo Drift pulled up on the screen (my favorite movie). On the workbench to my left, there's a cookie charcuterie board, popcorn, sandwiches, and rootbeer.

"Either way this would have been fun. But the fact that you won, not that I doubted you for a second, makes this so much better," he says.

Tears start to well up in my eyes. "How did you have time to do this?"

"Well, I couldn't have done it without a little help." As if on cue, the door to the camp trailer swings open. Out steps my tall, brunette best friend.

I scream and run to her, pulling Han into a big hug. Once she is in my arms, I squeeze her until my muscles can't take the strain anymore as I push back the tears that are threatening to spill from missing my best friend.

"When did you get here? And why didn't you come find me right away?"

"I've missed you too." She giggles. "I got in right before your competition. I'm sorry I missed it, I was a little busy." She puts her hands up and gestures to the set up on our trailer. "But I will be there to watch you kick ass at the Night Race comp!"

I can't believe she's actually here. This was just what I needed. We have a lot to catch up on. Nothing heals the heart like spilling your guts to your best friend.

I grew up my whole life not being able to make friends with other girls. Probably, the result of being raised by a single dad or because all my interests were in a male dominated hobby. Nonetheless, it still made things lonely growing up. I thought something was wrong with me.

I envied the women who had clans, best friends to do girly shit with. I have always enjoyed getting my nails done—even if it was always black—and shopping but I just couldn't connect on the level that other girls could. Still can't.

Until Han.

She accepts me for me. She never pushes me to talk about my feelings, she just stands in my corner as silent support knowing that eventually I will come running to her when I need help. In return, I let her gossip all she wants and accept her for who she is. A colorful, loud, somewhat obnoxious ray of sunshine to my dark cloud. Together, we don't make any sense. But it works for us. I ground her and she shows me how to be emotional.

Dad hitches a thumb over his shoulder. "I'm going to head inside and catch up on some reading. You two have fun."

I run over to him and pull him in for a hug. I look up from his chest and say. "Thank you"

"Of course."

He knows that I am going through a lot. That I just needed some time with my best friend and he somehow made it happen. His attentiveness and empathy has always made me feel heard and valued. I hope someday he will have an opportunity to bring love and happiness into another woman's life like he has done for me.

I join Han at the couch that is made out of cinder blocks and 2x2s. Outdoor cushions cover the seat and backrest. Multiple blankets litter the bench.

"Where did you get all this stuff?" I asked her. "And how did you have time to make this?"

"I have my resources." She winks.

"You've been in town for roughly two hours, you have no resources."

We both laugh knowing that she most definitely has resources already.

"Okay, your dad helped a little bit and he introduced me to a lovely woman named Tattie. She just happened to know a guy that has a trailer full of construction gear here on the beach. One thing led to another... and boom. Here we are." She pats her hand on the couch in a prideful manner.

Han has always been charming. Things seem to just fall into place for her, whereas I have to work my ass off for it. I'd be lying if I didn't say her unparalleled amount of luck makes me a little jealous. At the same time, whatever Han gets, she gives back to others tenfold. It is impossible to hate such a caring person.

Han has a rounded face with mid length brown hair that matches her eyes perfectly. She has the cutest dimples and a little mole on the top of the right side of her lip that couldn't have been placed more beautifully.

She was adopted by her family when she was four from her birth parents in Asia. She doesn't remember much about her birth family, only that they had a hard life.

She used to get nightmares every once in a while when we were little about strange people coming into her home. The dream always consisted of her birth mom hiding her under the floorboards, and she would peek up through a small split in the wood and see strange men holding guns. The last thing she remembered was a scream and she would wake up sweating and crying. When we would have sleepovers, she used to scare me so badly I would call my dad and ask him to come pick me up.

When we were about eleven she finally told me about the horrors she was living through in the night. The next time she had one while I was over, I just grabbed her and held her until she fell asleep against my chest and suddenly, I felt bad for all those times I had left.

She has gone to therapy for years. I think it's been awhile since she's had a nightmare but I know they still weigh on her.

Her parents, Charles and Vivienne Chambers, are mega-rich socialites that own a chain of hotels. Their headquarters are in Reno. One year when we were seven, my dad raised up enough money to send me to a summer camp. I met Han there and we have been inseparable since.

She has four older siblings, Charles II, Max (short for Maximus), Tobias, and Collette. All of them are equally as successful as the next and as equally insufferable. Collette was the only one who would ever spend time with us as kids, and even then, she had an aura of self righteousness. It was honestly surprising compared to their parents who were always so kind and humble. I was happy Han didn't turn out like her siblings. Don't get me wrong, she still has an expensive taste. All her clothes are designer, her favorite brand being Coach. She has a whole closet designated to her purse collection. It's almost comical seeing her sitting next to me on a makeshift couch in a hoodie and leggings, sand in between her toes. Although her hoodie is Fenty, and her leggings an expensive Italian brand, she fits right in. Growing up, she spent more time at our house than her own. I never understood why. Her parents have a giant garage with the coolest collection of old school hot rods, an ATV/ dirt bike track in the backyard, a hot tub, and a personal gym. Literally everything a girl could want.

Okay, or maybe just what I would want.

She also has a personal runway, a craft room, a fashion design room, and the biggest closet I had ever seen in my entire life. She has her own goddamn wing of the house. A whole ass wing. Still, she would choose our humble abode over hers any day.

"So, are we really going to spend the whole night watching this movie? Or are you going to tell me why your dad wanted to rush me up here so badly?"

I huff out a long breath. Then explain everything to Han. Starting with Dustin assuming I wasn't the racer, me reluctantly agreeing to the concert and then it being the most romantic night of my life, the morning after when he brought me my hair tie, his dad approaching me and telling me to leave Dustin alone, telling her my whole plan with winning the competition then my plan on telling Dustin after, the shrimp feed and how I broke down after he left, then no more than fifteen hours later seeing him hugging another girl at his campsite, the internal battle of riding for myself, but ultimately knowing deep down I was still riding for him.

"*And* now I'm here with you."

She lets out a whistle. "See what happens when you leave your best friend?"

My laugh breaks the silence of the night around us as I shove her playfully. "I mean you're not wrong."

"On a real note." She looks at me. "You need to talk to Dustin, Nae." She has been using that nickname ever since she found out my middle name was Reneé, after my mother. She only uses it when she's being serious. "I can see how much you care for him, not just by how your face lights up when you talk about the night on the beach, and the morning when he brought you your hair tie, but even in the moments when you're sad, your face lights up when you say his name. A lot of what you just told me sounds like miscommunication, or lack thereof. You're withholding from him. His dad has no right to ask you to step away, and he made you question yourself. I understand your plan, and it makes sense. But at the same time, you'd be giving Dustin his freedom just by telling him the truth as well. Let him choose if he wants to throw the race to show his dad who's boss. It's not your responsibility, love."

She's quiet as I take in everything she just said.

Why did she just make it sound so easy?

I had pondered that decision for hours and she had made it so simple in a matter of minutes.

"What about that girl I saw him with?"

"This afternoon when you saw him with that girl, he shouted at you saying *its not what it looks like* maybe it's as simple as that. Maybe it's a cousin or childhood friend. Or maybe something did happen but it means nothing to him. It's better to let him explain himself than you festering in hurt and anger because you don't have an answer. You two just need to talk and stop avoiding each other. Otherwise, you'll get comfortable with the distance and neither of you will ever know the truth."

She's right. She's absolutely right. We've been avoiding each other with our own secrets and making it worse for ourselves in the process.

"I still don't know if I'm ready, though. What if he gets even more angry with me? Or what if his answer about that girl hurts worse than I expect?"

"Then we will get through it together. I'll be here for the next few days. We will watch a ton of Fast & Furious and eat all the cookies. You'll crush the job interview, and I'll send you annoyingly ridiculous memes. And he'll be a thing of the past, just like JT." Hearing his name makes me cringe. The pain returns as I remember what happened that night. The night I left Han. She sees the shift in my demeanor. "I'm sorry, I didn't mean—"

"It's okay. You don't need to be sorry. I do... I left you."

"We've already talked about this, it's all forgiven, even if you wont tell me the whole truth." She glares at me.

"I'll talk to Dustin after the Night Race competition. They have a huge bonfire on the beach for the riders. That will be the perfect timing." My attempt at changing the subject. She is still glaring at me, and I know she wants to push, but she wont.

Her face finally softens in understanding and she lets it go.

"Okay, and I'll be right there having fun and maybe finding someone to go home with." She winks at me. I shake my head. "Or I guess to a tent, or maybe just in the sand. I don't know why but the idea of the roughness of sand on my skin while having sex has always turned me on." She shivers with excitement.

Han has always been more promiscuous than me. She is not afraid to embrace her sexuality. She knows what she wants and she's not afraid to tell you. Not afraid to share all the tiny details either. Where I'm more reserved and I like to keep those details between my partner and I. Only sharing myself with people I truly care about or genuinely like as a person.

She gets lost in thought and seems to shake herself out of it. "But I will be there in a heartbeat if you need me. Even if I'm running down the beach naked."

The two of us start cracking up laughing at the thought of Han running down the beach, post sex high, coming to rescue me. Both of us know that she would, without a doubt, do it if she had to.

My laughter gets interrupted by the ring of my cell phone. I look down and notice it's the same unknown number that's been calling me the last few days.

These telemarketers are relentless.

I press decline and continue to watch the movie with Han. When I look over at her my heart blooms with joy. I don't know what I did in life to deserve Han but I'd do it a thousand times again to make sure she was my best friend in this life and the next. "I love you, and I'm so happy you're here."

"I love you too." She smiles at me.

I jolt awake from a throbbing pain in my neck.

Sometime in the middle of the movie we must have passed out. I lift my head up from where it has been draped along the back of the concrete cinder blocks. When I finally blink away the haze of sleep I find Han draped across my lap. The beginning of morning light is peeking out through the vast opening of the ocean in front of us.

Besides the tight knot in my neck, I feel at peace.

I realize I am not only at peace in this moment but with everything in my life. For the first time in a long time I have accepted my past, my mistakes, and I welcome my future.

The first step, win the Night Race.

And tonight, I will race for myself. Under the moonlight, the stars, and against the crash of the ocean.

This will be my moment.

No questioning it this time.

Not a single piece of my riding—my passion—is going to be shared with anyone else.

Then I will talk to Dustin. I will tell him everything about the conversation with his dad, about my decision to race for him, and my plan that once felt like my only option.

I will lay everything out on the line and pray he does the same for me.

All I can do now is hope that these aren't lines we shouldn't cross.

Chapter Twelve

Dustin

The Night Race. The final competition for the SandMaster title. I have to win this in order to send Claire and I to a tiebreaker.

If I don't cross that finish line first, there will be a new face on the front of the local newspaper.

For the first time in five years someone new will hold that gold trophy. And I am oddly content with that.

No matter the outcome of tonight I have to talk to Claire. I have to explain myself and hope she forgives me.

Part of me is scared to death.

How would I react if she told me that she got blacked out drunk, from a broken heart, and let some guy go down on her?

I'd be pissed and hurt.

The guilt of knowing that knowledge weighs heavy on my chest.

My body begins to shake with nerves as I try to come to terms with the idea of confronting her with the truth. Yet, I can't bear the burden of keeping my infidelity from her any longer; it revs up my conscience like a finely-tuned engine at the starting line. Fueling itself off my anxiety and self-doubt. But I have to do the right thing, which means facing the consequences of my actions, even if it means losing her trust and any chance I had at being with her. If for some miracle she does forgive me, then this friendship needs to be based on honesty.

I know I can't expect her to forgive me right away, not after I might shatter any amount of confidence she has in me. But over time I will earn it back.

I will do anything to prove she can trust me again.

For the last few hours my eyes have had a mind of their own. I am unable to control where I find my gaze lingering. And everytime I catch myself, I always seem to be staring at her campsite.

Trying to steal as many glimpses of her as I can.

It's still morning and I realize she has a friend with her. I haven't seen them in town, so I assume they are from Reno. It looks like they slept outside from the blankets strewn across the makeshift couch. There is a white sheet pinned against the side of their camper; it is vaguely illuminated by the start up scene from F&F– a sick setup for a movie. I can't help but wonder if our lives had played out differently these last few days, if I might have been able to join them. It makes me sad thinking about all the pieces of her I have missed out on in the last couple of days.

I don't want to be known as the town creeper, so I reluctantly avert my gaze and decide to go wake up Axel. He is typically an early riser so it's not hard to convince him to go for a ride on the beach.

I walk my bike down to the bay and wait for him. He will be bringing his old 250 and I have my white Yamaha YZ250F.

Originally, we brought his bike as backup just in case something happens to mine, but I need this joy ride to settle my nerves.

I can already see the scolding we will get from our father for taking both my bike and the back-up out for a joy ride amidst a competition. Worrying about Dad's disapproval will just have to be saved for later. Luckily, this time I won't have to deal with his scowls and anger by myself.

Growing up, Axel would stick up for me all the time. As we got older, I think he realized by stepping in it only hindered our father and I's relationship, so he backed off.

I know it was the best choice.

But sometimes I really wish I wasn't in this alone.

There will come a time when I have had enough of his antics, just like Axel did. And I will finally have a much-needed conversation with my dad. But as of right now, because of the uncertainty of my future, I welcome the pressure.

At least I am working towards something instead of sitting on my ass, twiddling my fingers, and waiting for my destiny to fall into my lap.

Hell, riding is a great career option.

I get to do something I enjoy and make at least half a million dollars a year doing it.

Jackpot.

Except it doesn't feel like it.

I should be confident it's the right choice.

Shouldn't I?

I seem to not be making smart choices lately. Not only during DuneFest, but in life as well. I shouldn't make a decision like this while my mind is completely focused on the woman across the sand—and road—from me.

The world really wanted to shove her in my face and then tell me I couldn't have her, didn't it?

What a cruel punishment.

Waiting for Axel on the beach has my thoughts running wild.

I know no matter what preparation I try and make for myself, it will fail. No matter how carefully I plan it out—in the moment—I know my entire thought process will change. So there's no point in dwelling over it.

Right now, I need to decide for myself if I want to win the Night Race or not.

"What are you thinking about?" Axel says as he drops down the sand embankment with his 250.

"If I care about winning the Night Race."

He raises his eyebrows. "That's a big deal."

"Yeah... If you would have told me four days ago I would be considering not winning, I would have laughed in your face." I lean against my bike and watch as the waves crash along the beach. "But now... I don't know. It may sound stupid, but after meeting Claire I realize there is more to life than this tiny town and racing. Going pro just doesn't feel right anymore. Like I'm missing out on some other big opportunity."

He is mulling over everything I just confessed. I've never said that out loud before. It feels so good to have it out there. Just putting it into the world has taken a huge weight off my shoulders.

What's that word?

Manifestation.

It feels like I was able to manifest a better future for myself. One where I'm happy and there's no doubt in my mind that I'm living my life for myself and *not* my dad.

"You only have one life to live, D. You have to do what makes you happy. I don't know what that looks like for you, only you can make that decision."

I nod my head.

I sit in silence as I take in the orange and pinks cascading into the horizon. "I'm nervous about talking to Claire," I blurt.

It takes me a second to realize I actually said that out loud. "She's special, man. If I lose her forever, even as a friend, I'll never forgive myself."

Axel takes his time to answer, feeling the weight of my admission . "You made a mistake. The best thing you can do is tell her the truth. After that, it's up to Claire. You can't control her reaction no matter how hard you want to. Once you've been honest and apologized, you've done your part." He pauses. "I wish I could do more."

"You've helped me more than you know." I slip my helmet over my head and swing my leg over the seat of my bike. The only thing that's going to clear my mind is a ride– *without pressure*. I kickstart my bike and turn to him. "Let's ride."

<hr/>

The ride this morning with Axel was just the cure I needed.

This is the only moment since DuneFest started that my mind has felt clear. I left all my anxiety and nerves on the beach. Letting the waves roll over and pull them into the deep like a sunken ship hopefully never to be recovered.

I know my next steps.

I know the confrontation lying in front of me and I welcome the consequences of my actions.

I'm dressed in my riding gear and lined up at the starting gate for the Night Race Competition, Claire is only four riders away from me. Even from this distance I can feel her. Her warmth that I miss with every fiber of my being. The determination and drive that sparked passion inside of me.

Every time I see her in riding gear my cock twitches in my pants. But tonight the moonlight bouncing off her helmet and bike, giving the illusion she's glowing, just about has me on my knees.

Seeing her like this threatens to unravel the pieces of my mind that I carefully stitched together beforehand.

It makes my heart sink to think that I may never get to kiss her again. That no matter how hard I try, nothing will compare to her embrace.

The announcer brings me out of my thoughts and into the present.

"Welcome riders to the Night Racccceee!" Cheers and yells thundered all around me. "Yes... yes," he says while moving his hand up and down, telling the crowd to be quiet. "The Night race is everyone's favorite... but also the most *dangerous*. The racers tonight will be battling for first place on a five mile straightaway, on wet sand. The only problem?" He gestures to the audience to answer for him.

"NO LIGHTS!!" They shout.

"Correct. Riders will have to drive by moonlight and the lights of their competition." The crowd roars in excitement. "But don't worry, our lovely DuneFest hosts have EMTs on call, and a station every mile in case of emergency. With that being said... Riders... Are you readyyyyyy?" Every racer revs their engines in response. Sending vibrations out through the sand and into the hearts of everyone around. Adrenaline spikes into the air, encasing everyone in anticipation and the crowd feeds on our determination.

A woman walks out a few feet in front of us holding a rolled up green flag. She signals to the crowd to start the countdown.

"10...9...8...7...6...5...4...3...2...1"

She drops the green flag.

Bikes speed past her and cause her hair to flip in every direction.

I am a few rows behind the starting line, so I'm already playing a game of catch-up.

I can feel the tether that ties Claire and I together and see she's only a few bikes away from being first. I'm weaving in out of riders when we pass the first mile marker.

Only ten bikes away from first.

Claire is only two away.

She sneaks into second with only two miles to go.

I slip into fourth.

One mile to go.

She drops into 2nd and falls behind Dominic Linetti (who currently holds first).

What is she doing?

I pass Taylor Stevens and pull up side by side with Claire.

We are running out time there's only half a mile left.

I put my hand up—palm out—gesturing to ask her what she's doing. She points at her eyes through her goggles, and then she signals in Dom's direction. Just as I look in front of us, I notice his body posture shifts and he relaxes into his seat.

He is congratulating himself a little too early. Distracted by the fact he thinks she fell behind.

She let him think he was going to win.

Clever girl.

She is playing mind games and she just trapped me in one too.

I fell for it so easily.

Just like how I fell for her.

Quick, easy, effortless.

I look back over and she has already taken off. I notice her hand is down by her knee as she wiggles her fingers at me in goodbye. I shake my head and smile to myself.

Damn it. This girl has my entire heart.

She passes Dom with a quarter of a mile to go but no one is catching her now.

She crosses the finish line as Dom and I ride neck and neck.

I drop into 4th and thrust my throttle back.

I crossed the finish line and managed to pull ahead just enough to secure second place.

The patchwork I did on my feelings is completely destroyed. As soon as we had a silent communication while riding, I was completely wrapped around her finger again. I was naive to think I could bottle up my feelings and pretend like they weren't there.

The next few hours are going to be hell.

Chapter Thirteen

Dustin

Watching the title ceremony and seeing everyone congratulating Claire on her win while I can't, is its own kind of torture.

I am so fucking happy for her.

Not only is she the most exceptional rider I have ever met, but she effortlessly played on my emotions and perceived Dom's cockiness from a mile away.

I can't even be mad.

All I feel is an overwhelming sense of pride and admiration.

She looks breathtaking up there on the first place podium holding the gold trophy. She is wearing a black tank top, her riding pants, and boots. Her hair is strung across her shoulders in those beautiful black rings. Dirt glitters her collarbones and cheeks, highlighting her strong features making me think of how fucking gorgeous it would look if some of me was plastered all over her.

I thought people were exaggerating when they said they suffered from a broken heart. I assumed they were just being dramatic.

I couldn't have been more wrong.

My heart physically aches as I watch her get showered in praise and I can't be the one to hold her up and show her off to the world.

My anger boils over me as I watch men from my high school drool over her and pat her on the back.

My soul hates that I have hurt her.

My body hates that I've fucked this up because the only thing it wants to do is touch and lick every part of her, savor the taste of her forever. Show her just how much she deserves to be praised.

My whole being is against me in one way or another.

Not only am I at war with myself, but I still have a battle ahead of me. A battle of trying to convince her that I may have hurt her, but I will *never* make that mistake again.

She is stitched into my very being. Every emotion. Every tangible part. If I lose her, I'll lose myself in the process.

It's a race I have to win.

If I don't, every part of me might shut down.

The local news and DuneFest coordinators are wrapping up final pictures as a group of locals set up for the bonfire. A celebratory way for fans and riders to wrap up the final race for SandMaster. People all around me are dragging in coolers, blankets, footballs, and all the other miscellaneous objects that ultimately lead to a good time.

Out of the side of my eye I can see my family approaching me. Dad was missing when I found them after the race. Which was a breath of fresh air, honestly. I couldn't deal with him and my feelings for Claire at the same time.

But now I am ready for whatever he has to say.

He approaches me before the rest of the family. "Well, good news. David said the pros still want you for next season even with the loss of the SandMaster title."

I scoff.

You've got to be fucking kidding me.

This is seriously all he has to say to me. The first thing out of his mouth. No, *'congrats on second place'*. No, *'nice race son'*. Nothing. Just the fact that I didn't lose out on my opportunity at half a million dollars. I don't know why I expected anything different. I guess I'm still holding out for that *'I'm proud of you son'* that will never come.

"That's great fucking news Dad. Just fucking fantastic." I shake my head. "I am so *proud* to hear that."

"You need–"

"No."

"Excuse me?"

"I don't *need* to do anything. There's this funny thing called *being an adult*. It's when—all of a sudden—you get to make your own choices and your parents can either choose to be in your life or not. I'm sorry to break this to you Dad but... it's not *your* life. It's mine." I take a deep breath. Shock must be rendering him speechless so I seize my opportunity to continue. "While we're at it. I'm not accepting the offer. Before you ask, I don't have a fucking clue what I want to do instead... but I'll figure it out. And you know what? That's okay. All I know is that racing doesn't feel right." He shakes his head. The anger pulsing off of him is palpable in the space between us. "I know that sounds stupid to you, but it doesn't to me. All these years it would have been nice to hear a *'congratulations'* or *'I'm proud of you'*. But I should have known better than to expect that from *you*."

I mentally try to prepare for the repercussions of my trauma dump.

Instead, he storms off into the direction of our campsite. Mom follows suit with a quick glance over her shoulder and a solemn look on her face. Then they both disappear into the night.

I can feel Axels stare burning into me.

I hold a hand up before he can speak. "I know that wasn't the best way to go about it. I just couldn't take it anymore... I can't take the anger, the disappointment, the sadness. It's becoming too much."

"I'm not mad at you, D. I'm damn proud." I turn and look at him in surprise. "That was a long time coming. I love Dad, but sometimes that's the only way he hears things. The pressure he has put on your shoulders for the past few years has been fucking absurd." He smiles at me. "How does it feel?"

"Like I've been riding on chunder for miles and I have monkey-butt. Sore, but refreshing that it is finally over."

A weight has been taken off my shoulder but shortly replaced by a different one.

I didn't even get the chance to take a breath.

Claire is walking towards us, I see the sway of her beautiful hips just over Axel's shoulders. At first glance, my heart rate picks up and my mood instantly increases. It's short lived when my stomach plummets and I have the sudden urge to throw up. Axel watches my face blanch and follows my line of sight before huffing out a heavy breath.

He rests his hand on my shoulder and grabs my attention. "This is gonna be a big night for you. Two huge things back-to-back. Just don't forget to be in this moment with *her*. I'll be over by June's tent. When you're done, come find me. If you don't, I will send a search party." I nod just as Claire approaches us.

"Hey... can we talk?" she asks. I forgot how sensual and soft her voice is. "I hope I'm not interrupting." She glances between Axel and I.

"Oh, not at all! I was just leaving." Axel says as he pats me on the shoulder and whispers in my ear. "Breathe."

I hadn't realized I was holding my breath.

I exhale and respond to him, "I'm good."

He nods and then walks off towards June's tent.

"Want to go for a walk?" she says as she picks at her fingernails. It's excruciating being this close to her and not being able to kiss her.

"Yeah, that sounds nice."

Nice. That sounds nice?

I cringe.

She huffs out a small laugh.

Then takes a few steps away from the crowd of party goers. I follow suit and shortly our strides are in match as we walk side by side down the beach.

"I need to tell you something–"

"I'm sorry–"

We say at the same time then smirk at each other. The tension in the air is almost suffocating.

"You go first." I offer.

"Okay...I don't really know how to say this. I guess I'm just going to start and please try to listen before getting mad. At least until I'm done then I'll take whatever reaction you have." I nod as a fresh wave of fear runs through me. "After the FreeStyle competition we got invited to the Shrimp Feed by Tattie. I was trying to find you to ask if you wanted to come with us, and I also didn't know what the fuck a Shrimp Feed was."

We both laugh.

Her recollection also has me thinking.

Something big must have happened between the race and Shrimp Feed for her to change her mind so suddenly.

She stops walking and sits on a long piece of driftwood and waits for me to join her before continuing. "While I was looking for you... your dad stopped me." *I don't like where this is going*. "He told me—and I'm summarizing—to leave you alone until DuneFest was over so you could focus on your future. That if you lost this year's SandMaster title, you'd lose the offer from the pros. He told me that I was distracting you and that's why you were losing the comps." The grip on my knees tightens. The whites of my knuckles pop out through my skin.

Of course.

Of fucking course it was my Dad.

First off, he manipulated Claire into feeling like she was the problem and that she wasn't capable of winning on her own. Secondly, if he hadn't stopped her, she wouldn't have broken it off with me, I wouldn't have gotten drunk, and that night with April wouldn't have happened.

I take a deep breath. I don't want to scare Claire. I know it's too easy to blame my father for everything. Truth is, I still made a poor decision.

It makes me wonder, though. If I had told him sooner that I didn't want to race anymore would he have stopped Claire? Probably not.

Why didn't she tell me he approached her?

I gather my emotions and try to speak as level-headed as I can. "Why... how come you didn't tell me?" She still flinches. But I don't think it's because of my tone.

"I don't know. I should have realized how dumb it sounds, but at the time I made up this plan in my head. I'd pretend to listen to your dad and break things off, no matter how badly it hurt. I wanted your dad to believe that all your distractions were gone. I knew that you'd still have your offer, whether you won or not. If they are out here it is for a follow up, not to decide your fate in the pros. I thought your dad would know that, but I guess not." She sighs. " Next step was to win the SandMaster title and prove that I am a great rider, not a distraction. If I won, you'd get the freedom to choose your own future, not one your father was forcing on you."

It hurts so much more to know she did this with good intentions, and in return I just broke her trust.

Another reason I know I don't deserve her.

She hangs her head. "It sounds stupid out loud but when I was in the moment it sounded like the best option. I couldn't let another man manipulate me and not have any repercussions."

What does she mean by that?

I think she has a weight on her shoulder she needs to lift and that feeling is all too familiar. My intuition is telling me she wants me to push a little. That she needs to talk about whatever is on her mind.

I'll come back to this conversation later. All that matters now is letting her feel heard.

"What do you mean by that?"

She shifts her feet in the sand and her shoulders sink. She's trembling and it takes everything in me not to pull her into my lap and comfort her. I think she's about to shut me out, but then she starts speaking. Her words are broken up by her sobs. "If I share this with you... you have to promise not to tell anyone. Especially my dad. He must never know." I can hear the fear in her voice and I have a feeling I'll be trying to reign in my emotions for the rest of the night.

"I promise."

"Okay..." She takes a deep breath. "When I was in middle school, I met this guy named JT. He had just moved to Reno and was new at my school. My dad worked at a mechanics shop during the day and at night he worked on the transport team for the hospital. He met a lot of my teachers either through the hospital or from working on their cars. I was always a good kid, so any time a new student would enroll, they would ask me to show them around."

"I'm guessing they asked you to give JT a tour of the school." I already did not like this guy and his name felt like bile on my tongue.

She nods. "He had no friends. I felt bad, and offered for him to sit with my friend, Hannah, and I at lunch. He fit in easily and before I knew it he was hanging out with us every day. By the time we got into high school, everyone just assumed we were dating so we just kind of... started, I guess." She shrugs. "One thing led to another and he ended up coming to UNLV with Hannah and I. We had our own house, and he moved in about a month after we got there. My dad busted his ass working two jobs so that I wouldn't have to worry about working and being a full time student. If I wasn't in class, I was either at home cleaning or hanging out because I didn't want to spend unnecessary money. Han was in a sorority so she was gone a lot. Leaving JT and I at home alone together most of the time... I quickly found out he wasn't who I thought he was."

My jaw tenses and my knee starts bouncing uncontrollably. I am praying Claire can't feel the rage radiating off of me. I want her to feel safe while she is being vulnerable.

I steady my breathing. "What did he do?"

Her face twists in fear and she starts crying.

I swear to God, if I get my hands on this fucker I'll ring his neck.

She bites on her lip as she tries to regain her composure. "He... he came back drunk one evening after celebrating with some friends for passing a huge final. I told him I needed to talk... talk to him about something. Maybe it was my fault for not waiting until he was sober." I hate that she is trying to put blame on herself for any of his actions. "He said okay and then sat down on the couch. I told him... told him I wanted to break up and that we could just be friends like before... before things got complicated." She takes a deep breath. Her voice is shaky when she continues. "He didn't... say... say anything for a while, just stared at the... the TV. I got up... and told... told him I'd give him some time to think, but then... then he stood up really fast... knocked... knocked over my wine." She is breaking down. I can barely hear her through her sobs.

Fuck it.

I pull her into me and wrap her in my arms.

"It's okay, Angel. He's not here. You're safe now, and I promise... I promise with everything in me that I will protect you. I will do everything in my power to make sure you never feel that pain again. You are *strong*, and together, we'll heal."

She gains strength from my embrace, and god if that doesn't make me feel so damn good.

"It happened so... so fast I didn't even know what to... to do... he grabbed me around my throat and... he... he pinned me to the wall. He got in my face and said '*You think you can just leave me. Do you think you're anything without me? You're* mine *and you will always be* mine. *Do you understand*?' I couldn't breathe. The last thing I remember is the smell of the alcohol on his breath before my vision began to narrow and then all I could see was darkness. I knew I just needed to get out his hands, then I could figure out what to do next. So I nodded my head, and he dropped me. I fell to my knees and looked up at him as I tried to catch my breath. I remember at that moment it felt like I was trying to swallow sand. He said, '*Good, now that you know your place. Come to bed and give me what I* deserve'. Then walked off. I tried to stay in the living room for as long as I could but ultimately I got scared he would come back and... it would be... would be worse. By the time I'd gotten to the room he was passed out on the floor in the bathroom."

I didn't realize I was holding my breath until I finally let it out. It was bad enough that this asshole put his hands on her, but if he had...

Fuck.

I can't even think about it.

"I wanted to leave that night but I wouldn't have had enough time. So I waited till he left for his morning classes and packed as much as I could into the four duffel bags I had, and never went back."

I don't even know what to say.

What do you say in these situations?

Whatever response I can muster will never feel like enough.

"I'm so sorry." The only other thing that crosses my mind is '*I'll kill him*' but I have a strong feeling that won't be helpful. "You are *so* strong. Do you know that?"

"You don't need to be sorry, but thank you."

Oh, I do. More than you know.

I wanted to come clean to her tonight but this feels too big.

I need to let her have this moment. Let her have this slice of peace.

"Let's go jump in the ocean," she blurts out.

What?

"Did I just hear you correctly?"

She giggles, but it's broken up from the lump in her throat. "You heard me."

She gets up and slides her shirt over her head.

Everything ceases to exist. My brain stops functioning. The world stops spinning. The birds stop chirping. I'm mesmerized by her feminine fingers as she fumbles with the clips of her riding pants.

I finally shake out of my trance and come to.

I jump up so quickly that I trip over my own feet.

Her head falls back as her laughter breaks the silence of the night.

We continue to take off our clothes until I'm in my boxers and she's in her underwear and bra. My breath hitches in my throat as I drink in her beauty. This is the first time I've seen her almost naked. My imagination could never do her justice.

She is perfect.

She takes off running, her hair swaying behind her, her ass jiggles as she bounces across the sand. I can already feel myself harden as I admire every curve of her body. Her toes touch the water and I watch her shiver. She stands there for a moment as she slowly inches into the water. The moon descends in the sky behind her, touching the ocean's surface, creating a celestial canvas of light. Mother nature itself holds its breath as Claire stands before her. If there was one moment I'd want captured for eternity, it'd be this one. Even though the greatest artist, or the most expensive camera, could never do her beauty justice.

I want to plaster her beauty everywhere but at the same time hold it selfishly. Keep her away from the world because it doesn't deserve her.

She dives in.

The Pacific Ocean is not ideal to swim in. The water is freezing and the waves can be dangerous. But the way she adjusts to the biting temperature and moves along the waves is effortless, like she was born in the ocean. She resurfaces, her hair soaked, but her curls still visible. Her body is red from being stung by the bitter cold.

"Are you coming? Or are you *scared*?" she taunts.

She needs someone who will be just as wild as her.

I will swim in the most dangerous waters, jump off the tallest cliffs, and climb the highest mountains if that means I can make her mine.

I sprint into the water and scoop her into my arms. I sling her over my shoulder as she shrieks. Then I dunk us both into the freezing ocean. When both our heads pop up from the water she's laughing and her smile cuts right through my heart.

"You ass," she says, but her gaze is soft and she's holding back a smile. Every time I see her happy it fuels my soul and shatters it at the same time. The idea that I'm going to have to break her heart again, that I'm going to lose her again, hurts me all the way down to my bones.

Tears start to well up in my eyes, and confusion crosses her face. "What's wrong?"

I don't know if this is the right time. I want more than anything to ignore the nagging in my heart and just enjoy this moment with her.

She just shared a piece of herself with me.

She trusted me to help her heal and all I'm going to do is make it worse for her. But I can't keep my infidelity a secret any longer. I need to come clean now, so that it's all out in the open, and she can decide what is best for her. "I need to tell you something."

She is shivering and her teeth are chattering. "Okay...?"

Fuck, I'm a blubbering mess.

"You're scaring me, Dustin." A tear falls down her cheek.

I pull her in and squeeze her. "Shit. I'm sorry, Angel. I'm so sorry."

Our bodies warm each other up.

I choose to be selfish for a moment and just hold her.

Damn it, Dustin.

I speak into her hair as I hold her against my chest. "That night after the shrimp feed, I was so heartbroken. I felt ridiculous that it hurt so badly to lose you when we had just met... but it pained me nonetheless." I exhale. "I got back to my campsite and *begged* Axel to drink with me. I never turn to alcohol to solve my problems, but I was desperate. We drank a few beers and took a couple of shots. My original plan was to get drunk with my brother then pass out in my Bronco. But shortly after, a friend of ours, June, came over and invited us down to the pier with her and some friends. I drank way too much and blacked out. Axel told me the next morning that I...."

Oh, God this hurts so much.

My tears drop into her hair.

She must be able to feel the way this breaks me, because I can feel the tiny droplets of warmth spilling from her eyes. "Axel told me... he told me that he found some girl..." *Fuck.* "Giving me head. Once he told me I was-" She stiffens under my arm. Then she shoves me away and starts to storm up the sand. I follow behind her.

"Claire, please." She ignores me and continues up the shore. Grabbing her tank top and pulling it over her head. "Please, talk to me," I plead.

She steps into her riding pants, sand falls off her feet. She grabs her riding boots in her hands, not bothering to put them on, and begins to walk back to the bonfire. "Claire..." I grab her wrist gently.

She stops and inhales sharply. I let her go.

She spins around to face me.

Her eyes are rimmed in red. "I can't talk to you right now okay. God, Dustin..." She looks up at the sky then settles her eyes back on mine. "I just gave you a huge part of me, and you took it and stomped on it. I mean why the *fuck* didn't you tell me this before I gave you my trust?" She shakes her head. "Don't you understand? I have never told anyone about my past. And you know what the worst part is? I don't even want to be mad at you. Because... because partially it's my fault. If I just told you about the conversation with your dad you wouldn't have gotten drunk-"

"No. No you're not allowed to do that with me. You are not responsible for my actions. Mine, or anyone else's." I've never been so serious with her before and it catches her off guard. "Be mad at me, but don't walk away. I can't do it again. I can't live without the taste of you, the smell of you, the warmth of you. Please... stay and fight with me."

Tears are streaming down her cheeks, leaving trails that glisten in the moonlight. Even now she's the most beautiful woman I have ever seen. "I... I just need some time." She wipes away her tears and emotionally pushes me away. Again.

Then I watch as she walks off into the night. The only thing she leaves behind is her footprints in the sand.

And me.

I nod as I look off to the side. "Fuck..."

It's only now that I realize I'm still in my boxers.

Accepting defeat, the cold rushes into me. My body shuts down, refusing to warm me up, punishing me for letting her go again.

I walk back to the piece of driftwood that once held our clothes strewn across it. Slipping on my pants and shirt I look out to the point where the ocean meets the sky, a flashback of her standing there, welcoming me into the cold, comes flooding back.

Already a memory.

She's left her imprint in every aspect of my life, just like she left imprints of her feet in the sand as she walked away from me. From us.

I guess you have to drown before you can float.

Part 2

After DuneFest

Chapter Fourteen

Claire

It's been a week since DuneFest.

A week since I poured my heart out to Dustin.

A week since I walked away from him that night on the beach.

A week since I left my heart on the sand at his feet.

A whole week of wondering if I made the right choice. Questioning myself if I should have left or if I should have stayed and fought with him.

Running away seems to be my answer in times like these. Times where I feel weak. When I feel like I have no control, or too much.

Usually, in times like these I expect the world to stop spinning. The sun to stop setting. The moon to stop rising.

But none of that happened.

Life carried on, just like it always has.

Han went back to Reno and I went to my job interview. I made a good impression on my manager, June. I think I did a great job at hiding the pain her name caused me when she introduced herself. The memory of her being the one to invite Dustin to the beach that night, pushing itself to the forefront of my mind. I don't hold anything against her, it's not her fault. It's just the memory that haunts me. Angers me.

She set me up with a second interview, the owner of Big Fish Café, who just happened to be Tattie. She said it was a no-brainer and I was hired on the spot. I don't understand how I couldn't have known that Tattie owned Big Fish. But when I look back on our previous conversations they were always cut short. I never truly got to speak with her one on one.

Currently I'm getting dressed for the evening shift and today will make it an official week of working at Big Fish. June said they typically don't put new hires on the dinner schedule, but because of my previous experience and the fact that I have been such a hit with the morning regulars, she thought I was ready.

I am beyond excited.

Evening shifts get the best tips.

Even though I have been going through the motions the last seven days, I know when I need to put on the charm, and tonight I will be doing just that.

I sort of had a revelation a couple days ago.

I mean, it's something I've always thought about but it was never the right time, or I just didn't have the resources.

But I decided that I want to open my own mechanics shop. In order to do that I will need to be saving as much money as possible. Dad said he would help when the time was right, but I told him I wanted to do this on my own. He is helping enough by giving me a place to live and splitting the cost of groceries together. He doesn't charge me rent, which I've argued with him about numerous times, but now I'm grateful. It means I can save almost my entire paycheck and I only have to buy the necessities.

I fasten my name tag to the right of my plain black shirt. Tattie isn't super strict with dress code. She only asks us to be clean, wear a plain shirt, and no jeans with holes in them.

Today, I'm wearing a black skirt that hangs loosely down to my mid thigh and has bike shorts attached on the inside. Cute but classy. June recommended them for me. I have never owned a skirt or dress since I gained control of my own wardrobe, but she swore I would like this kind and she was right. *Of course.*

June has quickly become one of my favorite people.

I no longer associate her with Dustin and only recognize her as a friend now.

During our interview she said *'I know we are going to be best of friends, it will only take a couple days. You just watch'*. She was right about that, too.

In her own ways she reminds me a lot of Han. They would get along disgustingly well. They're both sunshine and rainbows with a dash demon. Together they could probably drown the world in glitter. I vow to make sure the next time Han comes into town that they meet each other.

I lace up my black high top converse and bound down the stairs to grab a quick bite before heading off to work.

My phone starts ringing in my hand.

It's that damn unknown number again.

Seriously, whoever this is, they're persistent. They deserve a raise.

I press decline.

They have been increasing lately. At first it was only once every couple of days. Now it's almost two to three times a day. Eventually I'll answer it and tell them to fuck off. I just don't have the energy right now.

Pocketing my phone, I look around and fully expect to find Dad down here. But he is nowhere to be seen and it is normally dinner time. I shrug and head for the front door.

He has been in the shop for the past week working on some project he won't tell me about. He also made me swear not to step foot into the garage, which is infuriating. The garage is my favorite place to be and he knows that.

This man and his surprises lately.

I really don't know what has gotten into him. He's been different since DuneFest, in a good way. He won't tell me any details. But I'd notice that glow anywhere. I think he is seeing someone.

Eventually he will tell me, but I just hate being patient.

I grab my microwaved burrito, wrap it in a paper towel, and head out the front door to my Ford. The parts I ordered showed up during DuneFest so they were waiting by the front door when we got home. It only took Dad and I a few hours to get my truck all squared away. Every time I see her in the driveway I fall in love with her all over again. She truly is a beautiful truck, especially now that she has all her pieces back and she's restored to her full glory. I guess it might be weird that I refer to my truck as a *she* but I love her like a best friend, so it makes sense to me.

My truck isn't the only thing I check out every morning.

I've gotten into the worst habit of looking across the street and checking for any signs of Dustin. Whether it's glimpses of him walking by his front window or getting the mail.

I've had no such luck.

His Bronco has been MIA for the past week, but Axel's truck is always in the driveway and I've seen him multiple times. It's always a silent wave and nothing more.

I was expecting at some point to hear from Dustin. I don't know why. It's not like he has my number. But I guess I was holding onto that last string of hope pretty damn tightly.

I pound on the door of the garage causing the metal to rattle under my fist. "Goodbye. I'm heading off to work."

Dads voice comes out muffled. "Bye, Mini! Have a great day." I hear a loud bang and shortly after he yells. "*Ow... Fuck!*"

I press my ear up to the cool steel. "Are you okay?" I shout.

"Uhh... yeah... I'm fine."

"You don't sound fine."

"I promise, I'm okay. Go to work before you're late."

"If you'd let me in I'd be able to help you."

I hear him shuffling around before he responds. "Not gonna happen."

I roll my eyes and shake my head.

Then I climb into the driver seat of my truck and head towards the café.

Big Fish is an adorable little building.

It used to be a Coast Guard outpost before it was converted into a restaurant a few years back. Even though it is fairly new, it has quickly gained an amazing reputation, making most nights busy as fuck– from what I've heard.

Joey, the head chef, is a wizard in the kitchen and also the most intimidating person I have ever seen. Until I got to know him and realized he is the biggest teddy bear known to man.

He is the definition of a silver fox. Tattooed from neck to ankles, full head of gorgeous silver locks, muscles big enough to squash your head. It looks like Posiden himself spit Joey out.

It makes no sense how he fits into that tiny kitchen at Big Fish, but somehow he makes it work. Every time he winks at me I blush, and I feel like I'm in middle school all over again. He has the same effect on June. Her and I constantly joke with him that if we were just thirty years older he would have to choose between us.

The three of us have fallen into an effortless rhythm. Coming to work has easily become the best part of my day. Which is weird, because I never thought I could be happy working at any other job other than being a mechanic.

Someday when I open my own business, leaving the three of them—including Tattie—will be the hardest part.

I pull into the employee's parking lot and take a second to admire the view. The sun is beginning its descent beyond the horizon, causing rays of light to bounce off the clear blue water. The café sits right at the edge of the Umpqua River, surrounded by a beautiful dock, making it the perfect destination for a date night. On many occasions I've pictured Dustin and I eating dinner here and then taking a walk along the wooden pathway.

I quickly push away the thought.

I've come to terms with the fact that I'll probably never hear from him again. I also don't know if I want to.

I feel betrayed but at the same time feel a little bit at fault. I know I can't control his actions, but if I had just told him the truth about his dad he wouldn't have gotten drunk, either.

But if he can't control himself while he's drinking, how am I supposed to trust him?

I don't know if I can.

I try to leave all my personal shit at the door as soon as I walk into work. But I'm not always successful. June has noticed my demeanor change a few times on shift and I've been brushing her off, but I think it'd be nice to talk to her. Especially because she's kind of involved.

I've talked to Han multiple times about it. She says he's a douche and I should leave him in the past.

But I can't seem to do that.

Nor do I believe that he is a douche.

Or at least I don't want to believe it.

June knows Dustin better than me, and she was there that night. Plus, it would be nice to talk to someone in person.

Next time we hang out, I'll talk to her.

I pull open the blue door to Big Fish and take the few steps down the small hallway that leads to the indoor dining area and bar.

As I'm about to descend the last step, my foot freezes in mid air.

My mouth drops open as I take in the decorations around me. There's blue and silver balloons tied to rocks at each corner of the Café, little bouquets of baby's breath and white roses at each table. The words 'We Love You' in silver balloons strung across the top of the windows that outlook the river. To my left is my crazy, blonde-haired friend bouncing up and down with the biggest grin on her face.

"Surprise!" She yells.

"What is all of this?" I finish my descent into the main dining area and gesture around the restaurant.

"It's your one week anniversary, silly." She shakes her head in disbelief like I'm the one being ridiculous.

Joey emerges from behind the kitchen door and leans against it. He has a towel looped through his pants and his flannel rolled up to his elbows. I pretend to drool and he laughs.

"I told her it was too soon, but she insisted," he says.

"It is *not* too soon. You just haven't partied since the war was over, and you wouldn't know a good time if it hit you in the face." June has a smug look on her face but she doesn't turn around to face Joey.

I cover my mouth with my hand as I try to hold in my laughter.

"You're just bitter because Taylor Swift lost the Best New Artist award to Amy Winehouse in 2007." His eyebrow hitches as Junes mouth drops open and she turns on her heel slowly.

I don't know whether to pity the man, or be impressed he knew that information.

"How dare you bring T. Swift-y into this. You know that's a sensitive subject!" Junes hands are in fists as she shoves them down to her sides. She looks like a six year old throwing a tantrum in this position.

"Don't mess with the bull or you'll get the horns."

We both give him a disgusted look.

"You aren't helping your case," I tell Joey.

He shrugs and then disappears back into the kitchen.

"It's beautiful. You really didn't have to do all this." I turn to June, appreciation in my eyes.

"Of course I did! You've been a rockstar since we hired you. You deserve to be recognized."

My last waitressing gig was when I was in high school, I worked at a Benny's down the street from our house. That job was awful. My coworkers were terrible and rude. My boss forced hours onto my schedule by threatening to fire me. This is nothing in comparison. I'm not saying that all Benny's are bad, but the one I worked at was horrible.

I was nervous about starting here because my first experience in service was so horrendous. Instead, working here has been nothing but a breath of fresh air.

The perfect distraction to keep my mind off Dustin.

Until it isn't.

I take in the scene around me one more time before starting my shift. My eyes begin to water.

When did I become so damn emotional?

"Thank you," I tell June.

"Of course, love. I wish we could stand here all day but we do have customers to attend too."

I giggle.

She leans in for a hug and then I head to the back to punch in.

Besides my problems with Dustin, everything about this move has been perfect.

I've never had this many people in my life that I genuinely care about.

Reedsport is home.

And it doesn't feel weird to say that anymore.

Chapter Fifteen

Dustin

When I told Claire that I wouldn't be able to handle losing her again. I was telling the truth.

That night, I picked myself up off the sand and walked straight to my truck. There's only one other place I go—besides sand dollar beach—when I feel broken.

After I stopped at the house, and loaded up what I would need for the week. I called Jeremy and cashed in my vacation time. Luckily, Liam and Michael needed the hours so they happily picked up my shifts for me.

Then I drove to Tahkenitch Lake.

Ever since I was a kid, our family would camp here for the Fourth of July weekend. It's one of my favorite family traditions.

The trees, lake water, and nature sounds are just as essential to me as breathing. Any time I find myself in a tough situation, where my spirit feels like it's suffocating, I wind up here. Right on the edge of this shoreline.

A part of me recognizes myself within these waters as a reflection of the emotions that live inside me. The parts of your life that are out of your control are like the jet skis and boats. Creating a wake that may surge, crash, or at times, be so still that the water looks like glass. And although the swimmers, fishers, and boats cast shadows into the depths, somehow I can still see the shimmer of hope amid the darkness.

It's easy to live in your self doubt, to continue to dance alongside your demons. To believe you are unworthy of anything good, anything beautiful. It's hard to pick yourself back up, dust off your pants, and keep moving forward.

In order to find the strength to stand back up, I imagine myself as the mountains, staring down into the lake–watching over it. I can choose to succumb to the pain, anger, and hurt, or I can embrace these feelings and discover the strength to plant roots like the trees and stand true to myself, to who I want to be.

It's easier said than done.

But healing begins with acceptance.

I have spent the last week out here in solitude learning how to embrace my mistakes, acknowledge my defeat, and find the courage to rise again.

Seven days of...

Thinking.

Breathing.

Crying.

Trying to figure out how to approach the woman I love.

Through my time out here, I have come to accept both outcomes; losing her forever, and the miracle of her accepting me back. I have thought of everything short of getting on my hands and knees and begging for her to forgive me. The only solution I have is to somehow find the strength to talk to her and hope we can move on from this.

But before I make the trek back to Reedsport, I have to get out of my head, and into my heart. I have to be honest with her, lay everything out on the track and hope we can cross the finish line together.

One last race I have to win.

I've spent enough time out here in these woods. Now, it's time to go home. Time to see an Angel, and hope she takes me to heaven with her, and not fly me to my own type of hell.

Chapter Sixteen

Claire

To say the shift was absolutely insane would be an understatement. June said tonight ended up cashing out as the busiest night of the year so far. The wad of cash in my pocket —from tips—would agree with her.

Besides spilling a soda down my leg, and constantly having to remind River to get off his phone, I would say the night was a success.

River has been working here for a little over two months. Tattie hired him as a favor to one of her friends. He is only eighteen, and was forced by his parents to get a job.

I don't have much say in the logistics of the restaurant business because I just got here. But personally, I think Tattie's favor has run its course.

River is only a host. All he has to do is show the customers to their seats, take a name down for each party, and note how many people are in each group. June and I even tell him when tables open up, even though that's supposed to be his job. Yet, all he does is sit on his phone and text his girlfriend or play *Candy Crush*.

He doesn't even greet people when they come in.

June said she's going to talk to Tattie this week and maybe see if we can move him to a dishwasher, give him janitorial duties, or fire him.

He really killed us tonight.

We desperately need someone capable as a host. Not someone we have to babysit. Due to the fact he lacks the ability to accomplish his tasks, June and I had to double our work load.

My feet are tired, I'm thoroughly annoyed, and I *cannot* wait to go home and take a bath.

June is closing out the tills, while I'm sweeping and mopping the floors, Joey is in the back prepping for tomorrow, and we sent River home because we just couldn't take it anymore. Plus, he would just get in the way as it is.

June has her face down as she's counting money and placing it into a deposit bag. "So... there's a big group of us heading down to the lighthouse to hang out. We are going to have a bonfire and roast s'mores. I was wondering... if you would like to come with me?" She lifts her head just slightly to read my expression. She's biting her bottom lip and her shoulders are lifted.

Her attempt at trying to convince me to go.

"I... I don't–"

"Before you say no," she cuts me off. "You haven't gotten out and met anyone yet, and every time I invite you... you say no. I love being your only friend. Trust me, I don't like sharing, at least not with my best friend." She winks.

I shake my head at her.

Just like Han, she's very open about her sexuality.

She continues, "But... I have some pretty cool friends. And maybe... just maybe you'll meet someone else there that gets your attention. You know, kinda help with the whole Dustin situation." The cash she's holding is threatening to come loose as she flicks her wrist in the air.

The idea of dating makes the fish and chips I ate earlier turn in my stomach. I'm definitely not in the mindset to meet another guy, but I wouldn't mind making some more friends.

I need to get my name out there so when I do start my own business, I won't be a complete stranger. Besides, I have said no the last two times June asked me to hang out with her and her friends. Granted, they do hang out like everyday, so it's not like this is my last opportunity. But I don't have work tomorrow and tonight is probably the best opportunity I'll have for the rest of the week.

My bath will just have to wait a little while longer for me.

"Stop thinking so hard and just say yes. You know you want to." June smirks at me and does a little shoulder dance.

I inhale and roll my eyes. "Fine."

She squeals, "Yay!"

I pretend to plug my ears and give her a playful smile.

She scowls at me in return. "It's going to be so fun! I promise."

I nod. "Mhmm."

June and I manage to close up pretty fast. Joey has a few more things to do in the kitchen so he is going to turn the lights off and lock up when he's done.

"Do you want to just ride together?" June asks me as we walk out to the employee parking lot.

Typically, I would say no because I like having an escape route. But my feet hurt and I can save money by not wasting gas, so this time I take her up on her offer.

June's car is exactly how I would picture it to be.

She has a purple Mini Cooper. Her car seat covers are rainbow and it looks like they are crocheted. On the dash is a bobble head Taylor Swift, and in each vent is a lemon shaped air freshener but the smell in her car is peaches and cream. She's got fake flowers hanging by her rear and front windows. Her floor mats match the purple of her car and she's got about four silk scrunchies on her shifter. Her car is abnormally clean, even though all the colors scream hectic.

I think I'm getting a headache.

This is every grease junkie's nightmare.

Not to mention the multiple safety hazards.

But I will give her points for knowing how to drive a manual.

June has chopped beach blonde hair that currently has highlights of pink, but they change every week. At work she wears a black shirt as well, but pairs it with some type of floral skirt with so many colors that they look like they are battling each other for who can stick out the most. Her staple accessory is always a food themed earring or hairpiece—that she makes herself out of polymer clay—and a cluster of necklaces around her neck. When she's not working she is usually wearing a crochet top, handmade by her. Even though they are totally not my style, they are beautiful. She usually adds gems to her masterpieces or the pattern itself is super elaborate.

She's really good at it.

I convinced her to start her own Etsy account. She had her first order the other day and we took celebratory shots after work.

I'm assuming she made her car seat covers as well.

Down both her arms she has an assortment of patchwork tattoos and some on her legs too. I asked her once what each of her tattoos mean and she said *'I saw something I liked or got one because it reminded me of something special'.*

She is the definition of a free-spirit.

She takes life by the day instead of worrying about what's to come. Her carefree personality is refreshing compared to my high-strung personality.

"I'm sorry it's such a mess," she says shyly as she moves a yellow Hydro Flask with a bunch of stickers on it to the back.

It's the only thing out of place in the entire car.

"You must be kidding." I say as I sit down in her passenger seat. All my black clothing is a drastic contrast to her colorful decor. I feel like a shadow covering her rainbow. "Have you seen the mud and dirt that cakes my Ford?"

She giggles. "Yes, but that's *so* you."

The drive to the lighthouse is only ten minutes away from Big Fish. June and I listen to her Taylor Swift playlist and then she begs me to connect to the Bluetooth and play some of my songs.

My Spotify consists mostly of My Chemical Romance, Evanescence—and I'm not ashamed to admit it— Nickelback. To my surprise June knows just about every song I play as we rock out in her car.

By the sight in front of me, I assume we are the last to show up. There's about twenty people surrounding a massive fire in the middle of the sand. It looks exactly like the one they held at DuneFest even though I only got to enjoy it for about five minutes before shit hit the fan.

Orange and yellow flickers into the darkened sky above while several people hover around with marshmallow sticks.

"Come on, I'll introduce you." June nods to the side and opens her door.

I grab the handle and follow suit, taking a few hurried steps to catch up with her.

Once we reach the beach, June is instantly engulfed by everyone here. They all seem to be trying to have their own conversation with her.

It must be nice to make friends so easily.

One person in particular stands out to me, I avoid eye contact.

She interrupts them by introducing me. "Everyone meet Claire!" She has to practically shout to get their attention. I wonder what it would be like to walk into a room and grab that much attention.

I would hate it.

"I'm not going to introduce you to everyone because that would take *way* too long, so I'll just tell you the important ones." She winks at the crowd and a few people *boo* her. "Claire, this is Tyler, Dom, Taylor, Sean, Jen, and..." She pauses, gulps, and says. "April." I recognized her instantly and have been dreading this moment.

I look around and notice everyone is waiting for my response.

I hate being in the spotlight. And this is so much worse.

I want to be mad, I want to hate her. But for what? It's not like Dustin and I were dating or that April and I knew each other beforehand.

This is a small town after all. I could give everyone a new story to gossip about or I could let it go.

I soften my glare and say. "It's nice to meet you." There's no emotion in my eyes when they lock with April's, and she looks down at the ground. "All of you," I say.

April lifts her head in surprise and mouths 'thank you'. I nod at her.

June has a prideful look on her face like she's saying '*That's my best friend. Go best friend*'. I'm almost one hundred percent positive that's exactly what is going on inside her head.

The crowd disperses and June and I walk off towards the back to get drinks.

This whole situation with April has made me realize there's no better time, than now, to talk about Dustin with June.

More like I need to.

She already knows the whole story thanks to April so I won't have to go into much detail.

"Can I talk to you about something?" I ask her as she grabs a pair of coronas from the cooler in front of us.

Thank god, the good beer.

"Oh, finally! I thought you'd never ask." Her enthusiasm makes me giggle. "Here let's go over here." She points to a large rock that's backed up against the shore. "There's a little cove and we will have more privacy. As long as some drunk couple doesn't try to come over and have sex in there."

"Is that one of the hook up spots?"

"Yeah. Mostly high schoolers but our crowd visits it occasionally when we are hanging out."

I love that she just called her friends *our* crowd. As if I have no other choice than to be friends with these people. Like I'm already a part of their group and I have been here the whole time.

Our conversation brings back a memory of flirting with Dustin on the beach after the concert. Back when times were simple and less complicated. The memory makes me sad and my emotions must be plastered on my face because June turns and looks at me as we are walking to the cove. "You're thinking about him again," she acknowledges.

I start picking at my fingernails. A horrible habit I've had since I was a kid. A coping mechanism I developed to try and comfort myself.

"Yeah."

We get to the cove and sit down on a large log that is wedged between both walls of rock. I try not to think about all the disgusting fluids that could be seeped into the wood.

My self control must be low today because a grimace crosses my face and I can't recover fast enough.

June catches it and laughs.

"Don't worry. During high tide the water fills the whole cave and basically washes everyone's nasty little juices away." She says as she flicks her fingers over the wood.

I relax a little with that information.

"Have you... ever?" I gesture around the small seclusive space.

"In here? God no! It's too common. I like to have my own experiences." She takes a sip of her beer as we both look out to the ocean in front of us. "I don't know how much I can help you. I mean I've known Dustin ever since I moved here but I know the situation and truthfully when I first heard about it I was completely shocked." I'm thankful that June just dives into the conversation. I had no idea how to start. "Dustin has *never*— I mean *never*—done anything like that before. The last person he dated was in middle school and I'm pretty damn positive he hasn't done anything with anyone ever since. I honestly wouldn't be surprised if he was a virgin. I guess there was that one girl..." She shakes her head. "Anyways, that's not the point. He is a good guy, always has been. But what he did was fucked up. I'm not justifying his actions at all. Even though he was professing every single feeling he had about you that night on the cooler in front of half the town." She sighs. "I can't tell you what to do, and I'll have your back no matter what." Her eyes meet mine. "If you decide to hate him... then we'll hate him. But I don't think you want to do that, do you?" She looks at me with suspicion in her hazel eyes.

I bite my lip. "I wanted to at first... but now I'm not so sure."

"Good! Because I think you should give him a second chance. You guys are totes adorbs." I furrow my brows at her. "Shut up! It's a thing, okay?" I scoff. "And if he fucks it up again, I'll kick him in the balls and we can do that dramatic movie scene thing when they throw their drinks in the guys face." She has a very animated excited expression on her face as she pretends to chuck her beer at an imaginary person.

I giggle. "What if we don't have drinks?"

"Then I'll find something. And you know I will!"

If there is one thing that June is, it's resourceful. Another thing she and Han have in common.

"Okay, deal."

I pull her in for a hug and she talks into my ear. "Now, let's go have some fun. Then we can get your man back after."

"He has been out of town."

She pulls away and raises her eyebrows at me. I swear they are so high they touch her hairline. "Have you been stalking him?"

I shrug my shoulders. "He lives right across the street from me."

She laughs. "Oh, right! Forgot about that part."

We both stand up to head back to the party.

On our walk back we share in our mutual annoyance with River and she tries to convince me to buy a dress. I told her not to push her luck. The three black skirts I bought with her a few days ago are all she's going to get out of me for the next year. She made fun of me by telling Siri to put in a reminder for this day next year: 'Get Claire a dress'.

I shove her playfully.

We both start laughing.

It's cut short when we look up and notice there are two new faces on the beach.

They are standing on the other side of the fire.

At first glance I can barely make out their faces.

Seems like Dustin and Axel decided to make an appearance after all.

I turn to see June looking at me apologetically. "I swear I didn't know they were going to be here... *but* I guess it's time to go get your man back sooner than expected." She nudges me.

The world must be listening pretty damn intently to my conversations if it works this fast.

I stand stone cold for a moment, I'm still not sure how I want to go about this.

The light from the fire dances in his eyes and I feel my knees begin to buckle. All my thoughts are distracted by the way the warmth has caused his cheeks to pink. He is the focal point of my fantasies when I lay in bed at night and touch myself, but my imagination could never do this man justice. The thought alone of him touching me, licking me, kissing me, already has warmth pooling in my core.

I can feel my nipples hardening underneath my shirt.

Fuck the hold this man has on me.

Even after everything we have been through, what we *are* going through. I have never wanted anyone more than I have wanted Dustin.

He finally feels my gaze drinking him in.

His emerald green locks with my icy-blue.

His jaw clenches and he whispers something in Axel's ear. Axel's head snaps up and he looks right at me. He nods in response to whatever Dustin just told him.

He starts to walk over to where June and I are standing.

"Well... I'm going to go get another drink."

She swishes around her half empty beer and walks towards the bonfire. Intercepting him before he can reach me, she whispers something into his ear.

Our eyes have stayed locked this entire time, I watch as his body stiffens at whatever June tells him.

He is closing in on me and my fists open and close in anticipation.

I have never been so nervous in my entire life.

He is so close now and I have to fight every urge I have to run.

Why is that my coping mechanism?

Chapter Seventeen

Claire

His beautiful, toned body towers over me.

The butterflies in my belly return under his gaze. His smell of evergreen and mint encases me. Heat pools in my core at the challenge of being close, but not able to touch.

"What did she say?"

"She said that if I hurt you again, she'd hang me from the lighthouse... by my balls," he says as he looks over his shoulder at June.

My mouth drops open. "I'm so sorry."

He shakes his head. "Don't be. I told her I would help her." I can see the regret etched on his face. "Can we take a walk?"

I nod.

We started walking down the beach together, towards the same direction June and I just came from.

He is wringing his hands together, and I can feel his heart pounding from here. I want to be able to reassure him, but I can't seem to find the words.

I don't know if I should jump into this. If I should let him speak first. Or if he even still wants to give us a chance.

I've never been so unsure in my entire life than I am at this moment.

We get to the cove and take a seat. He runs his hands up and down his thighs.

Just say something. Anything.

I don't know if I mean that for myself or him.

Luckily, he breaks the silence. "The entire walk here—well to be honest, this whole week—I have been trying to figure out the right thing to say. Trying to find the right words to explain how sorry I am." He drops his head. "But nothing is good enough. Nothing can possibly explain how much it hurts me that I hurt you. Nothing can describe the ache in my heart from making you question me... that I made you think you couldn't trust me." He lifts his head and looks straight into my soul. I take a deep breath. The anticipation of this moment catching up to me all at once. "The only thing I can do is tell you how much you mean to me. If you forgive me, I will spend the rest of my life proving to you that you didn't make the wrong decision. I will work my ass off everyday to gain your trust, and I'll never make you question me—us—again. I can't erase the mistake I've made but I am damn sure I can give you better memories. And I can promise that I will never let myself, or anyone else, hurt you. *Ever* again."

I'm finally able to breathe again. Deep down I was hoping this would be how Dustin felt. That this would be the direction tonight's conversation would go. Either way, I still tried to prepare myself for both outcomes.

It's better to expect heartbreak, and prepare for it, then to expect to fly and fall.

Truth is, I forgave him a week ago. "I know you won't hurt me again."

"I know I don't deserve... wait what?"

I smirk at him. "I forgave you as soon as I walked away that night. Even if I didn't want to."

He shakes his head. "I don't understand. Why didn't you text or call?"

I suck in air through my teeth. "I may or may not have thrown your note away."

"Oh. That makes sense. I mean, I don't blame you." He looks at the stone walls surrounding us. "Do you have your phone on you?"

I shift around in my back pocket and pull out my phone. After I unlock it, he takes it from my hand.

"Where have you been for the past week?"

I watch as he pulls up my contacts and starts a new one.

He smirks. "Stalking me now, huh? I've got to say obsession looks good on you." I shake my head and punch him in the shoulder. "Ow!" He laughs and rubs at his arm. "I was just at Tahkenitch Lake. It's where I go when I feel... lost."

It feels like my heart is at the bottom of the ocean. This whole time Dustin has been *healing*. From me, from us. I mean I have too, but I never thought he would have felt as broken as I have.

He turns his body to the side so I can't see what he's typing.

When he hands my phone back to me I look down at the caller ID. It reads 'Dustin (Forever in my debt)' with a black heart next to it.

"Why the black heart?"

"Because it's your favorite color and I want to be your favorite person."

My heart swells.

I smile at him. Then send him a text.

Me: Did you purposely take me to the hook up cove?

I hear his phone vibrate in his pocket.

He reads my text and panics. "No I swear... this... I... *fuck*." He rubs his hand on the back of his neck.

My laugh reverberates off the stone walls.

I love messing with him.

Making him sweat could easily be one of my favorite hobbies.

Suddenly, I want to see him sweat in other ways. I can't take the distance between our bodies anymore and I'm feeling brave. Maybe I'm rushing this. Maybe it's too soon. There's a possibility he won't reciprocate my feelings and he might want to take it slow. If that's what he wants, I will respect that. But it's been long enough.

I want him.

I want to feel his skin on mine.

I want to feel his warmth.

And God I want to feel those lips again.

I get up and move to stand in front of him, he looks up at me. I sit down on his lap and straddle him. He responds instantly, tossing his phone into the sand, and his hands find their rightful place on my hips. The way he reciprocates my desire makes me feel so wanted. I giggle at his theatrics.

Where his eyes once shone with panic, they now shine with lust. I like that I can flip his mood in an instant.

His gaze drops to my lips then slowly travels up my face, stopping at my eyes. "Claire?" He says my name like he is asking for permission.

I nod my head.

His arm instantly wraps around my lower back, pulling me into him as the fingers on his other hand thread themselves into my hair and he brings his lips to mine.

His kiss is so gentle.

We both savor this moment.

He pulls away and I instantly miss his mouth on mine. "God, I've missed you." He tucks a piece of my hair behind my ear.

"I've missed you too."

He pulls my forehead down to rest against his. "Never again." His breath tickles my lips when he speaks. "Never again, will I ever go this long without you."

I cradle his head in my hands and lift his eyes to meet mine. "It's me and you now. No matter what."

He kisses me again but this time fervently.

I push into him. There's no space between us, but I still don't feel close enough.

His fingers pull at the top of my shirt revealing my shoulder and collarbone. He leans in and leaves trails of kisses all the way up to my neck. My heart rate increases. I'm already panting with the warmth and fireworks that his lips place on my skin. He moves back down to my collarbone and bites gently. My head tilts back and a moan escapes my mouth. My reaction sends him over the edge. He stands up. Lifting me with him, my legs wrap tightly around his hips. We devour each other. This seems to be our favorite position.

A mouth should never taste this good.

Never feel this good.

I bite his lip.

"Fuck."

I pull away a little bit and kiss his neck, biting the upper half of his jaw before meeting his lips again.

The whole time he has been holding me against him, as we stand in the dark, the moon the only light that shines in.

It's euphoric.

He is hard and I can feel him pressing against my heat.

He sets me back down on the log and I lean against the cold stone behind me. The fire that's coursing through my veins against the chill of the wall, sends tingles down my body. Dustin stands above me and looks down at the rise and fall of my chest.

His eyes darken and he looks *hungry.*

His look is pushing me dangerously close to my own release.

He slowly kneels down in front of me and sticks two fingers out, and wiggles them side to side. Motioning me to open my legs. I spread them apart and he scoots in between, I squeeze my legs around him as he lifts up my shirt peppering my skin in tiny kisses. I lean my head back and exhale. Arching my back for him.

He stops just above my hip and whispers against my skin. "Fuck, Angel. If you keep pushing into me and making those sweet sounds. You're going to make me come in my pants." My walls clench together at the thought of him losing himself.

He bites down on my bone.

Fuck.

What is it about being bit that makes me lose my sanity?

My eyes roll back into my head as I lean against the stone.

He leaves a trail of bites and kisses all over my skin.

He stops when his mouth is close to my heat. The wetness in my skirt only gets worse with the anticipation of his mouth on my clit or his fingers inside of me.

As if he can read my thoughts he grabs the waistband of my skirt and yanks it down to my ankles. I yelp and when I look at him he has a devilish look in his eyes. He slides my panties to the side exposing all of me into the blackness of the night.

The view of me spread before him brings out the beast in him. He growls at the sight of me.

I let my head fall back.

He huffs out a sigh of disapproval, and releases my underwear. He stands up slowly, dragging his knee along my sensitive nerves. He braces himself with one hand by the side of my head and grabs my chin with the other. "If you look away, I stop." His eyes look depraved as he stares into me. "I want you to watch as I stroke your pretty little pussy. I want you to see how beautiful you look wrapped around my fingers."

I whimper at his words.

Satisfied with my response—or inability to respond— he drops back down and yanks my thong to the side for the second time. His eyes are purely sinful as he slowly slides his fingers inside of me. "Fuck, baby. You're so wet for me." It takes everything in me to keep his gaze when all I want to do is drop my head back and arch into his strong fingers. "Is this all mine?"

"*Yes.*"

"Say it."

He scissors his fingers back and forth as he plays with me. A smirk crosses his face.

This fucking asshole.

He wants me to push past my limit.

He notices the defiance in my face, but before I can give him shit, he thrusts his fingers into me relentlessly. "Say it, Claire. Tell me you're mine."

All my carefully held together resistance is gone. My head falls back instantly. Almost slamming into the stone behind me. He stands up and throws his left arm to the side of my head as he stares into my eyes, his fingers still diving into me.

Our breaths battling each other.

Chests rising and falling.

Mouths almost touching.

He slides a third finger into my wet heat and presses his hard bulge into chest. My breath catches in my throat at his size. Even in this position I can feel how big he is.

I can't wait to have him inside of me.

To have him in my mouth.

He reads my reaction. Read my thoughts.

He thrusts slow down and he lifts my chin with his other hand so that I'm staring directly into his eyes. I've never seen his emerald eyes so dark. So serious. "You may be the boss in every other part of your life. But when I'm fucking you, and your come is all over my fingers. I'm the boss." His tone catches me off guard. He has never talked to me like this before.

I like the challenge in his gaze. It blooms competition, and I love the idea of seeing who could hold out the longest.

A sassy response sits on the tip of my tongue. But I can't think straight with his fingers thrusting in and out of me.

The wet walls of my sex pulsate against his fingers. He groans. *I want this.*

I want this more than I want to be stubborn.

My head is spinning and it won't slow down and I have no other choice but to obey.

"I'm yours." I choke out.

"That's my good girl." He praises me.

His strokes quicken as he rubs his thumb along my clit. My vision blurs and I can tell I'm close to my release. He drops back down to his knees and replaces his thumb with his tongue, the warmth and wetness on my tender nerves makes me see stars.

He angles his fingers deep inside of me, hitting that spot, sending me over the edge. Before I spill over his fingers he takes them out and drinks me in. Making a figure eight motion with his tongue.

I dig my nails into his scalp. My legs trembling underneath me.

"Fuck. You taste so good, baby."

He leans over me and his lips meet mine with a gentle kiss. He opens my mouth with his tongue so I can taste myself on him.

Fuck, that was hot.

The act causes the need in my core to build again.

He wipes the back of his hand across his mouth, then slides my panties back into place. Bending down he leaves a gentle kiss on top of the thin fabric covering my sex. He grabs my skirt from my ankles and pulls them up my legs. I help by swaying my hips side to side to get them into the right spot. When he stands he has a wicked grin across his face, like I just gave him everything he has ever wanted. Even though I'm the only one that had relief.

"You are everything, Claire Gates. You deserve to be worshiped."

Dustin has healed so many parts of me in this moment and he will never realize the extent of how thankful I am.

Never in my life have I ever felt so cared for or appreciated. I feel like the only woman in the world. In one night he has made me feel so safe, cared for, and loved. More than JT had in two years.

I haven't told Dustin yet. But that day JT abused me was the day after I finally decided to have sex with him. To me it felt like I had given him permission to treat me like he did. It felt as though he had control over me because we slept together. I have been afraid to share myself with anyone ever since.

That is, until Dustin.

I don't know what it is, but I know I can trust him. Even though he made a mistake. I can feel all his emotions for me. I can feel his passion.

His intimacy.

His want.

His need.

His tenderness.

He is beyond comparison to any guy I have ever met. I want to show him how much I care for him, appreciate him. To tell him I feel all the same things he does. Even if I don't show them as well. I'm finally ready to give myself, all of me, to another person again.

The realization hits me so hard I almost stumble backwards.

He senses the small achievement I've had within my conscious but mistakes it as uncertainty.

"Are you okay, Angel?"

My face is cradled in his hands. His eyes are bouncing side to side trying to read my expression.

"I am *more* than okay."

His shoulders relax as the concern lifts from his body.

I can feel he is still hard as we stand chest to chest.

I want him to feel relief as well.

More than that, I want to have him in my mouth. I want to taste him. I want to feel my lips stretch around his size.

I reach for his zipper.

Stopping me, he grabs my hands.

"Trust me, Angel. I want more than anything to give you this." He takes my hand and rubs it along his hard length. "But tonight is all about you. Only you."

The fact he is so selfless makes me want to melt into his hands.

Then I remember his fingers aren't inside me anymore and now it's a free game.

I'm the boss again. I cross my arms over my chest.

"Fine. But I won't wait long."

"Hmm..." He shakes his head at me.

"What?"

"That didn't take you long." He lets go of our hands. "You're not even a minute past post climax and you're already being stubborn."

"Awe, Price. Did you forget what you got yourself into?"

He smirks and pulls me out of the cove.

"Never, I know *exactly* what I signed up for."

I smile to myself as we walk back towards the party. Although a fresh wave of nervousness takes over, alongside it, there's an unfamiliar feeling blooming in my chest. I want to focus on being happy and not on the panic that settles into my veins. I know I will be allowed to take this at my own pace, without being ridiculed or pressured, and that gives me a small amount of relief.

A new relationship scares the shit out of me, but I have never felt so safe. I look forward to our relationship growing. I look forward to learning more about him.

We are closing in on the group when Dustin leans in and whispers in my ear. The closeness of his lips against my skin sends lightning through my body. "I will punish you for that stubbornness later, Angel. Don't forget that."

I bite my lip and smile at his playful threat.

What I don't tell him is that I'm looking forward to it.

Chapter Eighteen

Dustin

If kissing Claire was enough to make me absolutely *obsessed* with her... there is no word in any language to express what I feel for her now. Watching my Angel's body writhe underneath me, and the beautiful faces she makes when I am pleasuring her, has me in a chokehold. I wanted more than anything to watch her beautiful lips stretch around me. But tonight needed to be about her, and her alone. I have a feeling we will have plenty of time to explore all the ways we want to learn about each other and I am happy to wait until I can hear her sweet moans in a place more comfortable.

I readjust myself in my pants before the glow from the fire shows everyone just how much we were enjoying ourselves in the cove.

Once we get back to the bonfire, the tension seeping off of the people around us is deafening. It's as if all conversations have halted upon our return.

I look over at Claire to gauge her response, and as expected, her head is held high as we make our way through the crowd over to where Axel and June are sitting on a large piece of driftwood. I smile at the fact she just doesn't give a fuck.

Claire takes a seat next to June, and I take the one on her other side, Axel brings up the end. Together my brother and I box the ladies in. As soon as we are comfortable June hands us both a stick with a marshmallow on it while 'Everlong' by the Foo Fighters plays in the background.

I watch as June leans over and very animatedly smells the air between us. Claire flicks her nose in response.

Giggling, June says, "You smell like sex."

I try to stifle my laugh but it's useless and Axel makes no attempt to quiet his own.

"At least one of us does." Claire snaps back.

June's eyes widen as she takes her eyes off the fire and looks over at her. "Is that a competition I hear?"

"Not even close, but one of us has to have some fun around here."

Axel looks down the line at me and raises his eyebrows as if to say *'you're in for it'*. In return I give him the same look to say *'I know I am'*. But I wouldn't want it any other way.

"Oh, you want to have fun do you?" June has a devious look on her face as she pulls the marshmallow off her stick.

"Don't. You. Dare," Claire threatens. I look down to see her own marshmallow, with melted chocolate, in the hand behind her back.

Well, this is about to get interesting.

June smirks, and I scoot down on the log so I am out of the cross fire. Axel does the same on his side. Then she begins to examine the sticky marshmallow strung between her fingers. "Surrender, and I'll think about it."

Oh, fuck.

Claire takes a deep breath. "If I was a nicer friend, I would have given you a headstart." She meets June's confused look. "But I am not." She says, then shoves the sticky mess into June's face. She squeals and then does the same to Claire.

"I can not believe you just did that!" June laughs hysterically as the pink and blonde strands of her hair bounce in every direction.

"What did you think would happen?" Claire says as she wipes at the marshmallow on her cheek.

Before June can respond, I take her face in my hands and spin her to face me. "Here let me help with that." I take a huge lick off her face. I savor the taste of the sugar and sweetness that lingers on her skin.

She shoves me playfully, almost making me fall. "Okay, I know that was supposed to be hot. But that felt so gross." Her smile brightens up her whole face, and my heart swells with emotion.

Claire bends down and rubs her cheek on my shirt, leaving behind a trail of marshmallow and spit.

"Thank you for that."

"You're welcome," she says proudly.

When she turns to face June again, they have a silent conversation between themselves and all of a sudden I feel the need to run. I meet Axel's gaze on the other end and I can tell he is thinking the same thing.

They both nod and then whirl on us so fast I don't have time to respond or save myself. Claire runs her fingers down the side of my face and leaves behind streaks of chocolate and marshmallow, giggling the whole time.

Axel grabs June's hand before she can reach his face. But unfortunately for him, she planned for that and another slab of sticky mess in her opposite hand lands on his cheek.

He looks at me and tilts his head. I nod in response and then turn my attention back onto Claire. "Oh, it's on."

Both the girls shriek and take off. Axel and I are on our own feet in an instant and chasing them down the sand. Everyone else at the bonfire has ultimately been forgotten.

In a few quick strides, I close in on Claire but she is surprisingly fast and slips out of my grip. "You can't run forever, Angel."

"Watch me." She shouts over her shoulder.

I shake my head then notice the bounce of her ass and the sway of her hair and think to myself. *Gladly.*

From behind us I hear a scream and two bodies hit the ground. My only evidence that Axel tackled June into the sand. *Good idea, big bro.*

I dig deep and increase my speed, within a few steps I'm on her tail and she begins to turn but before she does I leap and tackle her to the sand. I pull her body into mine and spin so that I am the one that lands on the hard ground.

Her sweet laugh sounds in my ear as I roll our bodies and pin her hands into the sand. Then I proceed to rub my face against hers and she squirms to get out from under my hold.

"Stop." Giggle. "Dustin..." Another beautiful giggle. "*Ew.* Stop"

I pull back and look down at her gorgeous face.

Her breathing is rapid as she tries to catch her breath, and the corner of her lips pull into a smile as she looks up at me. "I knew you would catch me."

"Good." I bend down and kiss her. She tastes like chocolate and marshmallows. She tastes like the girl of my dreams.

Chapter Nineteen

Dustin

These last few weeks with Claire have been heavenly. I never could have imagined how peaceful my life would be.

She's been staying over at my house pretty much everyday. Her clothes are scattered around my room and she has an extra toothbrush on my bathroom sink.

If someone would have told me a month ago that a girl would infiltrate my life and take over half my closet and bathroom, I would have thrown up. Commitment has never been my thing. I love having my own space. But I would be lying if I didn't say seeing pieces of her all over my life warms my heart and makes me feel whole. There's just something about sharing the most intimate parts of myself with her.

Currently we are in her room.

I'm laying on her bed with my legs hanging off the side, tossing a rubber basketball in the air. I'm still in shock from finding a small hoop hanging over her door. She claims it's completely normal but I have never met a girl who has ever owned one, even as kids.

I think it's bad ass.

Another piece of her that I am completely enamored by.

You would think by how obsessed I am with her that I would have asked her to be my girlfriend by now, but I haven't yet. I don't know why. It's not like I'm afraid of her answer. I guess, I just want it to be the right moment.

I look up briefly to see she is still frantically searching her room for some magical black top that looks both sexy and covers her completely.

I silently protested the latter.

She's getting ready for dinner at my parents house. While I could care less, she seems to be completely out of sorts. I told her it's not a big deal. It's just a barbecue with my parents and their friends, even her dad is coming. So, I don't know why she is freaking out so badly.

Although, I do understand her hesitancy when I first asked, especially because of the issue with my dad. Which I still haven't confronted him about. Actually, we haven't talked since I told him I didn't want to go pro. I told her we could mutually freeze out my father. She refused and said that I have to make up with him. I won't even entertain the idea of forgiving him until he apologizes to her.

The only reason we are going tonight is because I really want her to meet my mom. I know she is going to love her. Which is ultimately why she agreed to go.

Sometime while I got lost in thought, the sound of her rummaging around her room has stopped.

I catch the ball one last time and sit up.

"Claire?"

"In here." She shouts from her bathroom. It comes out muffled, she must have the door shut. I lay back down when the buzzing of her phone starts rattling her nightstand.

I lean over and pick it up.

Unknown number.

Weird.

I wonder if this is the number she's been telling me about. Her phone in my hand, I walk over to the bathroom door,

"Babe, you have an incoming call."

"Who is it?" she asks.

"It's an unknown number."

She lets out a frustrated sigh then yanks the door open.

Gravity takes my arms as they fall down at my side.

I didn't know my whole body had been tense, until it simultaneously relaxed at once.

I will never—*never*—get used to her beauty.

Her hair is in perfect rings as it falls down her back. Whatever product she's used makes her curls look extra shiny. Her eyelashes look longer and darker, making her icy blues bold and bright. Other than that, she's not wearing any makeup.

She is a goddess and I am her servant. Completely at her will.

She's wearing a red long sleeve top that swoops low, covering her breasts just enough, but also a little too much for my liking. The cinch in the middle stops just above her bra line and compliments her curves beautifully. The stitching hugging her boobs is trimmed in a delicate lace. She has two gold necklaces around her neck. One disappears into her cleavage.

I can't wait to find that later. I lick my lips in anticipation.

She's wearing black leather pants that are matte and not shiny, at the bottom she's wearing combat boots.

We are not leaving this house.

She grabs her phone from my frozen hand then looks down at her outfit. "I hope this is okay. I couldn't find that black top I wanted."

The fact that she thinks she is anything less than stunning pisses me off. "Shut the fuck up."

Her eyes shoot up. "Excuse me?" She says as her hands fall to her hips.

Her sass makes me laugh.

"I said–" I take a few steps forward and grip the doorframe above her head. Her lips are only a few inches away from mine. "Shut the fuck up." I drop my hands to cup her face and pull her in for a kiss. "You are the most beautiful woman on this planet and red... is my new favorite color." She softens under my hands.

She pulls up her phone and looks at the screen.

"*Shit!* We have to go. We are going to be late."

The phone call is forgotten. Whoever it is— if they keep harassing her— I'll be the one who answers next time and they will not want to be on the receiving end.

She darts back into the bathroom and grabs her purse.

"Their house is only five minutes away."

When she resurfaces she says, "If you are not ten minutes early, then you are late."

"What is up with everyone and these damn fortune cookie quotes?"

She tilts her head to the side. "What do you mean?"

I have a small flashback to Axel and I sitting in our living room eating pizza talking about Big Rich's warning.

If only I would have known then what I know now.

I smile. "Nothing. Are you ready?"

Arriving exactly in Claire's timeframe, we are ten minutes early. *And,* the only other people here besides my parents.

Jesse, Claire's dad, still intimidates the hell out of me. He seems cool but I can't get anything other than an emotionless stare or short answers. I think he is still waiting for me to fail again.

Jokes on him.

Now that I have her, I'm never letting her go.

He said he would meet up with us later.

Currently he is at the fire department filling out paperwork. Claire told me last week he decided to quit his job at the hospital and become a firefighter. I think it's pretty awesome. Although, she's worried for her dad. The west coast has major wildfires. At times, it can be dangerous. I understand her concern but Jesse is a smart guy, he knows how to play it safe when he needs to.

We are parked in the driveway of my parents house. Claire is sitting in the passenger seat of my Bronco, her legs bouncing uncontrollably. The arrangements of cookies I made sitting in her lap, about to spill over.

I put my hand on her thigh, her shaking instantly slows. She takes a deep breath.

"We don't have to go in if you don't want to."

"No, I'm okay. I want to meet your mom. I'm just a little nervous about being around your dad."

It makes me angry that he's made her feel this way.

I've dealt with my father, his unnecessary need to butt into my business, and his pressure to stay focused all my life. I'm used to it. But I don't want that for her.

"Do you want to wait until more people show up?"

Something shifts in her demeanor. She's back to the stubborn, bull-headed, woman I know.

"No. If he wants to say something let him say it. But the only thing I *will* be getting tonight is an apology."

"There's my girl." I lean over and give her a kiss.

I grab the cookies off her lap and step out of my truck. Closing my door, I hear her follow closely behind.

She links her arm in mine as we climb the stairs to my parents. I don't usually knock, but this time feels different, so I do. It only takes a few seconds before I hear my moms cheerful voice on the other side.

"Coming!"

The door swings open.

"Come on in–" She scrutinizes me, "Dustin, you know you don't have to knock."

"Hi, Mom."

She pulls me in for a hug before she glances at Claire.

"Well, aren't you beautiful!" Mom raises her eyebrows at me. "You must be Claire. It is so nice to finally meet you."

"It's nice to meet you too, Mrs. Price."

"Please! Call me Anna. I'm am so relieved to see him bringing over a girl, I was beginning to worry about Dustin there for a bit because he never–"

I cut her off, "Yeah, we can skip this part."

"Don't interrupt your mom like that! Where are your manners?" Claire says mockingly, shaking her head at me.

"Ooo... I like her already." They share a conspiratorial grin.

"See, this–" I point my finger between them. "This is not happening."

"I don't think you have a choice here, Dusty."

Claire raises her eyebrows at my moms nickname and tries to hide her smile. She fails. I mouth 'Don't even think about it'. Before she can respond, she is whisked away by my mom. She looks over her shoulder at me and shrugs. Leaving me on the porch standing by myself with a plate full of cookies, I watch the two of them giggle as they disappear into the kitchen.

"Welcome home, Dustin," I say to myself before stepping inside.

Most of the evening has been really fun actually.

Jesse showed up shortly after us and following closely behind him came Tattie, June, Joey, Jeremy, and Big Rich. Then a bunch more of Mom and Dad's friends.

Mom and Claire have been joined at the hip most of the night. They have already created a silent camaraderie. It's kind of scary how well they get along. I can't decide if I hate it or love it. I definitely don't like their secret giggles and glances, that I know for sure.

Claire and I have been silently avoiding my father, and luckily his feelings have been mutual. I know I'm going to have to talk to him at some point but every time he comes into my peripheral I get angry all over again.

He's had this aura about him all night that I can't quite place. His side glances, and how he looks at her apologetically, haven't gone unnoticed. If he was anyone else, I would have already cut him out of our lives. Even though he is a hard ass and his actions are borderline unforgivable, he is still my father... and I love him.

I know there are tons of kids out there who have lost their Dads or don't have one, and I won't take mine for granted.

Almost everyone has left by now and it's just Claire, Jesse, my parents, and I. All the men are cleaning up the back deck while the women are inside washing dishes and putting leftovers away.

The deafening silence mimics the suspense of being launched into the air after a challenging jump. All of us grappling for comfort in mid-air, so that we can land on solid ground and not get washed out.

I haven't had time to talk to Jesse about his opinions on the situation. But I bet he feels the same way I do, despite the friendly conversation he has held with my dad throughout the night.

"Hey, D." I turn and look at my father. "I was wondering if maybe you, Claire, and I could talk before you guys head out?"

From across the deck I see Jesse peek his head up and pause before he continues to grab the trash out of the can and tie it off. Then he disappears around the side yard.

I'd gladly switch positions with him.

"You know, Dad. I don't think that's a good idea."

"Come on. I just want to apologize."

It has been a month since DuneFest, at any point he could have said sorry. He could have called or sent a text, but he didn't.

"You had plenty of time to apologize to either one of us. Why now?"

"Tonight I noticed how much she really means to you and how much you mean to her. To be honest, I thought this would be a fling and you'd eventually come back and we would figure it out." He rubs the back of his neck with his hand. "I can see now that I was wrong. And I'm... I'm sorry." If I didn't know him so well, I could swear there were tears forming in his eyes, but that's impossible. "I also want to apologize for making you feel like you couldn't be honest with me about your future. I know I have been hard on you, but I only want what's best for you." He sighs. "I do realize you're an adult and I should back off. I guess it just took me a little bit longer to realize you don't need me as much anymore." He gives me a half smile. "And it doesn't matter that you don't know what you want to do yet. I just want you to be happy. I love you, son." His tone and demeanor tells me he is speaking from his heart. I want more than anything for this to be that easy. For everything to go back to normal. But I'm not naive. I know that this whole situation has shifted something between us.

He can feel it as well.

"Thanks. I love you too... this doesn't mean everything can magically go back to normal." He nods in understanding. "But this is a good start and you owe Claire an apology as well."

"I know." He rests his hand on my shoulder and takes a sharp breath. "I'm very proud of you."

Fuck, that felt good.

All these years I have waited for those five words and there they are. Funny how I expected them to be for racing, and instead I got them as praise for picking Claire. "She is a wonderful woman. I know you may not care to hear advice from your old man, especially right now. But, she is strong and independent, two very admirable traits in any person, but that also means she will try to take care of things by herself. Most of the time she will succeed. Just remember to always listen to your intuition, if you feel like something is off or wrong, make her talk with you. It may not seem like she needs you, but she does. More than you know. She reminds me a lot of your mom when we were your age, I think that's why they get along so well. They both have that fire."

We nod at each other, then he claps me on the back and we head inside.

Jesse is standing at the kitchen island, Claire at his side, as they talk with my mom. Dad shuffles in beside her and wraps his arm around her waist.

She looks up at him. "I was just telling them how nice it has been to have them over." She pinches him on his side. I've seen this many times before. It's her way of saying stop being an ass.

I smile at the interaction.

"Yes. It has been very nice to have both of you over. I do hope you visit again soon. Before you guys head out, Claire can I have a word please?"

I look over at Claire.

"Sure," she says.

I watch as they walk out back.

I continue to keep my eyes on them through the sliding glass door. Her arms are crossed and she has that look I know all too well. She put up her defenses. She's ready to argue and I'm ready to have her back if need be.

They are only out there for a couple minutes when I see her body relax and her glare soften. She's accepted whatever he is saying.

Shortly after, I feel a hand on my shoulder.

"I think they will be fine. Would you agree?" Jesse asks.

"Yeah, I think so."

"You two are good together."

I spin around in the bar stool and meet his gaze. This is the first nice thing Jesse has said to me since Claire and I have been together. "I guess I should put my defenses down too, huh?"

"I won't hurt her,"

He smirks. "Oh, I know you won't." There's a hint of a threat in his voice.

That used to scare me, but now I just respect it.

I give him a slight nod.

"Do me a favor and stop by my house before you guys call in for the night. I have a surprise for her."

"Sure. But you know she hates surprises."

He laughs. Honest to God laughs at something *I* said.

Hell yeah.

Major fuck-ups: 4. Dustin: 1.

"She'll get over it. Tell her I'll see her soon."

Before he leaves, he says goodbye to my mom and thanks her for the delicious food then slips out the front door.

Not long after, I see Dad hold out his hand in front of Claire, she takes it, and pulls him in for a hug. It catches him off guard at first and then the corners of his mouth pull into a smile.

This woman is fucking perfect.

"Don't let a woman like her go, Dusty. She's amazing. I'm pretty sure that if anything happens between you guys, I'm going to adopt her and we will have to say our goodbyes," Mom says playfully.

I scoff. "Honestly, I wouldn't blame you." I look over at Claire affectionately.

"You are equally just as amazing."

"Thanks, Mom."

The back door slides open and they step back inside.

It didn't take long for her to realize Jesse left.

We say goodbye to my parents, share a round of hugs, and promise to come back soon. Mom gives Claire her number so they can go shopping together. I know it's not her favorite thing to do, but the fact that she is willing to go just to spend time with my mom makes me feel all warm inside.

Originally, we were both worried about this night but I don't think it could have gone any better. I was able to spend the whole evening with all the people I love and care about—minus Axel because he was working— what more could a man ask for?

On the drive home I try to pry answers out of Claire about her conversation with my dad. The only thing she will tell me is that he apologized and they are both good now.

I could have figured that out by myself.

She equally grills me about the surprise Jesse has for her. Although, it's not really fair because I genuinely have no idea.

We pull into my driveway and walk across the street together, her hand in mine. Jesse is waiting at the garage door for us. I texted him earlier to let him know we were on our way.

"Okay, I don't know what has been up with you lately but I am tired of your surprises Jesse Jean Gates," Claire tells her dad.

Jesse puts his hands up and waves them in front of himself in a defensive motion. "Woah... woah... there is no need to bring my full name into this."

"I haven't been allowed in the garage for a month. A whole ass *month*. That's some bullshit." Claire sticks her leg out and crosses her arms.

I can't help but laugh at the whole interaction.

I'm also mentally taking notes. I will never tell Claire she isn't allowed into our garage.

I've been thinking about that a lot more lately, asking her to move in with me. We practically live together as it is. I should probably start with asking her to be my girlfriend first, though.

"You just better hope it's worth it," I tell Jesse.

"Oh... it is. I think you will appreciate it as well." Now I'm intrigued. Jesse has a satisfied grin on his face. "You ready, Mini?"

"I was born ready." She rolls her eyes.

Jesse pushes the large gray button on the garage door opener. The three of us sit back and watch as the steel door slowly creeps up. I know what it is before it even opens all the way. I think Claire can too.

It's badass.

"You didn't." She turns to Jesse.

"I built it from the ground up. Every single nut, bolt, and bearing. Now it's yours. It's an early birthday gift because I know you won't be able to wait that long."

"Dad, this is so fucking awesome." She runs her hand along the blue body of a Yamaha YZ 250 twin banshee. "I'm only a little mad that I didn't get to help build it."

This ATV has a lot of fucking power. It's going to be so fun to rip around on the sand. I don't know how I'm going to find a birthday present comparable to this.

"I figure you might want to take it for a ride. You still have about..." Jesse checks his watch. "Two hours of daylight left if you want to load it up on the F-250."

"Hell yeah! I'm down," I say.

"Let's do it." She chuckles then pulls her dad in for a hug. "Thank you, I love it."

Jesse and I finish loading up the quad and securing it with a couple of tie downs while she grabs a pair of helmets and an orange safety flag. Jesse reminds us to be safe and have fun as we climb into her truck. I still think it's strange, out of all the people who could have bought this truck, Claire was the one who ended up with it.

I guess it was just meant to be.

It fits her.

She looks better in it than I ever did, anyways.

Chapter Twenty

Dustin

We head toward Winchester Bay.

Neither of us have been back since Dunefest. I'm looking forward to being on the sand with her. It also feels like a chance to wash away the last memories we had there and build new ones. Better ones.

Claire eases off the sand embankment and parks the truck. Before we get out she says, "I'm just letting you know ahead of time, that you are riding bitch first."

I shake my head.

"You already know I love to hold your tits while we ride." I rub my tongue along my teeth as I admire her body.

I can tell she is thinking the same thing because she bites her lip in response, then shakes herself out of it.

"First, I want to unstrap this quad and take *it* for a ride."

I groan in defeat. "Cock-blocked by a quad. I've hit a new low."

She drums her fingers against the steering wheel impatiently.

"Okay, fine. Let's go."

We jump out of her truck and close our doors behind us. I walk to the back and pop open the tailgate as she climbs up from the rear tire and swings her leg over to straddle the seat of the banshee.

She cold starts the engine while I set up the ramps.

Not before long she backs down off the truck and is in the sand.

I admire her as she straps up her helmet.

It's pretty warm out tonight so she took her shirt off and is sitting on the quad in a black sports bra and her riding pants. Her tattoo is perfectly on display and I still haven't mustered up the courage to ask her what it means yet.

The ocean in the background showcases the sun slowly slipping behind the watery veil. The orange hues make her skin glow.

I'm so focused on her beauty that I don't realize she is staring right at me. Her body is twisted towards me, the light contouring her curves and muscles beautifully.

"Are you just gonna stand there and keep staring or are we going to ride?"

I shake my head. "You are so impatient."

"We already know this. Now get on, or I'm leaving you here."

I jump on the back and wrap my arms around her. I slide my hand down so that I'm right above her pussy. Playing with her through her pants, I start to rub my thumb up and down. She leans her head back onto my shoulder, our helmets bumping into each other.

"Just remember who will be the boss later."

She gives me a devilish laugh. "Is that so?"

Before I have time to respond she jerks her head back up and lays on the throttle. I'm scrambling to hold on as she pops a wheelie and takes off. She laughs maniacally as I whisper curse words under my breath.

This little shit.

"You good?" she yells over her shoulder, still speeding through the sand.

"Of course. No thanks to you."

"Sorry," she says but I can tell she is being sarcastic.

She hits a small jump and we fly through the air. We land and she takes off towards the tree line. There is something so tranquil about being here with her on the beach. The wind whipping her hair around, the smell of exhaust in the air, the roar of the engine underneath us, her ass pressed up to my dick.

This.

This is what I want my heaven to be like.

She slows down and pulls over. The trees tower over us, their branches providing a sense of privacy. She turns off the quad and takes off her helmet.

I unstrap mine as well. "What are we doing?"

"It's so peaceful out here. The way the dark green from the trees clashes with the color of the sand is beautiful, and then you add the ocean in the background and nothing compares. I think I want to stay here forever." She takes a deep breath. "I mean I want to travel, but this is *home.*" I watch as she picks at her fingernails. "I want to open my own mechanic shop." She looks at me and tries to gauge my reaction. As if I would do anything other than support her.

"I think that's a great idea, Angel." If anyone is going to be successful in this small town, it's going to be her. "I don't know what I want to do yet. I think I might want to be a chef."

I have never admitted that out loud to anyone before.

I don't even think I've officially admitted it to myself yet.

But I love cooking and I love how you can change a whole dish with one ingredient.

Making dinner for Claire these last few weeks has been amazing. Making those cookies for my parents' barbecue and everyone praising them made my heart sing. I still remember how perfect it felt when I stood in that kitchen at the local community college and took that Italian Cuisine course. I constantly think of my time there. I miss it.

Claire takes my hand. "Dustin, you would be an amazing chef."

I search her eyes for the lie, but when I look into her icy blues, I can tell she means every word.

I don't know why I have this terrible habit of thinking everyone is walking around eggshells with me. I don't know why I can't just accept the fact that she is being supportive and telling the truth.

Yet, no matter how hard I try something always nags at me, I think it's my own insecurities. But Claire's reassurance pushes all those negative feelings away.

There will never be enough words in any language to describe what she means to me. What she has done for me.

I wrap my arms around her and pull her in, making her back press into my chest. I tilt her head to the side and bring her lips to mine. I kiss her with passion, love, and tenderness. I use my mouth to tell her how much she means to me. She melts into me right away and swivels her hips so that we are facing each other. Our mouths never stop touching. Our tongues dance together as she runs her hands all over my body.

I slide my fingers along the muscles of her back and continue to reach up and grab a fistful of her black curls. Then I yank her head back gently so I can get better access to her neck. She whimpers in response.

I leave a trail of kisses down her neck to her collarbone. One of my favorite paths on her body.

When she starts to pull at the hem of my shirt, I lift my arms up so she can slide it over my head. I reach for the elastic band of her sports bra and yank it off. Exposing her perky breasts.

I release a heavy breath at the sight of her. I take one of her beautiful pink nipples into my mouth while I twist my fingers over the sensitive pebble of the other. Her head lolls back as she whispers. "Fuck, babe."

She fumbles around as she tries to find the zipper of my pants amid her pleasure. When she finally finds it and unbuttons them, I stand so that she can pull them off. Once she pulls them down past my hips, my dick springs from its nylon prison. She bites her lip at the sight of me. The look of pure lust on her face makes my breathing become rapid.

"I want you." She looks up at me. "Tonight, I want all of you inside me."

I drop down so fast it causes the quad to rock. Sitting next to her, I take her head into my hands and look directly into her eyes.

"Are you sure?"

She has been hesitant when it comes to sex and I completely understand why. Not only did that asshole abuse her, but he strangled her the day after she decided to sleep with him. I am completely content with waiting as long as she needs. I can't imagine the pain she has gone through, all the steps she has taken to mentally recover from a situation like hers.

If she was ready—ready now—then I won't tell her no.

"Yes, I'm sure."

"If you need more time I completely understand. I want you to know you make me completely happy just like this. That you are perfect. You don't feel pressured, do you? God, I don't want you to feel pressured at all. Are you sure you want it *here*?" I gesture to the scenery around us. "You don't want to be in a bed, or I can make a special–"

She giggles and puts her hand over my mouth. "Dustin... I'm sure." She stares into my eyes. "I love you."

The breath gets knocked out of me and my body goes entirely limp.

It's a struggle to swallow the lump forming in my throat.

We haven't said those lovely three words to each other yet. I know we have both been feeling it, masking it with an over exaggerated *'I really like you'* back and forth.

But hearing them come out of Claire's mouth is such a sweet, *sweet* victory. Better than any trophy I have ever won.

"Dustin?" There's uncertainty in her voice. She seems scared that I won't reciprocate her feelings.

She is so fucking wrong.

"Angel, I love you so much. So much that it hurts. You will never have to worry that I don't feel *everything* you feel for me... and more."

Her eyes are glimmering in the moonlight, the angle creating that familiar blue halo on top of her head. A welcomed illusion made from the night sky.

She's finally *my* Angel.

She smiles as she wraps her arms around my neck pulling me in for a kiss. Then slowly moves a hand down my abs, gently scratching me with her nails, and palms my dick. She pulls away just slightly to whisper against my lips. It's not until this moment that I realize while we were talking, I have been sitting in my underwear and she has been topless.

"We have some unfinished business."

A thousand responses come to mind, but the best response I can give her is my actions.

I reach my hand around to the underside of her left knee and swing her leg over, making her sit on the seat of the ATV like a chair. I jump off the banshee causing the quad to sway a little. I notice the movement makes her breast jiggle and my cock twitches in response.

Moving to stand in front of her, I let her legs wrap around me. My feet on the sand and her ass on the seat. I slide my tongue across her bottom lip before I sink into her kiss. That familiar scent of vanilla and cherry filling my senses. I unclip the straps of her pants.

"What do you want, baby? Do you need me to take it slow? Or can I show you just how much I've been imagining myself inside you?" I whisper in her ear.

Her breathing quickens and I feel her shiver under my touch.

"Shut up and fuck me already."

This woman is going to ruin me.

I pull her pants off completely, and throw them to the side. I grab the black lace that clings to her hip and rip it in half, causing her to gasp, then continue to toss them aside to join their vexatious partner.

"Hey, I liked those," Claire protests.

"They were in my way."

She slips her hands down my sides, her soft touch tickles my skin.

The feeling of her pressed into me sends sparks of lightning throughout my body. Her fingers slip into the waistband of my boxers. Pulling them down halfway, she stops and uses the top of her foot to drop them all the way to the ground.

Fuck, that was hot.

Her legs are spread apart in front of me and my eyes land on the beautiful apex of her thighs. Her back is arched and head tilted back, her hands are on either side of her hips as she braces herself on the quad. The whites of her knuckles popping out as she grips the seat. The glow from the night sky travels along the planes of her muscles and accentuates her alluring curves.

I don't know when she pulled her hair up, but now her black curls sit in a messy bun on top of her head.

Behind her I can see rolling hills of sand broken up by islands of evergreens, the waves of the ocean crashing against the shore just beyond that. The moon is full tonight and the stars are illuminating the sky, the Milky Way peeking through the dark.

The scene in front of me is out of this world.

And yet the most beautiful thing tonight is the woman sitting in front of me.

Naked.

Ready and waiting for me.

"Where did you go?"

"Nowhere, Angel. I'll always be right here. I'll always be with you."

I get on my knees, and rest her foot on the top of my shoulder. Gripping her ankle I slide my tongue along her leg up to her knee. Her foot slips, causing her knee to hook over my shoulder. Her hand finds its way into my hair, scratching gently against my scalp. I'm so close to her. I can smell her, feel the warmth radiating off of her, can see just how wet I make her, and she's all mine.

I swing her other leg over my shoulder and line myself up at her entrance.

"Once I make you mine, you will belong to me, and *no one* else... ever again. Do you understand? I am going to mold you into my own sweet obsession. Your taste, your come, your kiss, it will all be mine now, Angel. There's no going back."

I slide my dick along her sex letting her wet heat coat my shaft.

"I need you to tell me you understand. I need you to know I will *hurt* anyone who touches you again." I run my hand along the side of her face, through her hair. Leaning over I whisper into her ear. "You were worth the wait."

She's having a hard time keeping her eyes open. But I hear her when she says, "You were worth the pain."

I ease into her, allowing her to adjust to my size.

When I get all the way to the hilt, she moans my name.

My heart rate spikes.

I savor this moment. I look down at the spot we are joined, and brace the back of her neck with my hand. "Look, Angel. Look how beautiful you are wrapped around me. Look at how you were made for me."

I rock my hips back and forth. Moving slowly in and out of her. I'm trying to hold on for as long as I can, but I'm already threatening to come undone.

Her hands stroke my back, her nails run along my muscles. The small pain makes me quicken my strokes.

"More," she pleads.

Fuck.

Her desire sends me over the edge. I ease out of her and flip her around. She grabs a hold of the seat. Her ass is displayed perfectly in front of me. I smack her cheek, leaving a slight red imprint of my hand. She whimpers, I pulsate in response. The sight of her tattoo trailing the ridges of her spine, turns me on even more.

Whether it's the sex in general, or the fact we are about to fuck in public, I can feel she is tense. I want to reassure her. I need to make sure she knows that she is safe with me. That I will only ever take what she is willing to give.

"Thank you for trusting me with this piece of you, baby. Are you okay?"

She exhales and her body relaxes significantly. "Yes."

Our feet planted into the sand. Her legs between mine. I ease back into her entrance.

My strokes are slow as I hold onto her hips.

"Please, baby. I want you to fuck me," she begs. "Hard."

God, I love that she is comfortable telling me what she wants.

I grab her waist and thrust into her. Her body instantly responds and tightens around me. Her fingers dig into the seat as she screams my name. My strokes are fast when I feel her release encase me. Her body shudders and I quicken my thrusts, feeling my own release building inside. I bury myself so deep that I completely disappear inside her.

I'm about to pull out to come on her back when she reaches behind and grabs my wrist.

"Don't. I'm on birth control. Stay inside me, I want all of you."

I growl. "*Fuck,* you really are going to ruin me aren't you?"

I thrust back into her.

It doesn't take me long, I'm already way past my point.

I let go, unloading all of me inside her.

My knees are about to buckle as I struggle to hold myself up. The endorphins coursing through my body are too much to handle. Nothing has ever felt *this* good.

I wish I could stay here all night. Buried inside of her and sharing the most intimate moment with her. But I can't, not here.

Slowly, I slip out of her and she turns to face me.

I pull her into my arms, and squeeze her hard. I try to fill her up with all my love. At the same time, I need her strength to continue to hold myself upright.

She fits perfectly into me.

Her warm, sexy, body is completely attuned with mine.

Our chests rising and falling together.

I reach over and grab my shirt from off the back of the quad. "Lean back, Angel."

She listens as I proceed to gently clean her off.

Watching me spill out of her makes me hard again. "Will you be my girlfriend?" *Damn. I did not plan for that to happen.*

Her laugh is so loud, so full of life. "Dustin, I think it's a little late for that."

I chuckle. "I guess you might be right."

She smiles and her whole face lights up. "But... of course. I would love to be your girlfriend."

I wipe my forehead of imaginary sweat. "Phew."

She playfully punches me in the shoulder. Taking a quick glance around she says. "I think we should probably get dressed now."

I scan the scenery around us, realizing how out in the open we are. "Yeah... probably."

I place both my hands on each one of her ass cheeks and pull her in for one more deep kiss before getting dressed.

Once we are fully clothed, Claire starts up the Banshee and we ride back to her truck. This time I drive and she holds on to me. I don't think I'll ever get enough of her body wrapped around mine.

The drive back feels shorter than the drive to the clearing. I realize from this distance how easily someone could have spotted us. An odd thrill of almost being caught shoots through me, I'm not sure how I feel about that yet. I don't necessarily want to be caught, I don't want anyone seeing Claire the way that I get to. But there is something that spikes my adrenaline with breaking the rules.

When we pull up to the truck, I park the quad so it's facing the tailgate.

Claire hops off the back, takes her helmet off, and sits on the open door; waiting for me to join her. "I don't want to go home yet. I want to enjoy this night a little longer."

I slip off my helmet and take a seat next to her. Wrapping my arm around her, I pull her in. In the process, I catch a glimpse of her back tattoo again. My curiosity getting the best of me, "Can I ask you something?"

"Of course."

"Your back tattoo. What does it mean?" I have seen it plenty of times while we've been together. I can tell its script but

I haven't been able to get a long enough look at it to read what it says.

She takes a deep breath. "It's for my mom."

Chapter Twenty-One

Claire

"I knew you would ask eventually." I look down at my hands and pick at my fingernails. My nervous tic. I really need to get a hair tie to snap instead.

We haven't talked much about my mom. I told him her name is Reneé and that she passed away shortly after I was born. I've wanted to share her with him for a long time, but there's a part of me that feels like it's sacred between Dad and I.

"We don't have to talk about it if you don't want to."

"No, it's okay. I think it would be nice to talk about her with someone other than my dad." Han is the only other person who knows the basic details of my mom. Even then I don't think I have explained to her the meaning of my tattoo. This is the second big moment that I have shared with Dustin. Something about being with him makes me feel safe, secure. I know he will always be by my side while I conquer my demons.

"My tattoo says '*Sometimes you will never know the value of a moment until it becomes a memory*'. It's a Dr. Seuss quote. When my mom was pregnant with me, my dad told me she would read me one of his books every night before she fell asleep. I still have the whole collection in the attic somewhere, apparently she has written notes to me in every single one." I look up at him. "But I haven't been able to bring myself to open them yet." I pull my eyes away from his as I try to hold back the tears that threaten to surface.

I shift into Dustin's lap and lay down across his thighs. My true place of comfort. He runs his hands through my hair. "She died when I was born. Dad told me when I was born the umbilical cord was wrapped around my neck three times, so the nurses and doctor rushed me off. He said when I let out my first cry, my mom took her last breath. The doctor told him that she had a severe postpartum hemorrhage and lost too much blood after giving birth. Her labor and delivery team did everything they could to try and prevent the blood loss, but there was nothing they could do." Tears silently spill down my cheeks, wetting his jeans under my head. Even though I didn't get to know my mom or build a relationship with her, the pain is the same. Losing a parent is never easy, no matter the circumstances.

I remember what it was like to be a girl growing up without a Mom. To watch as Han's mom braided her hair for a volleyball game, or when they invited me over to make crafts and jewelry, how Han told me her mom taught her about makeup and fashion, all the womanly things that I know my dad would have helped me with but I felt too awkward to ask.

When Dad sat me down—around the time of my sixth birthday— and told me what happened to my mom. I remember being sad and confused, but also feeling a massive amount of respect for him.

The fact that he had to be in the labor and delivery room, and instead of celebrating with my mom for bringing me into this world, he had to deal with conflicting emotions of pain and grief, mixed with gratitude and love. I never want to know what that pain must have felt like.

Dustin's quiet while I have this moment. I know he wants to say something but is having a hard time finding the words. So instead, I continue to share everything that's going on inside my head.

"My dad did an amazing job at sharing her with me. I know her favorite color, animal, fruit, restaurant, hobbies, and how she grew up, what her personality was like, *everything*." I take a deep breath. "She played volleyball and won a bunch of awards, until she got pregnant with me her senior year. He told me that even after all her trophies, I was her favorite accomplishment. She was strong and stubborn, wasn't afraid to show how proud she was to have me, and never let anyone tell her that her choices were wrong. People tried to tell her that she was messing up her life by keeping me, and she gave them the middle finger. She *owned* her pregnancy." I smile.

"Sounds like you take after your mom."

I shift to look up at him, a tear falling down my cheek.

"I miss her." I can't keep back the sob that escapes my mouth. Dustin takes his thumb and brushes the tears away.

"I know you do."

"I never even got the chance to meet her. It feels ridiculous sometimes to feel so empty, when technically, nothing was missing in the first place. I have never known the difference between her being here and her being gone, but it still hurts all the same and I don't understand why. No matter how hard I try to."

His eyes start to water and a rogue tear falls into my hair.

All these years of being angry, sad, confused, hurt, jealous, it all stemmed from my own confliction. I battled—still battle—with myself constantly. *You have a dad who loves you. You have a great life and you should be grateful. Why do you feel sad for a person you never met? Kids who lost their mom later in life have every reason to cry over the loss,* but you don't.

I've googled it enough times to know those thoughts are normal, that my grief is mine to handle, however I see fit. But I have never been able to say these words out loud.

"You have gone through *so* much and you're still the strongest person I know, Angel. Truth is, I don't think you'll ever feel whole. I know that sounds mean, but what I am trying to say is you were robbed of something—someone— so important. It's okay to feel whatever you need to feel." He inhales and wipes his tears away. "You will be okay no matter what. I mean look at what you've done already. From what you told me, I think she still lives within you. That you may have lost her physically but she has always been with you spiritually. I believe she is proud of you. Proud of who you have become, what you stand for, and that she loves you *so much*."

I press my hands against my face as the rest of my self control disappears. He puts his hands under my armpits and sits me upright, so that I'm straddling him. He pulls me into him and squeezes all the pain away as I cry into his chest.

"I'm sorry." My words come out distorted between the fabric and my sobs.

"Are you apologizing to me?"

"Yes. This should be a good moment. We just had sex together for the first time. We should be having a good night. I shouldn't be crying on my tailgate."

He pulls me away from his chest and gently lowers my hands from my face. "Angel, every moment with you is precious to me. You being vulnerable with me, trusting me, is far more valuable. Getting to know about the pieces of you that make you who you *are,* that is important to me. I want to know everything about you. The good and the bad. You're sexy ass body, and tasting absolutely delicious—" He rolls his eyes and licks his lips. I laugh at the childishness. "That's only a bonus. The real prize is having this." He places a hand over my heart.

I fall against his chest. This time I soak in his warmth and the feeling of his strong muscles holding me. Grounding me.

"I love you. I don't think I'll ever get tired of saying that."

"I love you too. I don't think I'll ever be able to say it enough."

I smile into his embrace. The weight of everything rushing into me. I struggle to keep my red-rimmed eyes open.

"I'm tired."

"Me too, Angel. Let's go home."

Chapter Twenty-Two

Claire

Dustin and I's time together has been limited these past couple of weeks.

He has been extremely busy down at the shop with Jeremy, and I have been picking up every shift I can at the café.

Tattie hired another waitress. Her name is Ashley. She's very sweet, but she has only shown up for half of her scheduled shifts. Every time there's a different excuse. She's a single mom, so I'm trying to give her the benefit of the doubt, but she's making it really hard. Her reasons just don't always add up. This is the first time she's had to be away from her baby though, and I bet that's extremely hard. I'm just hoping she can find a way to make it work.

I'm not entirely complaining about it. I need to work as much as I can if I want to reach my goal of opening a shop in the next two years.

This is the fourth date that Dustin and I have scheduled. The last three were canceled, and I'm really hoping that it doesn't happen again. I miss him and we desperately need this time together. The plan is to drive over to Roseburg—which is only an hour away—and have dinner at a steakhouse in town.

I've never been on a fancy date like this.

JT never asked me out. Being that we have known each other for so long, he just would bring home dinner for me or buy me flowers here and there. I guess he never thought it was important to take me out.

To be fair, I did tell him I didn't want to get dressed up and go out, but the effort would have been nice, anyway. It's easy to notice all of the other fucked up parts of our relationship, now that I have a healthy one.

Dustin is showing me what it feels like to be loved and cared for. Even if that means being pushed out of your comfort zone here and there.

I am so unbelievably nervous about tonight that I had to call in reinforcements.

June is coming over after she gets off work to help me with my hair and makeup. I have no fucking clue on how to put on makeup besides the little amount of blush and mascara I do for rare occasions. I've never really had the desire to learn. But I don't think it's just that. I think it's because I didn't get to grow up and watch my mom get ready. She didn't get to teach me how to put on makeup, or how to braid my hair.

I knew if I asked Dad he would happily watch an endless amount of YouTube videos and learn everything that he possibly could to help me. But for some reason, it felt more sacred.

I mean, Dad already taught me about my period and helped me when I bled through my underwear at Gabby Carmichael's thirteenth birthday party. I remember him and I rushing to the bathroom and he had no shame as he bulldozed through their bathroom cabinets till he found a tampon. Apparently he already did the research. Other than the twinge of red on his cheeks, he told me in perfect instruction on how to put it in and take out, what to expect and what getting a period meant.

Surprisingly, it wasn't uncomfortable or awkward at all.

That was a pivotal moment for me. In that small, dimly lit bathroom I knew I could trust Dad with everything.

I told him about my first crush.

I told him when Kyle in the eighth grade called me a boy and told me no guys would ever like me because I was '*too*' manly. After I climbed into his truck at the end of school that day, I finally dropped all of my defenses, and tears streamed down my face. He didn't even need an explanation, he slammed on the brakes and threw the truck in park, right in the middle of the parent pick up line and stomped up the stairs into the main office of my middle school. To this day I don't know the extent of what he had done, all I know is that Kyle never bothered me again.

Even though I keep some things from him—to protect him—and he undoubtedly keeps some things from me as well. Dad and I's bond is unbreakable.

Makeup was just not a line I wanted to cross with him.

I'm thankful that I now have June to help. A small part of me has been desiring to tap in more with my femininity.

The doorbell sounds off throughout the house.

Dustin made reservations at the Parrott House for six tonight, meaning we would have to leave my house by four-forty-five at the latest. I told June to be at the house at four o'clock to help me get ready, but she insisted we would need more time than that. So, here she is, ringing my doorbell at *three*.

Why on earth do we need an hour and forty-five minutes to get ready?

Pushing myself off my bed, I jump to my feet, and bound down the stairs. I yank the door open and stand baffled as I look upon my friend.

"What. The. Fuck. Is all of this?"

June looks through her heart-shaped sunglasses to the large, highlighter orange, wheeled case at her left side, a neon green duffel bag with swirls of blue sitting on top of it, a bright pink tote bag with sunflowers on it under her right arm, then looks back up at me.

"Oh, I know," she says as she shrugs and barrels past me into the house. Almost knocking me over in the process. "It's not enough, but I only had the two bags so I had to make do with what was available."

"You've got to be kidding me. *This* isn't enough? You look like you've brought your whole closet with you,"

She lets out an obnoxious laugh. Tiny snorts leave her nose as she pulls the sunglasses off her eyes and hangs them on her shirt right between her boobs. "Oh honey, my entire closet wouldn't even fit in the bed of your truck."

I shake my head. Then grab the large case from her to help carry it up the stairs.

"What is this, anyway?" I ask her as I inspect the abnormally large and strange looking thing in my hand.

"That's my makeup train."

"*Train.* A makeup train?"

"Yes?" She furrows her brows at me as if to say '*duh*'.

"So there's literally only makeup in here? That's absurd, who needs that much makeup?"

"My mom used to be a makeup artist… this was the only thing I kept from her."

Well, shit. Now, I feel like an ass.

June and I haven't talked about her parents yet. She mentioned back when I first got hired that Tattie was all the family she needed. I didn't pressure her to talk about it either because I know how it feels to be on the other side of the endless questions.

As we round the top of the staircase and walk into the small family room that sits across from my bedroom, I turn and look at my friend.

"I just want you to know that I am always here for you. I know what it's like to lose someone special, and I know how hard the battle inside is. I won't ever push you to talk, but I will *always* be here. No matter what."

She smiles at me. "Let's get started on your makeup and then I would love to talk."

I have a large floor to ceiling mirror on the far wall of the room, the one Dustin and I used to watch him slip inside me. The memory of seeing him behind me, naked, and panting as he leaned me over the couch makes my body heat. I remember him thrusting into me causing my boobs to bounce relentlessly. The sound of skin slapping skin. My cheeks blush and I smile at the thought of being able to do that again.

"This is perfect!" June says as she examines the space I have set up in front of it. I'm relieved she didn't recognize the flash of emotion on my face. I sit on the swiveling bar stool, one I brought up from downstairs. The small console table I stole from the living room stands in front of me. The perfect width for June to set things on but not big enough to get in the way.

"Okay, so I'm thinking with your icy blue eyes that a classic smokey eye would look beautiful on you. Then, I have a very light, wispy pair of eyelashes to really bring the whole look together." June is standing behind me playing with my hair. We both look at my reflection in the mirror. "You still plan on wearing that short black dress—the backless one—that has those chains crossing over your spine right?"

"Yes, absolutely."

Earlier in the week, June and I went to a small boutique in town. I found the most gorgeous dress.

I guess it didn't take her a whole year to convince me to buy one.

It felt like butter on my skin and hugged my hips so perfectly. I didn't even step all the way out of the changing room before June walked me over to the cash register, and demanded I buy it, the dress still attached to my body with the tag poking my side.

I haven't tried on a lot of dresses in my life, but the few that I have, never felt so... *me.*

Kinda how I am with my past and secrets, the low cut in the back reveals just enough but not everything. The chains that cross over my back remind me of my bike and the black is an obvious staple.

I can't wait to see Dustin's face when he sees me.

"I would have fought you if you didn't. That dress was made for you."

We both giggle, knowing she wouldn't stand a chance.

She walks over to her makeup train and swings the door open. "Here we go."

My eyes go wide as I take in the never ending palettes, tubes, and brushes.

"Holy shit!"

"I know! Pretty impressive right?"

"You hardly do your makeup, why do you need all this stuff?"

"I do makeup for locals who can't afford an expensive artist. I do graduation, prom, wedding, really any kind of special event. It's my way of helping the memory of my mom live on." She pauses and takes a deep breath. "She taught me everything she knew. I'm good at makeup but she... she was great."

I take note of the way she uses past tense when she talks about her mom.

"Can I ask what happened?"

She squirts a small amount of lotion-looking stuff in her palm before putting it on my face. I ask her what it is and come to find out it's primer with SPF in it. Apparently, I am supposed to be putting sunscreen on my face everyday. I'm given a very thorough background on why it's important, after June chastises me for not knowing about the damaging effects that the sun and blue-light have on the skin.

She carries on from our previous conversation like there was no break at all. "Well, my dad is a drug addict and has been in jail my whole life. I can't even tell you what he looks like." I catch her eye contact and she gives me a half smile, then turns around to grab an eyeshadow palette. "And my mom... she was a big league makeup artist in L.A. Until she was killed in a car accident by a drunk driver. Close your eyes for me." My body jolts at the feather-like sensation to my eyelid. "I moved here when I was eighteen. I lived almost my whole life in Cali, up until the last six years. Tattie was the only one that would take me in... give me a job."

"I'm so sorry. I know it doesn't help, but I am so sorry you went through that."

"Hey, it's life. We can't control the hand we are dealt."

"What about the rest of your family?"

"My mom's parents died before I met them and she was an only child. So, no aunts, uncles, or cousins on her side. And as I said I don't know my dad. But my mom told me he was from Australia and apparently I have family there." Switching out her palette for blush, and some brown-colored stuff, she continues. "I didn't want to leave the states, though. I don't know them anyway, so either way I would be living with strangers. Instead, I asked my social services officer if I could get emancipated. She advised me against it, but I had already made up my mind. After I had full rights over my future, I sold as much as I could from our apartment in L.A., and some of my moms client's gave me a rather large check, so I took all my money and hitchhiked along the 101... until I got here."

My heart hurts for my friend and everything she has gone through at such a young age. I never truly understood how strong June is until this very moment. I understand the pain of not having one parent, but both? *God, I couldn't imagine.* And losing a parent as a teenager? Would that be worse than losing a parent before you got to know them? I have no idea. But it sure seems like it.

"Why did you come here?"

"This is where my parents met. And I don't know... it just felt like the right place to be. It must have been the right choice because here I am, almost a decade later." She shrugs.

"Well, I'm glad you're here."

"Me too." She grins at me with affection in her eyes. "Now... no more depressing talk we have a date to finish getting ready for." She walks over to the stereo in the opposite corner and turns up 'Uptown Girl' by Billy Joel.

The next hour and half fly by.

My bathroom, bedroom, and living area look like a cosmetic bomb went off. There's clothes strung over every surface from our impromptu fashion show, makeup all over the console table, various hair products, and a small curling wand on the bathroom counter.

This will be fun to clean up tomorrow.

My phone buzzes on the side table next to my bed as June pins the last piece of my hair into place, pulling back just the left side of my hair.

"And done." June says and steps back to admire her work.

I pick up my phone and see a text message from Dustin.

Dustin (forever in my debt)

Him: Walking over now. I can't wait to see you!

Me: Okay, sounds good! See you soon.

My stomach jumps into my throat. A fresh wave of nerves taking over my body. I glance down and start picking at my nails. My knee bounces as the black heels I'm wearing tap against the floor.

June notices the shift in my mood.

"Hey... hey none of that. Here stand up, come with me." Before I can protest she grabs my wrist and yanks me to the mirror across the flat. "Look at yourself. You have me fucking questioning my sexuality right now."

I do really love how I look.

June did my makeup beautifully. My hair cooperates with me, for once, and falls in perfect bouncy curls. The dress is absolutely stunning, even more so now with the complete look.

I run my hands down my sides and take everything in.

"It just feels so... different, not in a bad way, just... different."

Would I have been more accustomed to this if my mom had been alive? I don't know. But I can't get hung up on that because it's not how my life is now. My mom isn't here so I don't have answers to the what ifs, and for the first time, I'm okay with that. I have people in my life who are there for me, who can help me with all the missing pieces.

I pull June in for a tight hug and whisper into her ear.

"Thank you so much."

Caught off guard, her hands hang down at her sides before she returns my embrace.

"I was going to give you some words of encouragement but it seems like you got it. You're so welcome, love. You truly are *so* beautiful. Inside and out. Don't forget it."

Just as we pull away there is a knock on the front door.

June looks at me with excitement in her eyes before she grabs me by my shoulders and leads me to the staircase. I can hear muffled voices coming from below as we near the edge.

Dads voice booms from the bottom of the stairs.

"*Claire!* Dustin's here."

I take a deep breath and straighten my back before I walk down. Step by step. The anticipation of this moment causes goosebumps to rise on my arms. As I get closer to the bottom—June right behind me— I see his shoes first. A pair of black leather Oxfords.

Then, his pants, dark gray dress pants.

Next, his button down black shirt—untucked—the first two buttons undone and a silver chain around his neck. Both of his hands are in his pockets.

Then I see his face and...

He's gleaming.

He is so incredibly handsome.

His dirty blonde hair is loosely slicked back giving it the perfect done-undone look. His emerald green eyes shine with both lust and love.

He licks his lips before he says. "Holy shi-" then thinks better of it and whips his head towards my father. Dad crosses his arms over his chest. Dustin clears his throat then looks back at me. "I mean... you look so beautiful." I giggle at the somewhat juvenile interaction. "Seriously you look like a dream. The best kind of dream." Then he winks at me. I bit my lip as heat rises to my cheeks.

I hear the cracking of knuckles and grab Dustin by the wrist leading him to the front door.

"Okay, time to go." I say in a rush. "Thank you J. Love you. Dad."

Before I can reach the door Dustin stops dead in his tracks.

"Angel."

"What?" I turn to face him, but he grabs my hips and spins me back around.

"The back. Your back... just... holy shit." Hands still on my hips he pulls my ass into him and wraps his arms around me then whispers into my ear. "So, you like the way chains feel on your skin. Does my Angel like to be tied up?" Heat shoots through my body, straight to my core.

Someone clears their throat behind us. I step away, startled. But when I turn around I can tell it was June. I notice that she is pretending to hold my father back.

"Umm... you guys should probably get going, you know, before I can't hold this guy back anymore."

I laugh.

Smiling, Dad rolls his eyes and shakes his head before he tells us to have a good night. I remind him to be safe while he is training for the fire department this evening. Then, Dustin and I jump into his bronco and head for Roseburg.

Chapter Twenty-Three

Claire

We make it about halfway before Dustin and I can't take it any longer and he pulls off the road.

He slams the shifter into park. "If you don't get in that bed right now, I will throw you back there."

I giggle and climb over the passenger seat. I sit down on the air mattress he still has back here. "I guess, we are lucky you're a procrastinator."

"If the bed wasn't back here I would have just laid you out on my hood."

Mmmm.

I kinda wish the bed wasn't here now.

Dustin scrambles over his seat and unzips my dress.

"Damn, straight to it then?"

"We are going to be late."

"I thought I was the punctual one."

"Shut up, and let me fuck you."

I reach behind and unclip my bra. "Yes, boss."

He pauses on the zipper of his pants. His gaze slowly lifts to mine, when he growls. "Say that again."

I get on all fours and crawl to him. "Whatever you want... *boss*."

"Fuck." He hisses. Then rushes to take off the rest of his clothes. I admire the cut of his muscles and how they flex as he removes piece after piece. "Give me your dress."

I narrow my eyes. "Why?"

He raises his eyebrow at me, and god dammit I love the intimidating side of him. The side only I get to see.

I obey and grab my dress from behind me.

He takes it. "Give me your wrists."

I do as he says. He loops each of my hands through the chained straps then takes the dress and twists it so the restriction on my wrists tighten. There's a decent space between the dress and where my impromptu handcuffs are. If I was wearing the dress it would be where you could see my lower back. He takes the dress and slips it over the headrest of the driver seat. Hooking my hands in place.

My arms are above my head, my hands are completely confined, my boobs are on display.

I'm completely at his will.

His eyes travel up and down my body, causing my cheeks to blush and heat to rush to my core.

I pull my knees up to my chest and tease him with the sight of me.

He licks his teeth and finally meets my gaze. His eyes are so dark, I can't see any of the emerald green that usually blesses me.

"Beg."

"I will not."

He smirks, knowing he will get exactly what he wants. "Beg, Angel."

I have two options here. I can give him what he wants, *or* play this game a little longer and see who gives in first. He reads the challenge in my expression and starts to stroke himself. My breath hitches. *Fuck, he's good.* I see a small bead of liquid leak out of him. My mouth salivates.

"Please, Dustin."

When did I become so weak?

He has a satisfied look on his face. "That's my girl."

I roll my eyes. But secretly I love being bossed around. He grips the headrest above my head and nudges his way between my legs, then thrusts home.

I gasp and I go to run my hands down his body when I realize they are still tied up.

He chuckles at my attempt then continues to slide in and out of me, building up my release. "Fuck, you're so wet." He rasps out, hastening his strokes.

"*Dustin.*" My eyes roll into the back of my head as he hits that spot.

The sound of skin slapping skin and our panting, the only sound in the quiet woods. The car rocks back and forth with our movements, our breath fogs up the glass, and I try to hold on for as long as I can to keep this moment from ending. But all my will-power vanishes when he bites on the lobe of my ear and moves his hips in a circular motion.

"*Dustin, oh fuck.*" My release comes and he grunts as his own release follows mine. Both our bodies spasm as we come down from the high.

He grabs my face and rubs his thumb along my lips. "I love you so much. I will never get enough of you." He thrusts into me one more time, my sex throbs. "Of this." Then he kisses me, a soft and loving kiss, and unties me from the seat.

"I love you too."

We clean up with the sheet he has over the bed and finish getting dressed. I end up having to take all the bobby-pins out of my hair because I can't figure out how to pin my hair back the way June had it.

She would be so proud.

Now my curls just hang in an undone mess while Dustin loosely fixes his hair in the mirror. He starts up his Bronco and we take off again for Roseburg. His hand rubs little circles on my thigh as I massage the back of his neck. I look over at him, and just really *look* at him. For the first time in my life I feel full, loved, and cared for. I don't understand how I've lived so long without this feeling. Without him.

As we pull into the restaurant's parking lot, I finally get the opportunity to fully register how disheveled we look. I say as much to Dustin and we take a couple minutes to fix each other before we walk inside.

The restaurant is gorgeous.

Chandeliers hang from the ceiling to give it the perfect ambiance. The tables and floors are made of dark wood that perfectly match with the bar, and are accented with black leather seats. There's tea light candles flickering from each table, and the servers are wearing tuxedos or black dresses. I have never been to a place like this before.

As the hostess leads us to our table, Dustin takes my hand in his. We end up getting a booth in the back, giving us a little privacy from the rest of the crowd.

We take our seats, and the waitress asks us what we would like to drink—water for both of us— then says she will be right back to get our dinner order. I'm looking over the menu when Dustin breaks the silence. "You truly do look so beautiful tonight."

"Thank you. You look very handsome, as well. We clean up nice, don't we?"

"We definitely do." All of a sudden he looks extremely nervous. He rubs his hands together under the table. "A nice dinner wasn't my only motivation for taking you out tonight."

I put my menu down. "Oh, it wasn't?"

"No, I was wondering if–" My phone starts ringing in my purse, interrupting him.

"I'm so sorry, I thought I put it on silent. Let me just turn it off real quick." I reach into my purse and pull out my phone, it's another unknown number, but this time it has an Oregon area code.

That's odd.

All the people I know that have Oregon phone numbers are already programmed into my phone.

"Everything okay?"

"It's an Oregon number... I'm gonna answer it. I'm sorry, It could be an emergency."

Dustin nods. But he looks disappointed. "Don't be sorry."

I tap on the little green dot in the corner of my screen then hold the phone up to my ear. "Hello?"

"Hi, is this Claire Gates?" A female voice I don't recognize asks on the other end of the phone.

"Yes, this is Claire."

"This is Katie from the Emergency Care Unit at the Lower Umpqua Hospital here in Reedsport." I'm on my feet in an instant and Dustin follows suit. He's already grabbing his keys and we are both heading for the door. "I have a... Jesse Jean Gates here with us, he's been in an accident while training at the fire department. You're listed as his emergency contact. Is that correct?"

My ears are ringing and everything around me has become black except the few feet in front of me. I vaguely notice Dustin telling the waitress that we will be leaving and us walking out the glass door. I'm trying to rein in my breathing so I can respond, but failing. He places his hand on my lap as he starts his truck. His small touch gives me the strength I need.

Not Dad.

I can't lose Dad too.

I fight back tears when I say. "Yes, that's correct. Is he okay?" My voice is cracking but Katie miraculously hears me.

"I can't provide that information over the phone. Are you able to come down to the ER?"

I take a deep breath.

"Yes, I will be there in about an hour."

Another deep breath.

Just keep breathing.

"We will see you then, just ask for me when you get here."

The line goes dead on the other end, and a part of me was hoping she would stay on the phone until we got there. No matter how unrealistic that is.

Tears are streaming down my face as I try to hold in my sobs. Praying to God that he allows me to keep my Dad. That he doesn't take him from me too. I don't know if I could survive without my father.

Dustin hasn't said a word to me yet, hasn't asked what's going on. He just holds my hand, my leg, whatever he can to keep me here on this earth. I assume he can feel my panic and already has an idea of what might be happening.

He is already driving as fast as he can, within reason.

The minutes tick by and the trip back feels *so* much longer than the trip to the restaurant.

When we pull into the hospital parking lot, I'm already jumping out of the truck before Dustin can put it into park. I run through the automatic doors straight to the check-in window of the ER. I'm vaguely aware of his footsteps behind me.

When I reach the desk, the older woman behind the plexiglass looks up at me.

"I'm here for Jesse Jean Gates."

Chapter Twenty-Four

Dustin

I've been staring up at the ceiling for the past two hours.

Why do hospitals always have the shittiest lighting?

Claire finally passed out on my lap about ten minutes ago. The adrenaline and panic fueling her body finally running its course.

The doctor came by shortly after we arrived and informed us that Jesse had fractured his leg in three different places during a training exercise at the fire department, and apparently he suffers from a condition called Deep Vein Thrombosis (DVT). Between the break and an already progressing case of DVT, he experienced a pulmonary embolism, causing him to pass out. If he hadn't broken his leg, he could have suffered from more fatal complications later on. The accident was actually a saving grace.

We were both relieved when Dr. Shank informed us that Jesse would be fine. His broken leg would heal in about three months and the doctor prescribed him some blood thinning medication to help take care of the DVT. He also reassured us

Jesse would be able to keep his job, and that everything should be back to normal soon.

Even though the outcome could have been way worse, Claire was still on edge the entire time Jesse was back in surgery. Insistent that anything could happen and that there was no way she would sit down until after the doctor came back and told us he was out of surgery. Despite my effort to try to get her to drink some water and breathe, she refused. Instead she paced back and forth on the checkered linoleum and asked for an update from the nurse at the front desk every twenty minutes.

I completely understand her concern.

I also knew that if she continued to worry herself she would only drain her own body instead. I was right. Eventually she couldn't hold her body upright anymore and she had no choice but to relent with her determination. Bringing us to this moment, her fast asleep on my lap, and my mind running wild.

I wanted to ask Claire to move in with me tonight at dinner. Now I don't know when the next opportunity will present itself. It was already hard for Claire and I to find time together. Now she will have her Dad to worry about and we will both be heading back to work soon.

None of these thoughts crossed my mind until after we found out that Jesse was going to be okay. But I still feel selfish for being sad that I didn't get to ask her. To be fair, this moment has shown me that life is too short, that anything could happen, and I don't want to wait any longer. I want to spend every day with Claire. But her dad needs her more than anything right now, and she needs him.

Our time together is just going to have to begin later.

My train of thought is interrupted by the sound of footsteps entering the waiting room from the surgical wing.

"Claire..." A nurse in blue scrubs looks down at her clipboard. "Claire Gates."

I gently shake Claire awake. "Angel, time to wake up."

Her body shoots up, unaware that she has fallen asleep. "What! What is going on? Is he okay?" She frantically looks from me to the nurse in front of us.

"He's fine, hun. He just woke up from surgery and is asking to see you," the nurse responds.

Claire runs her hands through her hair and takes a deep breath. "Okay. Can... can he come too?" She motions toward me.

"Are you sure? I'm fine, really. If you want to go alone I totally understand."

"I need you there." The look in her eye makes my heart swell in my chest. I'll never get used to the fact that she needs me just as much as I need her.

I nod. "Okay, then I'll be there." I look at the nurse to ask for permission. "If I'm allowed to be?"

"Absolutely, follow me. He's in room 218."

Claire and I follow the nurse—who happens to be Katie—through a series of hallways, until we reach Jesse's room. On our walk, Katie warns us that Jesse might be a little bit out of it since he is coming down from the anesthesia. Claire completely ignores that as we round the corner and room 218 comes into view. She books it, and blows through the door.

"Thank you." I tell Katie before I push open the door to Jesse's room and go inside.

When I step past the privacy curtain the first thing I see is Claire leaning over the hospital bed, Jesse holding onto her and his face buried into her shoulders. Tears are streaming down his face when he says. "I'm okay. I'm okay."

She lightly shakes her head against him. "I was so scared."

I can feel this is a private moment so I take a step backwards.

I'll just wait in the hall to give them some space.

Before I can step out Jesse calls me back into the room.

"Hey, D. Where are you going?"

I peek around the curtain again. "I'm just going to take a couple minutes in the hall, let you guys have this moment."

"No, we are good. Aren't we, Mini?" Jesse looks at Claire for confirmation and she shakes her head then sits up on the bed next to him. "Plus, I would rather you be here with us."

Even though Jesse and I get along for the most part, there's always going to be a part of me that doesn't feel like I'm good enough for Claire. The fact that Jesse asks me to be here helps settle those insecurities. It gives me a little bit of confidence that he doesn't think I'm entirely bad for her. This moment feels pivotal. One that I can't entirely explain yet.

"Alright, then I'll stay."

Once the moment settles a little more and she comes to terms that Jesse isn't going anywhere, she begins bombarding him with questions. *'What happened?' 'Why were you up that high without a harness?' 'Why didn't the fire department call me?' 'How long do you have to stay here?' 'When do you get the cast off?'*. It feels like I am watching a game of twenty questions. Jesse fires back answers and it continues on, for at least half an hour.

It gets worse when the nurse comes in and she wants to double check that her dad has all the information correct. Seeing her so protective so... nurturing, creates a permanent smile on my face.

We find out that Jesse has to stay for at least two days. I offer to drive over to their house and grab them both an overnight bag. They happily accept and send me out with a list of what to grab and where I can find everything.

I am actually thankful to leave, only because I am ready to take a shower and change out of last night's clothes.

When I pull into the driveway I notice that Axel has finally returned from his trip to Vancouver Island. I turn off my truck and head up the steps to our front door.

Once I'm inside, I yell out for Axel. "Hello?"

"Hey, D! I'm up here."

I run up the stairs two at a time and find Axel sitting on the edge of his bed sliding on his Romeo's.

"What's up, bro?" I huff out a breath and slide down his bedroom wall, the full weight of today finally catching up with me. "Oh shit. What's going on?"

"Well... Jesse is in the hospital and it's been just a hectic night, and morning, I guess." I look up at Axel and see that familiar look of panic. "Jesse is okay! She's there with him now."

He lets out a heavy breath. "Is that all?"

"No... it's just that Claire and I haven't gotten any time together in the last couple of weeks, and it has been weighing on me. We finally got the opportunity to go out on a date together, so I took her to that steakhouse in Roseburg, Parrott House." I run my hands through my hair. "Do you remember how I was going to ask her to move in?"

Axel nods. "I'm guessing it didn't go over well?"

I shake my head. "That's not it. The drive there and the night was perfect. But she got a call from the ER and they couldn't give her any information over the phone. She was on edge the whole drive back and the whole time we were in the waiting room. I was trying to be the support she needed."

His eyes widen. "Shit, D. I couldn't imagine. I would be pissed if they wouldn't give me information on the phone. I'm glad he is okay though."

"Me too. I just think the stress of the day finally left once I got here and saw you."

"Awe." He sticks his bottom lip out. "I love you too."

I smirk and shake my head at him.

"Shut up. You know what I mean."

Leave it to my brother to make me smile when I don't think I have it in me.

"What did she say when you asked her to move in with you?"

"That's the thing. I didn't get to. Her phone rang right when I was about to ask, and now I feel selfish because I'm disappointed. I mean, it's not the first thing on my mind. The first thing was making sure Jesse was okay. But after we knew he was fine, I couldn't help but be upset. I know it's stupid considering the circumstances, and I've been trying to talk myself out of these feelings. But if this whole situation has taught me anything it's that not everyday is a given, and although I don't want to take any time away from Claire and her Dad, she feels like home to me. She is who I want to wake up to every morning and come home to every night. I want to be there for every laugh, every sassy remark. I don't want to miss any more precious moments with her. I want her to consume *every single* minute I have left on this earth."

"Fuck. You got it bad."

I sigh. "Yeah... yeah I do."

"To be fair, I dont think it's selfish. You took care of her when she needed you. You were there for her in probably one of the hardest moments of her life and you are continuing to help her now. You have every right to be disappointed with what didn't happen as long as you are still making decisions that help the present... and you are doing that." He smiles at me. "Last night isn't the only opportunity you will have to ask her. It may not be in such a nice setting, but either way it will be special, because it's the two of you. Don't hang your head, just focus on now and the timing will come all by itself."

"You're right."

"I know I am."

I scoff. "I better get going. I have to stop by their house and grab some stuff for them to stay overnight, and I desperately need a shower." I stand up and pull Axel in for a hug. "Thanks, man."

"Anytime."

I turn to leave but before I do I remember that Axel was trying to set up an account with one of the docks in Vancouver Island and didn't even ask how it went.

"Hey. How was the meeting with Nanaimo?"

Axel's face lights up. "It was good! They offered me a position. I'll be going up there once a month to host tours. I'll be stationed strictly at Port McNeil. It's the best crabbing spot on Vancouver Island, I couldn't be more stoked."

"That's amazing! I'm happy for you."

"Thanks, you'll have to come with me on one of my trips. There's an amazing chef there who hosts cooking classes in his restaurant on the weekends. I met him when I was up there."

"Absolutely, I'd love to go."

This is the first time, in a long time, that I've thought about my potential cooking career. I've been so focused on my job down at Jeremys —and Claire— that I haven't had the time to think about if I want to take culinary classes or go to school. This seems like the perfect opportunity. I could learn some more about the art of cooking, maybe pick this chef's brain about how to start/run a restaurant, and it wouldn't have to be a full time commitment.

Axel gives me the restaurant's name, and tells me to call and ask for the head chef. My next step is to introduce myself, ask how much his classes cost, and what weekends they are on.

But first, I need to head back to Claire and Jesse. I say goodbye to Axel and jump in the shower. After getting dressed, I jog over to Claire's house and stuff all the things they need into a black duffel bag I found in her closet.

Before I head back to the hospital I run by Coopers Fried Chicken to pick up some lunch. I figure they will be hungry, and hospital food is not the best. Then, I swing by Bestie Brew to grab coffees for all of us.

If anything is going to turn their day around it will be a great lunch and a good coffee.

Chapter Twenty-Five

Claire

"I've got it I promise."

Dad protests as I try to assist him up the stairs to our house.

"You're on crutches! Stop being so stubborn."

"The crutches are there for *support* and you are just making their job difficult."

"Fine. Do it yourself old man. But if you fall down the stairs I won't feel bad for you. That will just be the product of your ignorance."

"Whatever you say."

When we reach the top of the stairs, we both stand there in silence for a moment until he nods towards the handle.

"*Oh*" I draw, "so this I can help you with." I roll my eyes and lead him through the front door. "The doctor said to elevate your leg and try to stay off of it for at least a month until it's somewhat comfortable to stand on." I scan the room. "Until then, I set up this little area in your room and I put the TV in there because I won't need it. Is there anything else I can grab? I do have to work tonight so Dustin is going to come by after he gets off work to see how you are doing and if you need anything."

"Mini. I love you and I am so thankful for all your help. But this is not my first broken bone and I will be okay."

"What if your DVT flares up? And I'm... I'm not–"

"Mini, the doctor said I will be fine. I have my medication. I set an alarm on my phone to make sure I take it everyday." He sets his hand on my shoulder. "I am going to be fine."

My eyes are starting to water and I don't trust myself to sound coherent so instead of responding I just nod.

"I'm going to head upstairs to take a shower, hopefully nap, then I have to head to work. Do–"

He reaches for the TV remote. "Sounds good, Mini. I'll be here rewatching Prison Break."

I smirk, then close his door and head to my bedroom.

These last forty eight hours have really taken a toll on my body. Between praying to God every minute on our drive from Roseburg back to Reedsport, and not getting an ounce of sleep at the hospital because of the sound of my dads heart monitor beeping, I know I am going to look like a walking corpse at work today, but I need the hours.

June told me I could take another day off, in fact she insisted. Tattie was able to give me paid sick leave for the last couple days, which I am extremely thankful for.

My hourly wage was nice, but nothing compared to the tips I make during my eight hour shifts. We are going to need all the money we can get in order to pay for his hospital expenses. Luckily, he signed his paperwork with the fire department a few days before his accident so his insurance will cover most of the surgery, but that still leaves the issue of the copay and remaining balance.

Fuck, my head hurts.

I slam face first into my pillow. My eyelids attempting to fall completely closed, the black slowly closing in on me.

Finally, a little bit of peace.

Bzzt. Bzzt. Bzzt.

Damn it.

I pull my phone out of my back pocket and check who is calling.

Oh, for fucks sake.

It's the unknown number again. I do not have the energy for this right now. I press decline and get up to go take a shower. I guess sleep will just have to wait till later.

After I get dressed, I grab an apple, check on dad, and head to work. Before I jump into the driver's seat I see Dustin walking towards me from across the street.

"Hey, Angel."

The breath gets knocked out of me.

He's wearing tan Carhartt's with grease wiped all over his pants. A black shirt hugs the ripped muscles in his chest and arms, his black boots have scuff marks all over the front, and gloves hang out of his back pocket. He is the most handsome man I have ever laid my eyes on.

I know what would make me feel better.

Riding this man like a 500cc on an uphill full of boulders.

"Hey, handsome."

"I'm on lunch right now. I was hoping to catch you before you headed in. How are you doing?" His support these last couple of days have been amazing.

He pulls me into his arms. His embrace warms me from the outside in. I could spend eternity right here, wrapped up in him.

I take a deep breath, savoring his evergreen and mint smell with a hint of motor oil. "I'm fine. Dad's good, I just need some sleep."

He pulls away. "Will you stay the night tonight? I'll run a bath and give you a massage to try to relieve some of that stress."

"You know that sounds perfect. But I don't know if I should leave Dad alone."

"I'm sure he will be fine. We can check on him as much as you want. Even if it's at two in the morning."

I giggle and bite my lip. "Okay, deal. I have to get going though, or I'll be late."

"Okay. I love you, Angel. Try to have a good day. If you need anything just call."

"I love you too."

He turns to walk back to his house and I can't help but admire how good his ass looks in those cargo pants.

Yum.

"I feel you staring!" he yells over his shoulder.

"Just enjoying the view."

He swings his hips side to side, exaggerating his movements– doing his best catwalk.

I laugh hysterically and then climb into my F-250.

Gripping the steering wheel and smiling to myself, I realize as long as I have Dustin, everything will be alright.

Luckily, tonight is relatively slow. The perfect shift to come back to after a few days off. Especially after all of the chaos from the past couple days.

Everyone seemed very generous tonight with tips, most were either the same amount as the bill or more. I chalk it up to the locals knowing about what happened to my dad. Although I hate the thought that people are only being nice to me because they feel bad for my family.

Tonight June tells me to go home early. She told me in a not so inconspicuous way that I look like death walking and that we would all benefit from me getting some rest. I happily oblige, remembering that Dustin promised me a bath and massage.

I finish clocking out, and say goodbye to the others.

I haven't taken one step out of the building before my phone starts vibrating in my pocket.

Excited, I pull it into my hands, fully expecting it to be Dustin. Until I realize it's that same fucking number.

That's it, I'm done.

Instead of pressing decline, this time I press the enticing green circle.

"Listen, I don't know what you're selling or who the fuck you are–"

"Claire?"

My entire body freezes.

My heart rate picks up.

I swear I'm going to pass out right here on the wooden deck of Big Fish.

"Claire? It's JT... damn are you a hard person to get a hold of." My breathing is erratic and I'm struggling to stay upright. I haven't heard this voice in a little over a year and I was hoping I would never hear it again. "Hello? Are you there?"

Somehow I'm able to form words, but it feels like someone else is speaking for me. "What do you want, JT?"

"You need to come back to Vegas. That whole thing that happened between us, you've been overreacting."

"It's been a whole fucking year and you're just now begging for me to come back?"

"It's not like you answered your phone calls before. Plus, I saw your pretty picture in the news. Congrats on winning the SandMaster title, seems like you moved to a sweet little town called Reedsport. No wonder you weren't home when I came to look for you. Why did you move?"

"That's none of your business. And that *thing* that happened between us was you choking me and almost raping me."

"Bullshit. But I'll allow you to live in your delusion. Listen, you can either come back on your own or I'll come fucking get you and ruin your life... and your *dad's*."

"Are you drunk?"

"Why the fuck would that matter?"

"Because there is no way you could be this stupid without the influence of alcohol. I'm not coming back, JT. Not ever. Not to you, not to Vegas. Hell, not even to Nevada. You need to let me go."

"That will never happen."

The line cuts out.

Fuck, I could have gone my whole life without answering that phone call.

It has to be just threats right.

JT has no way of ruining my life or my dads.

Fuck.

FUCK.

Sometime between my consuming thoughts, and pacing along the front deck of Big Fish, my phone connects with the ground. When I bend down to pick it up I notice there's a spider web of cracks across the screen.

June slams the door open in panic. "Is everything alright? I heard you yelling then something slammed to the ground. What's going on? Who were you on the phone with? You look sick. Are you okay?"

"Nothing, sorry I... I just need... need to get home." I'm tripping over my words while running around the railing into the parking lot. "Thank you for taking the extra work for me." I shake my head. "I mean finishing up the last hour. I'm sorry. I just need to get out of here."

"Claire, I'm worried. I'm calling Dustin."

I throw my hands up. "No, don't!" Her eyebrow hitches. She knows that if I'm hiding something from Dustin, then it's serious. Which only fuels her concern. "I just... that's exactly where I'm going. So you don't need to call him."

She crosses her arms over her chest. "I'll give you fifteen minutes. That gives you time to get to his house, talk to him, then I'm calling either you or him to make sure you're actually there. No games, Claire. You're done shutting people out. You don't have to fight your battles alone anymore. Do you understand?"

The anxiety pulsing through my veins makes me speak without thinking. "You don't know me, June. You don't know my past. Who the fuck are you to tell me what to do? You're not my goddamn mom." On that note I jump into my truck and slam the door. I peek at her through my windshield and her body slumps. I've hurt her and all she was trying to do was help me.

I'm a fucking bad friend.

I'm going to have to make it up to her later.

Right now I just need to get to Dustin before I break down in my workplace parking lot.

When did he become my sanctuary?

The whole drive to Dustin's house I'm fueled by rage and frustration.

Mad at myself for snapping at June.

Mad at JT for getting under my skin.

Mad that my past is still catching up with me despite how hard I try to run away from it.

Mad that my dad was in the hospital.

Mad that I don't have a mom.

"Please give me a fucking break!" I shout.

By the time I pull into his driveway I'm a ball of fury. I'm thankful that Axel's truck isn't here because I definitely don't want him to see me like this. I step through the front door and close it behind me. Then proceed to take my shoes off.

My footsteps are heavy as I climb the stairs.

"Dustin?" There's a crack in my voice. He doesn't respond but I can hear running water in the bathroom. Once I reach the top, I check inside but he's not there. What I do notice is the full bath and candles lit along the side. "Dustin?"

Please answer.

Fuck, I'm about to lose it right here.

"Claire? In here." He calls from his bedroom.

I continue down the hallway and when I reach his room I see a massage table set up in the middle. On a bench to the side he has an assortment of lotions and oils.

Seeing this is the final straw.

The flood gates open and next thing I know I'm sobbing and curled up in a ball in the middle of his carpet. Dustin rounds the corner from his closet and drops the pillow he is holding. He scoops me up into his arms and pulls me into his chest. "What happened?" I can't find the words yet. I just need to cry. "Who hurt you?" When I don't answer, Dustin doesn't push anymore, he just grabs me by my arm and pulls me up. "Come on, Angel."

Leading me into the bathroom, he closes the door behind us, and helps me get undressed. I'm still crying uncontrollably, and an overwhelming feeling of embarrassment racks my body, causing more tears to flood. I'm not usually one to cry. I'm stronger than this.

"I'm so... sorry." I choke out.

"Claire, I've told you this before. Don't ever be sorry for your feelings. You and I, we are a team. We will hurt as a team, build as a team, *heal* as a team." He helps me step into the claw foot tub. Once I'm settled he starts to take off his clothes.

"I'm going to get in with you. Is that okay?"

My head is in my hands, my knees pulled up to my chest, and I nod. "Please."

The only indication he's gotten in with me is the sloshing of the water around my body. He slides his legs on either side of me then grabs a soft towel that is resting on the edge of the tub. Dipping it into the water, he begins to run it along my shoulders. I finally feel a little bit of relief. "Take deep breaths for me baby. I'll do them with you." I follow his breathing and my heart rate begins to slow. "How are you feeling?"

"Better."

"I'm going to wash your hair now okay?"

"Are you even real? Or am I making you up to deal with my trauma?"

He chuckles. "I'm real and I'm right here, always will be. I promise."

I slide down so that my head is resting between his legs. When I look up I notice the skylight above the tub.

I've been in this bathroom over a hundred times and I don't think I've ever appreciated it as much as I do now.

The moon is peeking in from the edge of the window. The stars are dancing in the sky, as light twinkles all around us from the burning candles.

No other moment will ever compare to this one. And dammit, it could have been so much more special if I didn't come into this house as a messy ball of emotions.

He grabs a bottle—I'm assuming shampoo—from the wooden shelf that hangs off the edge of the tub. He massages the soap into my head. His fingers are heaven.

I already knew that.

"God, this feels so good. Almost better than sex."

"I really need to step up my game, then."

I smile. It fades just as fast as it came.

"Do you want to tell me what's going on?" He grabs the hand shower and begins to wash the shampoo from my hair. I take a deep breath. I feel safe here with Dustin.

"You know that unknown number that's been calling me?" He nods. "Well, I finally answered it after work today. I finally had enough of the harassment, and the stress from my dads injury just pushed me over the edge. The voice on the other end... it was JT."

Dustin's hand stops briefly. If I didn't know him so well I probably wouldn't have noticed. I look up to catch his eyes and his jaw is tense.

When he responds his voice, and face, is the poster of calm. "What did he say?" He reaches over to grab the conditioner, I sit up a little so he can run it through the ends of my hair.

"He said I need to come back to Vegas, that I've been overreacting... then continued to threaten my dad and I, saying he was going to ruin our lives." Dustin's breaths increase in speed. "I told him to fuck off and that there is no way in hell I would be returning to Nevada. I told him he needs to let me go... he said 'That's not going to happen' and then hung up."

Dustin rinses out the conditioner in my hair. No sign of his emotions on his face. Except his eyes flared when I told him how JT ended the conversation. "Did you block his number?"

"Shit... no, but I'll do that as soon as we get out."

"Good. Do you think he will come here?"

"I don't know. No one knew we were here besides Han and her family. He said he saw the SandMaster article in the news."

"I still don't want to risk it. With your permission, I would like to give Sheriff Toby a picture of him and just ask to keep a look out for anyone matching his description."

I shake my head. "You know I don't like favors."

"You're in a small town now, Angel. We look out for each other around here. Whether you like it or not."

I sit up and face him. "I yelled at June tonight. For almost that exact reason." I drop my head and pick at my fingernails. "Do you think she will hate me now?"

Dustin grabs my hands, stopping me from my nervous habit. "No, I don't think so. But you will need to do something extravagant, knowing her."

I laugh. "Yeah, you're probably right. Can we just enjoy the rest of our night now? Go back to what we originally had planned?"

"Whatever you want, Angel. Tonight's all about you."

My past might be full of shitty things. But without it, I wouldn't be sitting in a bathtub under the stars with the sexiest guy I have ever met. So in a way, I guess I have to be thankful for all the rocks that have been thrown in my lane, because now I don't have to fight my battles alone.

Dustin has taught me how to accept help, to be open with the people I love, how to love myself in ways I never thought I could.

Knowing that my past brought me to this moment; bring it on, future.

I'm not running anymore.

Chapter Twenty-Six

Claire

"Nope. No way. There's no chance I'm going to a karaoke night."

"I don't think you have a choice. It's three versus one."

It's been two weeks since my dad's accident.

Two weeks since JT's phone call.

We are sitting around Dustin's kitchen table as June, Axel, and him try to convince me to go to a 'Twos for Tuesday' night at Tides. Apparently, along with it being karaoke night, it's also two dollar margarita night.

According to June *'she's a slut for a cheap marg'* and that should be all the convincing I need.

"I'm sorry, but no. Someone needs to be available for my dad. He is still bedridden for at least two more weeks and if I'm drunk, I won't be much help."

"I already called in reinforcements." June says with a sly smirk.

The day after I yelled at June, I showed up to work with an apology basket filled with three rolls of her 'fancy' yarn, a new pair of crochet needles—ones with tiny sunflowers on them—and a gift card to Bestie Brews. Then, I loosely explained the situation to her, and Dustin was right, she forgave me right out of the starting gate. She told me to never keep things from her again and we would be fine.

"What did you do?" I scrutinize her.

"I promise you'll approve."

"What. Did. You. Do?" I put emphasis on each word.

"I may or may not have told a certain *boss* to go over there for a movie night." She lifts her hands up and bounces them up and down like she's weighing options.

"Tattie?! You didn't!"

"And here I was going to guess Jeremy," Dustin plays.

Axel laughs.

June and I glare at him.

He throws his hands up in response.

She turns to face me again. Her head is bobbing up and down with a grin of satisfaction on her face. "I did."

"I'm impressed. I've been trying to get them together for a month now."

"So this is what girls do in their past time." Axel mocks.

"Ugh, do they have to come? We could just do a girls night."

"You're just mad at men right now because of what happened with Derrick." June's eyes widen and she shakes her head at me.

"Whose Derrick?" Dustin asks.

"No one," June and I say at the same time.

There's a look on Axel's face that I can't quite figure out.

"Well, are we going or not?"

"Oh, we are going," June responds for the whole group.

Dustin looks to me for confirmation and I shrug my shoulders.

After waiting on June for about half an hour, we load up into Dustin's Bronco and drive towards Tides. He claimed the role of DD (designated driver) but I have a feeling Axel doesn't drink much either. So it's most likely just going to be the Claire and June show tonight.

The place is small, exactly what you would picture a local bar to look like. I will say that this place is *packed*. I didn't know that this many people lived in Reedsport.

June ushers me over to the bar for Margaritas while the men snag a pool table for us in the back.

About three margaritas and two games of pool later, I'm definitely starting to feel it and June is too. But I'm still present enough to notice the protective stare Axel has had on her all night.

I slide into the booth. "I see the way you look at her."

"You've got, Dustin. She's got me. At least for tonight."

We both look in her direction.

"Mhm... I'm not buying it."

"You're drunk."

I glare at him. "I'm buzzed, there's a difference."

June has been on the dance floor all night. A mix of guys and girls stepping in behind her. Her partners have been changing faster than the songs.

"You know if you want to go dance with her, you could just ask."

"I don't dance."

"Okay, fine. Then continue to be the creeper in the back watching her from a distance."

His eyes snap to mine. "That's... I'm not–"

I giggle. "I'm going to go grab another drink. Where's Dustin?"

Axel throws his thumb over his shoulder. "Bathroom."

I walk up to the bar and ask for a jalapeño pineapple margarita on the rocks. As I'm waiting for my drink, 'Dreams by Fleetwood Mac' comes on.

Fuck, this is my song.

I start swaying my hips a little bit. Letting the music flood my veins. The chorus comes on and I automatically follow along. Someone puts a hand across my low back and settles in on my hip. I swing around and it's an older guy, probably in his late thirties. I've never seen him before.

I shoot him a warning look.

He doesn't move his hand, instead he slips his finger through my belt loop. "Hey, gorgeous. I haven't seen you around here before. My name is Barry."

"Get your hands off me." I have way too many margaritas in me to care if I beat the shit out of some guy in front of half the town.

"You were dancing over here all alone. I figured you could use–"

"You better remove your grimy ass hand before I remove it for you." His familiar voice thunders from behind me. A grin tugs at my lips. "Hasn't anyone taught you not to touch a woman without her permission? " Dustin is standing at my side now, and Barry finally removed his hand. "I suggest you leave before I break your fucking nose in front of all your bitch ass buddies over there in the back corner." Sure enough, there's a table of about four men watching this whole thing go down.

Barry puts his hands up. "Sorry man. Didn't know she was with someone."

"Even if I wasn't, that doesn't give you the right to put your hands on me, dog breath." Dustin pulls me into him. "He'll break your nose and I'll break your wrist if you touch anyone else in here without their consent."

"Dog breath?"

"Yeah, because you're a bitch. Now go sit like a good boy."

Barry rolls his eyes and walks away, back over to his friends. I'm sure the story he tells them will be different than what actually happened, but hopefully he has learned his lesson nonetheless.

"I have had enough of shitty men mistreating you." Dustin fists are clenched at his side.

I rub my hand down his arm. My attempt at trying to soothe him. "Thanks for having my back."

He lifts my hand to his chest. His heart is beating a million miles a minute. "I will always have your back. I will always protect you. You are my reason to breathe, Claire."

I take his cheeks into my hands. "And you are mine."

He removes my hand from his face and threads his fingers through mine. When we look upon the crowd we see June and Axel dancing together. She looks *tiny* standing next to him.

We share a conspiratorial look.

Looks like we aren't the only ones having a good time tonight.

Chapter Twenty-Seven

Claire

My head pounds against my skull as I get dressed into my work clothes.

"I'm never drinking again."

Dustin laughs then rolls over onto his side. The sheet from his bed barely covers him. "Says every single person after they wake up from a night of drinking."

"Yeah, well I mean it."

"I'm sure they say that too."

I narrow my eyes. "Are you trying to piss me off?"

"Come here." I glance down at his toned body, my gaze snagging on the bulge peeking through the black sheet. I lick my lips. Then force myself out of his trance.

"No... no! Last time you made me late."

"I promise I'll be quick this time. I'll pay you double what you make if you stay behind."

"You said that last time, and no." I snag my purse from the floor and pull my last converse on.

I'll tie them in the car.

I lean in to give Dustin a kiss goodbye and he pulls me onto his lap so that I'm straddling him. I shriek. His thick size pushes against the thin layer of fabric between me and him. His eyebrow arches and the lust in his eyes just about drives me into madness.

"Please stay, something feels off."

"I can't." He deflates. I run my hand along him. "Save this for me after work."

"Promise?"

"Promise."

I give Dustin a long kiss then head downstairs.

I grab my name tag off the kitchen island and head out the front door.

Evanescence blasts from my stereo as I pull into the parking lot at Big Fish. After I finish tying up my laces, I strut through the front and I'm greeted by River, or lack thereof, he's playing on his phone.

"Hey, River."

He only nods as a hello.

We really need to fire you.

I'm about to take the steps into the seating area when River stops me. "Oh, hey. Some guy is looking for you." I jolt backward and swivel my body to face River. "He said he would be out on the pier, fishing... I think. Said it was about your dad." He shrugs his shoulders. "I don't know, I wasn't really paying attention."

I'm gonna kill him.

"Did he leave a name?"

"Don't remember."

"Did he say what time I should meet him?"

River sighs and leans over to glance at the clock on the check-in machine. "Now, actually."

"Fuck." I grab a post-it note from the hostess desk and write a note to June.

Hey, something important came up.
Please cover for me, I owe you big time.
I'll be back soon. Promise.
Love, C

I stick the note on June's server book. Then head out the door. I hear the click of it closing behind me and stop.

Fuck it.

I pull it back open and peek in. "Hey, River."

Surprisingly, he looks up this time. "Quit or I'll make you quit."

His face goes slack as the door slams closed behind me.

I know what I'm about to face. It's time. This needs to be over for good. I can't move on to the next chapter in my life if I'm constantly being dragged down by the past.

I won't live in fear anymore.

Dustin helped me get my strength back and I'll be damn if I let an asshole like JT tear me apart again.

Time for one more lesson to be taught.

Chapter Twenty-Eight

Dustin

I have never felt rage like I had at Tides when a stranger, Barry, put his hands on Claire. I could have snapped his neck right then and there and not felt any remorse. The only thing that was keeping me grounded was her. I know she doesn't need any more violence in her life and I want to be a man that deserves her.

So instead, I tried to get my point across by words, or threats in my case, before pummeling the guy. Luckily, he listened and walked away. Back to his—probably just as douchey—friends.

I was determined to give her the night off she deserved, and I think she definitely got it. We danced all night with Axel and June. She finished off two more margaritas and then we came home. I tasted her until she came in my mouth and passed out from pure bliss. She wanted to have sex but I won't sleep with her while she has alcohol in her system. Even if she wasn't drunk, it doesn't feel right.

This morning Claire got ready for work and I tried to sneak her back into bed with me, but I was unsuccessful. And rightfully so. Last time I made her late. I was enjoying being inside her too much. *Who could blame me?*

Today I'm off and she is working the afternoon shift, so tonight we will be all alone. I'll finally get another chance at asking her to move in with me. It won't be as fancy as the Parrott House, but I am setting up a nice little scene here and cooking her favorite dish—chicken saltimbocca.

I've been feeling uneasy since Claire left for work. I have this gut feeling I need to go check on her, but I know she'd kick my ass for being overbearing. Instead, I grab some ibuprofen and a Gatorade, deciding to drop it off to her so I can check in without making it obvious. I need to stamp out the stirring feeling in my stomach that something is wrong– off.

I finish tying up my converse, and head for the front door. A bag with the perfect hangover cure dangling on my wrist. Before I can reach the handle, I'm almost knocked on my ass.

Something is wrong. Not like an illness, just wrong. I can't explain it.

I rush out the door and jump into my Bronco, heading straight for Big Fish. I'm trying to talk myself down, that it's only in my head. It has to be because of that perv from the bar last night, that's why I'm overreacting.

When I pull into the parking lot for Big Fish my hunches are proven correct. Claire's truck isn't here. She was supposed to clock-in at least fifteen minutes ago.

I throw the truck into park right in a fire zone, I don't even pull the keys out of the ignition. I bolt through the front door.

"Where's Claire?" I demand.

"Woah. Chill man."

Not the right thing to say to me now.

Before I know it I'm on the other side of the room and I have River pinned up against the wall by his shirt. His feet dangling off the ground, his eyes wide, and his hand over mine trying to pull on my grip.

"I'm going to ask this *one more time* and you're going to give me a straight answer."

In my peripheral I see June sprinting up the stairs. "Dustin, what's going on?" She looks between me and the customers waiting to be seated. They must have fear written across their faces. When June speaks to me next her voice is more calm. "Please, put River down."

"Tell me. *Now.*"

"She went to the pier. Some guy had inform–" I'm already out the door before he can finish his sentence.

I jump into my truck and slam the door. I shoot a quick text to Toby at the station,then speed out of the parking lot.

I'll never ignore my instincts again. I knew something was wrong. I could feel it in every fiber of my being. And now I've probably lost her.

Fuck. Fuck. Fuck. Please be alive.

I repeat in my head as I slam my palms into the steering wheel of my Bronco.

I swear if that fucker touches one piece of hair on her beautiful head. I'll end him.

I'm driving ninety down highway 101 when I look in my rear view mirror and see a swarm of red and blue fluorescents flash by. There have been very few moments in my life where I've been thankful for this small town, and this is definitely going to be one of them.

It's a damn good thing the cops are going to get there before me, because if they didn't, they would be zipping up a body in a black bag tonight. But it wouldn't be mine or Claire's they'd be hauling out.

I'll never forgive myself if I'm too late.

Hang on, Angel. I'm coming. Please, just hold on.

Chapter Twenty-Nine

Claire

My palms are sweating as I drive towards the pier.

I don't know what to expect.

I don't know how this conversation is going to go.

All I know is I need him gone. For good.

The pier is off Salmon Harbor Drive in Winchester Bay, about fifteen minutes from here.

How did he find me? How does he know the area?

Do I think he actually has any information on my dad?

Possibly.

He wouldn't reach out to me, especially out of the blue, if he didn't think he had something he could use against me. It's been a year and a half since I've seen or talked to the guy. He wouldn't think he could convince me to come back if he didn't have good enough leverage. Would he?

I have thought about calling or texting Dustin a dozen times already. But I can't. If I told him where I was heading he would undoubtedly show up and then all hope of getting information out of JT would be gone. I have to do this alone.

One last thing, and Dustin and I can finally have the future we deserve.

No more interruptions. No more distractions. No more fear.

One more turn and I'll see the man that has haunted me for too long.

I take a right and head onto the pier. I drive all the way down until the road stops. It's just me and him. River was right about one thing, he is fishing.

It's odd seeing a psychopath act so humane.

I hop out of my truck and walk his way.

He doesn't turn around when he says. "I'm glad you decided to come. I have so much to tell you."

"Just tell me what you want, JT."

He slides the handle of his fishing pole into the rod holder. When he turns around to face me, I feel... *nothing*. I tilt my head to the side to get a better look at him. *Hmm... still nothing*. A smile crosses my face. It's strange to see a man who was once your best friend, was once someone you loved, become nothing but a monster. Someone who you only associate with fear and disgust even though you share a mountain of memories from your past.

A part of me was always scared that if I saw him again, I would want to go back. After I met Dustin, I knew that was no longer the case.

"I can tell you're just as relieved to see me as I am at seeing you. You look beautiful, Claire."

"Law school really made your ego blow up, didn't it?"

An evil laugh escapes his throat. "I see you're just as sassy as ever."

"Make this quick. I need to get back to work."

His eyes widened in shock. "Work? So you're not having daddy pay for everything anymore? I'm proud of you. Claire is a big girl now."

God, I fucking hate this guy.

"I'm about ten seconds from walking away."

"I wouldn't do that if I were you." He takes a step closer, I step back. He scoffs. "You see I found out some interesting information a couple months back." He's waiting for a reaction but I'm not going to give him one. "Going into law school has its perks."

My face is the epitome of boredom but he continues anyways. "I stumbled upon a set of small crimes. Ones that at a first glance you wouldn't think could be related at all. But once you looked closer... *mmm* you found some good stuff." He rubs his hands together. "Connections, darling."

"Don't call me that."

Tsk. Tsk. He clicks his tongue to the roof of his mouth. "I'm being nice right now. If you keep up with the attitude you won't like where this ends."

"What? Are you going to strangle me again? Fuel that male bravado of yours. Congratulations, you took down a woman half your size."

He huffs out a breath and anger flashes across his face.

I gulp but continue to hold my ground.

His tone is more hoarse, more serious when he speaks. "These small crimes I found were connected to a black market selling racing parts. Guess what company those sales were coming out of."

Fuck.

Dad, what did you do?

"I see you piecing it together, but let me finish it for you. The shop dabbling in botched parts was... Born Ready Auto."

I really want to slap the smugness off his face.

There's no way, Dad would never do this. Why would I believe a psychopath like him anyways?

"You're lying."

"I wish I was."

I cross my arms over my chest. "Let's say, hypothetically, you're telling the truth. What would punishment look like for a shop dealing in black market pieces?"

Without batting an eye he says, "At least fifty thousand dollars bail and five years in prison."

I want to scream so bad but I can't play into his hand. If he believes even for a second that I think my dad is guilty, he'll use it against me.

"You need to go home, JT."

"Not without you. Want to know my price for keeping my mouth shut? It's *you*. You come back with me and all is forgotten. I can even make these petty crimes disappear, if you're *nice* enough." He winks at me and suddenly I want to vomit.

"No. I will never go back with you. Not ever. I'm happy here."

His jaw clenches. "I will ruin your precious life here."

"No you won't. You know why? Because you can't." I laugh and my head tilts back a little bit. "You literally have no power here. Move on, JT. Let me go. You've been spending a whole year obsessed with me, trying to find a way to drag me back to you. When this whole time you could have moved on... found someone else."

"Is that what you did? Move on?"

I don't respond. My silence is answer enough.

"I see." He turns around and grabs his fishing pole along with his tackle box. When he turns to face me again, he has that same blank look on his face that he did when he pinned me to the wall in our apartment. My adrenaline spikes. I enter fight or flight mode and last time I ran, this time I won't.

"JT." I say his name in warning. "You deserve to be happy. Just not with me. Go home."

"You see, Claire." He glances down at his tackle box, slowly taking steps towards me. "I didn't spend a year of my life, working my ass off to walk away empty handed. On the phone I told you..." he looks back up at me. "I told you. You either come with me willingly or I'll *make* you."

It's too late, I know that look. There's no talking him down off the ledge he has put himself on.

Damn it.

My only regret is that I didn't get enough time with Dustin. That we spent so much time being mad at eachother and not enough time loving each other.

I have to make it back to him.

"I'll go... I'll go with you. Just don't–"

It happens so fast. The world goes black for a moment.

I slam to the ground.

The light fades in and out as I try to open my eyes. Something is making it hard to blink. I reach up to touch my head, because *God* it hurts *so* bad.

I flex my fingers.

What's in my hand?

I look down.

Oh, I'm on the pier. It's sand in my hands.

How did I get here?

I reach up to rub my eyes.

I just need to open my eyes.

When I pull my hand away, through slits of light, I notice they are red.

Blood.

Lots of blood on my hands.

My head is heavy as I try to keep it upright.

His voice seems distant but somehow so close at the same time. "See, I don't trust you anymore, Claire. You lie. You make up things in your head. You live in your *delusions*." He crouches down so he is face to face with me. I pick up bits and pieces of him as my vision fades in and out. I think I can hear the faint sound of sirens but maybe that's just my ears ringing. "See what *you* made me do?" He runs his finger along my hair, moving the strands out of my face. I try to turn away but I don't have the strength to. "You'll always be *mine*. All you had to do was listen and we wouldn't be in this position."

"Fuck you." I spit.

JT rubs at his face as he stands up. "You little bitch. You got blood all over me." He lifts his foot over my head. "Ready to go home?"

Home.

I'm sure this is the end. If he kicks me in the head there's no way I'm making it out of this. He will drag me back to Las Vegas. Hide me. Torture me. I'll be his, for good.

He lifts his knee. His boot inches away from my face.

The first thing that flashes through my mind is... Dustin.

His emerald eyes, his smile, and goofiness.

In my head I see...

Two people at a concert, him cracking a sand dollar into my hand, crying on his lap as I told him about my mom, me wrapped in his arms as we took a bath, dancing with him under neon lights in a bar.

Every memory we have shared together throughout the past few months.

"You were worth the pain." I whisper before I close my eyes.

"I've waited a long time for this." I feel the rush of air as his boot comes rushing towards my face.

"FREEZE! STEP AWAY FROM THE GIRL! Hands behind your head." I can feel the faint pressure from his sole frozen above my head.

Oh, good. The cops.

Here comes the darkness again.

Sleep sounds good.

Yeah, I'm just going to rest my eyes a bit.

Red and blue flashing

Flashing flashing flashing

Why do they flash so fast?

So fast.

Fast.

Fast.

F

     A

          S

              T

Someone....

Is that my name?

It's really dark.

Dark.

Dark.

D ...A... ...R   ... K

D

     A

         R

            K

Chapter Thirty

Dustin

I can see Toby's patrol car in front of me as we follow a squad of cop cars.

Why does it feel like we've been driving for hours?

I need to text Jesse.

Oh, god. I feel like I'm going to throw up.

Fuck, I need to pull myself together.

Why would she go off alone?

I can't determine where my anger ends and my anxiety begins.

My mind wants to go to all the dark places. It wants to think of all the worst case scenarios. That's not an option, not right now. I can't break down, not when Claire needs me.

My hands are sweating, my whole body is shaking, I'm struggling to keep the tears at bay. My knuckles are white as they grip the steering wheel. Memories of Claire flash through my mind, my body's response at trying to savor every piece of her. From the first time I saw her bent over working on her bike, to when she kicked my ass at the Infiniti Huck then agreed to go to a concert with me, her eyes shining under the moonlight, her laugh when she breached the surface of the ocean after I dragged her in with me, her body under mine in a dark cove. My angel.

Fuck. My Angel.

I can't lose her.

One single tear escapes as I follow the police cars down the pier.

I'm almost there.

I'm almost there, Angel. I promise.

Apparently, two of Toby's officers were closer than the ones I have been following. They are parked and jumping out of their vehicles, guns pulled, when I fly into the parking lot at the pier.

I roll my window down praying I can hear something, anything.

I hear a policeman yelling but I can't see past the cars in front of me. When we get closer I see one of the men in blue pinning a man down, JT, the other man is tending to...

Oh, god.

All the self control I have evaporates. Wet hot tears stream down my face as I take in the sight in front of me. The other policeman is tending to Claire. She's lying on the ground unconscious.

There's so much blood.

So much blood covering her face, I can't tell where it begins and ends.

I slam the gear shift of my Bronco into park, right next to Toby's cruiser. As soon as my feet touch the ground, I take off for her. But before I can get past the front of my bronco a body slams into me.

"You can't, Dustin. I know it's hard, but this is a crime scene now. You can't go past the squad cars." Toby's voice comes at me from a distance even though I know he is standing right next to me. My entire focus is on Claire's slack body about fifty feet away from us. The other officer straps an oxygen mask around her head and covers her nose and mouth.

"Please," I beg. "Please, Toby. Please. I have to see her." I turn away from her just for a few seconds to meet his eyes. "Please."

He shakes his head. There's a sympathetic look in his eyes. "I can't do that, Dustin. I'm sorry."

The whine of the ambulance goes off behind me and a group of EMTs and paramedics rush to her side. "The best way to help her now is to go inform her dad and meet the team at the hospital."

The officer pinning down JT lifts him to his feet and ushers him to the back of a police car. White hot rage takes over my entire body. JT glances in my direction and we catch each other's stare. I fling my body in his direction, but Toby stops me from going anywhere. I point my finger at him. "You're fucking dead! You hear me? *Dead.*" I can tell he hears me, because this fucker smiles.

Fucking smiles.

I thrust my body at him again, but Toby holds me back.

The officer shoves JT's head down into the back seat and shuts the door.

My focus returns to Claire and the EMTs. They are strapping her body into a gurney. I'm trying so hard to see the rise and fall of her chest. Praying for that indication of life still in her. Beating into my beautiful, stubborn, intelligent, adrenaline junky. I can't tell from this distance if she's still breathing and it kills me.

They haul her into the back of the ambulance.

"Dustin. I'm going to let you go now." Toby's hands release me and I feel weightless.

If you take her please take me too.

"Dustin you need..." He is still talking, I can tell because his lips are moving but the ringing in my head got too loud and I can't hear anything. I failed her. I failed to keep her safe when she needed me.

I wasn't there when she needed me.

The ambulance pulls out of the parking lot and drives past us, sirens blaring. I try to catch a glimpse of her through the window but all I can see is the EMTs.

Toby pats me on the shoulder, snapping my hearing back into function. "Did you hear me?" I shake my head. "You need to go tell Jesse before the station calls him. He would appreciate it more from you than us. Then you two should go to the hospital." I'm zoned in on the spot where Claire was laying on the pier. The only remnant of her is a large crimson spill. "I have to go. Are you going to be alright?"

No. No, I'm not.

But I nod my head anyway.

Toby retreats to his car and drives away.

My knees slam into the ground as the sound of my Bronco hums behind me.

Chapter Thirty-One

Dustin

Death.

Usually when people talk about dying they are referring to the part when your heart fails, when you stop taking breaths, and ultimately when that machine flat lines.

I think there's two types of dying.

One is the former and the second one is the death of your *soul*.

When you lose someone you love—or the fear of losing someone you love—your heart shatters but doesn't stop beating. Some part of you leaves with them. Some part of you that you will never get back, and you're glad you won't, because you know that piece is with them and it was worth every *damn* ounce of pain to experience sharing it with them.

The memory of Claire's body on that gurney flashes by as I kneel in the sand.

There was so much blood.

The other half of my soul.

The other half of my heart.

The other half of my *world*.

My head falls into my hands. Tears stream down my face as I beg, beg to anyone and everyone who can hear me.

"Please, don't take her from me."

<hr />

I give myself approximately five minutes to break down in the sand before I hop back into my truck and haul ass to Jesse's. I call him on the way there and inform him of everything I know. Including Claire's background with JT. I can deal with her being mad at me later. Right now, all that matters is her safety and the fact that she *has* to be okay. So, I tell Jesse. His reaction is as expected, a few cuss words, and threats thrown JT's way. All the same things I threatened to do to that slimy bastard.

Without the squad cars in front of me, the usual fifteen minutes from the pier to Claire's house only takes eight. I have no time to think about how different the last twenty minutes could have been if I got there before the police.

I would probably be in a jail cell right now.

When I pull up to Claire's, Jesse is already waiting on the curb for me. He hops in fairly quickly for a guy with a broken leg, then we speed off to the hospital.

The drive from their house to the ER is even quicker, a total of five minutes. Now, Jesse is sitting in one of the chairs in the waiting room, his uninjured leg bouncing up and down. His injured leg in a cast elevated on a chair directing in front of him. Meanwhile, I'm pacing back and forth against the far wall, closest to the large swinging doors that lead to the back of the ER wing. Back to where Claire is.

Fuck, I have been in this hospital way too many times for my liking in the last few weeks.

Although, this time feels a lot heavier.

God, there was so much blood.

One of the details I kept from Jesse. That image of Clare's body frozen, unmoving on the splinter wood, blood pooling around her head. I wouldn't wish that on my worst enemy. And I sure as hell wasn't going to talk to Jesse about it.

The sound of the automatic doors to the ER opening snaps me into place. Dr. Shank walks out. "Hey, Dustin. Let's go have a seat." I follow him over to where Jesse is sitting in the waiting room. I take the chair next to him and Dr. Shank sits across from us. "Claire is stable." Jesse and I both let out a huge breath of relief. "She is suffering from major blunt force trauma to the head. From the information we received from the station, we know an old metal tackle box was the cause of her injury." I don't know what's worse: the thought that JT beat her with his fists, or that he hit her with a heavy object. "She's in recovery now." Dr. Shank takes a deep breath. My jaw tenses in response. I know what's coming is going to be the worst part.

"Please, doc. Just say it." Jesse pleads.

"The location of her injury is going to cause... complications with her recovery. Her injury resulted in major swelling, and the way her body was laying on the pier applied a significant amount of compression to a major part of her reticular activating system. The brain's arousal system. She is currently in a state of comatose." That familiar deafening sound is back, my vision is narrowing to a point. It feels like the walls are caving in on me.

My back slams into the seat.

Claire is in a coma.

Claire is in a fucking coma.

"Do we know how long she will be... unconscious?" Jesse asks.

"Unfortunately, there's no way to know for sure."

Jesse sniffles next to me as his fists clench and unclench at his side.

All of a sudden the room feels like it's trying to suffocate me. I stand up with so much force my chair screeches along the vinyl and falls over. I storm towards the bright red exit sign and burst through the door.

As soon as I am outside..

I scream.

I scream so loud the birds in the bush to my left take off into flight.

I scream so loud and so long until all the anger leaves my body.

Until all that's left is a body racked with pain and heartbreak.

Until I have the strength to walk back into that hospital and watch as my girlfriend takes breaths everyday but doesn't open her eyes.

Until I can face her dad again and tell him I'm sorry for not taking care of his daughter.

Until I can come to terms with the fact that hope is all I have left now.

※※※※※※※※※※※※※※※※

"Dustin, you look like death has knocked on your doorstep at least ten times today."

"*June*," I shoot a sharp, cautionary look her way. "I'm not in the mood."

"No, Dustin. No one is. Doesn't mean you shouldn't take a shower."

"I'm not leaving."

"I didn't ask you to, they have one here you—"

"Just drop off your flowers and leave." June has been here everyday since Claire's injury. Bringing gifts of all different kinds; flowers, crocheted blankets, healing herbs/oils, pretty much anything she can get her hands on. And everyday she gives me shit about my looks and smell.

"D–"

"Stop. I don't need your pity, June. Claire does. And maybe if you stayed here every hour for the past week, you would look the same way I do." I run my hands through my hair. "I'm not going anywhere until she wakes up. Do you understand? So stop asking me." I look down at my lap. The dirt stains from the sand catch my eye but I don't care.

"That's not fair. All my free time has been here. You know I still have to work." She scoffs and rolls her eyes at me. "Not everyone can live off of family money."

I'm on my feet in an instant. "What the fuck did you just say to me?"

"Woah... woah!" Jesse looks like he wants to stand up but then remembers his current state. A frustrated look crosses his face before he continues, "Everyone needs to calm down. This isn't helping anything. We are all under a lot of stress and Claire wouldn't want us coming at each other's throats like this. Especially, not on her behalf." He says from the bench across the room from us, his eyes narrowing in on me.

I take a breath and sit back down.

"I'm sorry, D. You know I love her too and if I could be here every hour I would be." June's head slumps from her shoulders and she rubs at her eyes. "Do you know I blame myself? If I had just been at the front desk when she came in I could have stopped her from going."

My response is almost instant. "Yeah, you could have."

June glances at me then nods her head up and down.

God, I'm an asshole.

"Dustin!" Jesse hisses at me.

I hold my hand up, to stop him from lecturing me. I shouldn't have said that. It's not June's fault.

I know the stress of this whole situation has really amped up my emotions. But I thought I had a better handle on them.

"You know that morning she was hungover. I *begged* her to stay behind with me. *Begged* her to call in sick." June lifts her head and looks at me. "I told her I would pay her double what she made if she stayed behind because I missed her so much." I let out a half laugh and look over at my beautiful fallen angel wrapped up in her hospital sheets. My eyes begin to water. "If only I was more convincing, then she wouldn't have left in the first place. If anyone is at fault, it's me." Jesse opens his mouth to interrupt me but I stop him again. "At least that is what I told myself for the first three days. Then I remembered two things. One, I'll never be able to convince Claire to do something she doesn't want to do. And two, it is no one's fault except JT's for her being here... don't blame yourself."

June nods at me as if she understands the darkness that has consumed me for the last several days, then she proceeds to thank me before she leaves flowers on the windowsill, kisses Claire on the forehead, and says goodbye. Leaving, Jesse and I sit in the silence of a single beeping monitor.

"You're a good man, Dustin. Even if you look like shit."

I laugh. "I wouldn't say you look much better, old man."

He smirks. Then the present moment drags both of us back into its unrelenting grips.

"Toby called, said JT was charged with attempted..." Jesse chokes on the next word, "murder." He straightens his back against the wall. "Stalking, and a few other minor charges that Toby threw on to lengthen his sentence and increase his bail. He got ten years."

"That's not enough."

"No, no it's not." He takes a deep breath then looks over at me. I've seen this expression before. He is trying to decide if he wants to tell me something, or if he can trust me. "I have a way of potentially getting him more time."

My eyes snap to him. "I'm listening."

"Apparently, JT was about to finish law school. Turns out he got access from his internship to a lot of information he wasn't supposed to have." He pauses, looks me over, then continues, "Back when it was just us, I was fresh out of high school, a single dad and struggling paycheck to paycheck. Let's just say I made some choices that weren't... ideal. In that course of time, I made some really good connections though. Connections that will make what I want to do easy. This would benefit not only Claire and our peace of mind but also me and some unfortunately shady things I got into. It won't be easy. But if you want to help, I won't say no."

My mind is swarming with questions. Everything I thought I knew about Jesse goes out the door.

What could Jesse possibly have gotten himself into? What is his plan? What would we need to do?

Then I look over at Claire, unconscious, stitches across her forehead and down the side of her partially shaved head. I made my decision the second I saw her under that night sky, the moonlight creating a blue halo around her head, that I would do anything to keep her safe.

I turn toward Jesse to give him my response, my mouth hangs open, the answer right there on the tip of my tongue.

Then time stands still.

"D... Dustin?"

Epilogue

Claire

Three months later...

"I think that's the last box."

I shuffle through the doorway into Dustin's house, or I guess I should say my house now. I squeeze past Dad as he takes the box out of my hands. We had to finish up a couple of things before I moved in—like dealing with JT's sentence—and now the time has finally come.

For three months I have been waiting for this moment.

"Are you sure?"

"Yeah, I double checked both rooms and the bathroom. I'll head over there after the weekend and clean up."

"Don't worry about it. Tattie is already coming over on Saturday to help."

"Oh... is she now?" I raise my eyebrows at him.

He rubs the back of his neck. "Yeah we are kinda.. I don't know, I guess-"

I put my hand on his shoulder. "Dad. It's okay, I'm happy for you."

"No more secrets."

"No more secrets," I repeat. This is our new promise to each other. Ever since my *coma*. That still feels so strange to say, to think about. After he told me about his shady business deals and I told him about JT's abuse, we swore to never keep anything from each other ever again.

He smiles at me then leaps up the stairs to drop the box off in my room. His leg fully healed.

I look around the house, still in awe that I get to live here, that Dustin and I get to have our time. That I get to wake up next to him every morning.

As soon as I woke up in that hospital bed, he rushed to my side. Before I was able to form full words he asked me to move in with him, he told me he doesn't want to waste any more moments, and I couldn't agree more. It was the fastest '*yes*' I have ever nodded.

Dad returns from upstairs, stands next to me, and puts his hand on my freshly cut bob. I couldn't live with one half of my hair being significantly shorter than the rest.

"Are you sure you want to move out?"

"I'm literally across the street. Is it still considered moving out?" He has been overly protective since the whole '*incident*' which I prefer to call it instead of a coma. Or I say '*my really long nap*' which pisses Dustin off.

I understand why all the men in my life have been extra cautious around me, but I hate it. Dr. Shank gave me a clean bill of health, and told me I can go back to normal life, for a reason.

"Don't worry, Jesse. I'll still be sending you hourly photo updates like we discussed." Dustin teases from the kitchen.

"Hourly photo *updates?*"

Dad laughs. "Thank you, D."

Dustin rounds the corner of the kitchen wiping his hands on the apron I got him for Christmas. It says *'Once you put my meat in your mouth, you're gonna wanna swallow'*, I laugh everytime I see it. "Do we have everything moved over?"

"Yeah, pretty sure. She just handed me the last box."

"Sweet, are you still coming over for dinner tonight?"

Are they really just going to ignore the whole photo thing?

"Yeah... I was wondering if you made enough food for maybe one more mouth?" Dad asks him.

Oh, my interest is piqued now.

"Of course, who would you like to bring?"

"Tattie, if that's alright."

Dustin looks over at me, eyes wide, and I shrug my shoulders. After making sure I am comfortable with it, he turns back to my father, "Absolutely."

So it's serious enough that he wants to bring her to dinner. I love that.

"Hold on. We are not going to ignore the fact that you have been taking hourly photo updates!"

"It was just a joke, Angel."

I point at the two of them. "If I find any shared messages between the two of you with my face in them, I will throw both of you—and your phones—into the ocean."

They laugh and we all walk out onto the back patio to join Axel, June, and Dustin's parents. I smile as I look at the scene in front of me. I never really understood the meaning of family. It was always just Dad and I, sometimes Han, and we were perfect for that period of my life. That was all I needed and it never felt like anything was missing. Until I look at my life now, and then look back at my life then, and realize how quiet and lonely it seemed.

I spent hours building my skills on the motocross track, but little did I know that my passion for racing would lead me to a love I never expected. To a family I never expected.

As I look around this table and see multiple people who care for each other and would lay their lives down for one another, I'm overwhelmed with a sense of gratitude. I don't know how I came to have so many people that hold a piece of my heart or how I was blessed with a second chance, a second life. All I know is that I will not take this one for granted.

No more running,

No more hiding,

No more fighting alone.

Together we can conquer the most daring lines we should cross.

Bonus Chapter

A year and four months later...

Dustin takes a hold of my hand. "It's going to be okay. I am right here."

I take a deep breath and look at the box in front of me. The cardboard is falling apart and the script is unfamiliar, even though it shouldn't be.

I don't know what finally gave me the courage to take the twelve steps leading into *our* attic.

It could be that today is her birthday, or it could be that everything feels so *real* lately. Dustin and I have just moved into our new home, we are getting married in less than a year, and someday in the *distant* future, the pitter-patter of little feet will bless this house.

It could be that once again, I have somehow managed to find a way to continue to grow, to continue to live life, and even though something always feels missing— I still find the strength to continue to move forward.

I run my fingers along the worn edges and stare at the writing addressed to me. *'For my baby girl, may all your wishes come true and all your dreams be forever within your grasp'.*

Maybe she somehow knew something would happen to her. Maybe she knew that our time would be limited. Maybe she had an intuition that this would be the only way that I would get to meet her.

Dad said she finished the twenty-third book in the series and stashed them away until the craziness of having a newborn wore off and the plan was to bring them back out when I was about six months old.

Maybe it's because my twenty-third birthday is coming up and it somehow felt like fate.

My tears are already threatening to spill at the simple thought of my mom, but I bite my cheek and blink them away.

Dustin places his hand on my thigh in silent support. "Take your time. Even if it's not today, you have made it one step closer, and that is all that matters."

I take one more deep breath and peel back the tape sealing it shut. The first book I see is 'Oh! The Places You'll Go'. Instantly, I feel the warmth and wetness flooding down my cheeks.

I pull out the somewhat worn cover and flip it open. *'My dear Claire, this is the first note I have ever written to you. I haven't even met you yet and you are already the most wonderful thing on this planet. I am currently six months pregnant with you, and by the way you kick me in every direction, I know for a* fact *that you are going to keep your dad and I on our toes. That's okay though, he would have never been able to keep up with us anyway (;'* I giggle, and somehow it hurts a little bit more and a little less at the same time. *'All jokes aside, keep it easy on him. He may look all hard and rough on the outside, but really he is the biggest teddy bear you will ever meet. I love you my darling, three more months and that's it. See you soon, baby girl. I can't wait to see all the places you will go'.* I close the book and squeeze it against my chest.

I take a moment to myself and Dustin runs his hand along my back, anchoring me, keeping me tethered to this universe. One without her in it.

I place the book back into the box— right into the same spot— and grab the next one, 'The Cat in the Hat Comes Back'.

'Seven months pregnant and we already need to have a conversation about the amount of sweets you consume'. I guess some things don't change. 'Perhaps another time. For now, I want to tell you one thing: In this book, the cat comes back to visit Sally and Jack, over and over and over again. Even when they tell him to leave. I just want you to know that this will be me. If you are even half as stubborn as I am, then I already know that you will try to push everyone who loves you away, and try to solve your problems by yourself. Darling, if someone loves you, or when you find that someone that makes you glow inside, let them in. Let them fight your battles with you. It can be a dark world when you don't allow yourself to experience unconditional love. Take it from your momma, let them in! I love you baby girl, two more months'.

I look over at Dustin and kiss him on the cheek. "Thank you. For always fighting for me and always being there."

"Until my last breath, Angel."

I smile at him but it comes out a little strained. I slip the book back into the box.

We stay up here in this cramped room until I have read almost every single one. The last one stares back at me, burning into my soul, the last piece of my mom.

"You could save it."

"No, I need this. *Needed* this piece of her."

Somehow I know this is going to be the hardest one, but I don't know why.

He hasn't asked to read any, and I know he won't until I offer it to him. Someday I will share these with him and our future children. Just not today. It's too raw– too fresh.

I reach in and pull out 'The Lorax'.

When I flip open the book, my heart skips in my chest. *There's no way.*

I look at the book, then at Dustin. "It's for you."

His eyebrows pull together.

I hand it over. He stares down at the passage addressed to ᵼd then closes the book. Looking back up at me, he asks, ⎧ou sure?"

I nod. "You were worth the pain."

Dustin

Claire saying those words at this moment, hit me like a freight train. "You were worth the wait," I tell her as I reopen 'The Lorax'.

'To the one my daughter decides to hand her heart over to. If she's chosen you, then I know I don't have to tell you how precious her heart is because she already knows you cherish it.

The Lorax protects the forest with everything he has. He sings and dances and tries to convince a very stubborn Once-ler that saving the Truffula Trees is worth the sacrifice of riches. I am not naive, and neither is Claire. She will have someone from her past that will try and use her, try and dim the light she shines, and try to bleed her dry for their own benefit. Unfortunately, the world is full of these people. She will mourn and fight and struggle until she's just about to give up hope. And that's where you come in, The Lorax. You are the protector of her light, of her beauty (And I don't mean on the outside, even though I know she will be striking). She may seem strong and independent—self-sufficient. But in actuality, she needs you more than anything else. So once you step into her life, do not let anymore Once-ler's come in and cut her down.

I can't wait to meet you. When that day comes it will be an honor *to meet the man who won over the other half of my soul.*

So thank you. Thank you for being everything she needs and so much more. Love, Reneé Elizabeth Gates.'

A sob escapes my throat as Claire wraps her body around mine and buries her face into my chest. I sniffle and wipe the snot from my nose with my shirt then look up at the roof. In my head I make my own promise.

A promise to her mom.

I tell her that I will never let anyone cut her down, or dim her light, that I will protect my Angel with everything in me. And that I will see to it that she knows for the rest of her life she will *never* have to fight alone.

I pull Claire in tighter and take a deep breath.

The wind rushes outside, sending a low whistle into the dimly lit space and I can't help but think that maybe this was the last thing Reneé needed to be able to move on. That she needed to say goodbye in her own way. That Claire opening this box, and being filled by the love that she felt was missing, was the final step.

I know Claire thinks it too when she looks out the window and whispers, "I love you, Mom."

Acknowledgements

cannot believe this day has come! Holy shit! You are ...lding my book in your hand, this is so surreal. Okay, ...ing out now and talk about all the people who made this day possible.

To all the people who helped put Dustin and Claire's story out in the world.

First and foremost, I want to thank all you readers. Thank you so much for taking the time to read my debut novel. This dream of mine wouldn't be possible without all of you.

I want to thank my mom and my boyfriend, Sam, without your help none of this could have been done. Sam, my partner in crime, thank you for financially supporting me through this process, and helping me with the kids so that this story could actually be on paper one day. For being my ultimate love, our story is my favorite. Mom, you are always there for me when I need you and without you I would have lost my mind a long time ago. For letting me cry and encouraging me to be vulnerable. For showing me the strength in kindness and compassion. Thank you both for being my rock against the raging river of my emotions. To Kori, my bestest friend and the best MIL I could ask for, thank you for always pushing me in my faith and listening to me rant for hours on end about everything in my life. For encouraging me to always stick it out and be the best person I can be. To my dad, for always pushing me to be strong and independent. For giving me the backbone I needed to get through life. For showing me what hard work and dedication can get you. And, last but most importantly, my God. Who designed me, who made me become the woman, Mom, and writer that I am today. All my glory is for you. I love you all so much.

My valkyries, my best friends who have become my family, Steph & Sarah. Without the two of you, this book would probably be spending an eternity in my google docs. Thank you for making me believe this was possible. Sarah, for answering all my publishing and author questions and letting me learn from your own journey, for showing me what the future could look like if I stayed determined and strong. Steph, for constantly reassuring me that LWSC was worth sharing and encouraging me on my lowest days. For our FaceTimes calls, that lasted hours, and weeks of editing with me. For rewriting the same sentence over and over and over again. LWSC is what it is today because of your help and love.

My fern, Jen Jen, for putting together the best playlist and being my friend from the very beginning. Thank you for giving me the best feedback, and hyping me up. You brought me back to myself on some of my lowest days. There's too much I want to say to be able to put on here, but I'll leave it as I miss you so much. Tay, for answering all my motocross questions and making sure my riding scenes didn't sound completely ridiculous, and for letting me use your name and riding number!

My early beta readers, Joc & Mel, for looking at a very *rough* draft and seeing the story past its mistakes. Your time and opinions matter so much to me. Thank you for taking a chance on an indie author from bookstagram.

My Arc readers, who got excited when LWSC was just an image on an iPad. For, flipping through page after page and continuing to read about Dustin and Claire. For leaving your reviews and for supporting me in my author journey. The Book Community is my favorite place to be because of people like you.

Now go cross all the lines you shouldn't because there's a beautiful life out there waiting for you!

Love, Cece.

Need more of Dustin & Claire?

Read Axel and June's story in the next book of the
Winchester Bay Series!!

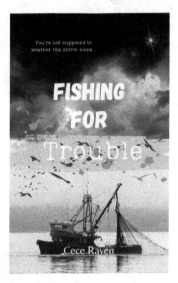

Release day set for February of 2024

Hope to see you then!

In the meantime you can follow Cece Raven on instagram
@authorceceraven to stay up to date on current information and
ARC opportunities.

Welcome to Reedsport

Chapter One

June

"Oh, come on, come on. Pick up." My knee bounces uncontrollably as I try to get ahold of my landlord. He can't just leave me an email saying I need to move out and then not answer his phone ten minutes after he sends it. "You piece of–"

"Hello?"

I sit up straight.

"Hey, Mark. It's June. I just got your email, and I'm a little confused. It says I have two weeks to move out." Nyx barks in the background and I move into my bedroom so that it's quieter. I rescued the husky-wolf mix about three months ago and it was the best decision I have ever made.

"What are you confused about?"

"It says 'failure to abide by pet restrictions' but I have been paying the pet deposit and got approval from Jan before I rescued Nyx."

"In your agreement, there are certain... restrictions to the size of dog you can get. I'm sorry June, but you're going to have to move out, no matter what my wife told you."

"I checked the agreement four times before choosing Nyx, and there were no details about what size he had to be, just that I would need to pay a deposit and a monthly added expense."

"I don't know what to tell you, we have our copy of the lease right here. Again, I'm sorry June, but you have till the end of the month to move out."

The line disconnects. My hand and phone land in my lap as a stare at my bedroom wall.

What am I going to do?

I don't have enough money right now to pay another deposit. Tattie is already renting out her apartment to Joey. I can't live out of my car with a dog.

I just adopted Nyx and now we are going to be homeless.

I hang my head and cry into my hands. Shortly after, I feel a large weight sink in next to my leg. Nyx whimpers. I take a deep breath and scratch the black hair behind his ear.

"We are going to be okay. Aren't we, baby? Mom will figure it out."

I lift my phone back up and hover over *his* contact.

No. I can't.

I can't go back down that road. I know he would be here in a heartbeat, but that's not fair to him. I may not be able to ask him directly but I can ask someone else.

I pick up my phone and call my best friend.

She's kind of breathless when she answers. "Hey, love. What's up?"

"Claire! Oh my god. I need a huge favor. My landlord kicked me out and I have until the end of the month to move, I don't have any money to get into a new place, and I can't live on the streets with Nyx. You know, because I want to give him a good life and what kind of dog-mom would I be if I let us sleep in the car and–"

I hear her shuffle around in the background. "Woah, okay, slow down. You have to move out?"

I sob. "Yes, and I just got Nyx. What if they take him away?"

"That's not gonna happen. You know we have the extra room here, and it's yours. We can start moving your stuff over after work today."

"What about Dustin, don't you need to ask him first?"

"Right here!" He shouts in the background. "Thanks for interrupting, June."

"Shut up! *Oh my god*. I've always wanted to cock-block."

Claire laughs and Dustin yells profanities.

"He is... frustrated, but he already agreed."

"Thank you so much! I promise I won't be in your way for very long. Just a few months, so I can save up some money and get into my own place."

"Don't worry about it." She shrieks and starts giggling. "I'm sorry.." Laugh. "I have..." Another laugh. "To go."

I pull the phone away from my ear and hang up on her. *Gross.*

But good for her.

"See baby, we will be okay. We are going to go live with your aunt and uncle for a little bit, doesn't that sound fun?" He barks in response. "I thought so." I take a deep breath. "We are just going to have to figure out how to live with Axel. Now, *that* might be a difficult situation." Another bark.

I'm not fishing for any trouble so everything is going to be A-OK.

I hope...

Printed in the USA
CPSIA information can be obtained
at www.ICGtesting.com
LVHW020556081123
763363LV00050B/242